THE DEVIL
YOU KNOW

MONIQUE SINGLETON

By Monique Singleton

The Dominion Series

The Devil You Know

I AM the Storm

To Hell and Back

Insurrection

I would like to dedicate this book to everyone who dares to ask:
Why?

Vinci Books

vinci-books.com

Published by Vinci Books Ltd in 2025

1

A CIP catalogue record for this book is available from the British Library.

Paperback ISBN: 9781036705152

Never grow old.

Chapter One

'Leave, all of you.'

The voice came from the dark corner.

A big shadow filled the area. Unruly, long black hair and a full beard hid most of the man's face. From the length of his torso and his legs pushed to the side of the table, I gauged him to be at least six-foot-six. His t-shirt under the faded jeans jacket was tight over a muscled physique. The torn and frayed sleeves showed traditional tribal tattoos covering equally powerful arms. But in this light, the defining characteristics were the eyes; fierce brown-green rimmed black irises.

'He's here for me,' he declared.

As one, the patrons abandoned their drinks on the tables, hastily made their way to the door and escaped out to the relative safety of the street.

I observed the figure in the corner. Not exactly what I'd expected. Damn Michael and Rafe. Damn their stupid games.

Maybe I should have taken back-up with me.

I turned my attention back to the reason I was here in this god-forsaken hell hole. The piercing eyes never left me.

A glint of light reflecting on a metallic surface against the wall next to his chair distracted me momentarily. I could just make out the contours of a double-headed axe. Viking style. Times ten, by the look of it.

I really should have brought back-up.

His hands stayed on the table, one holding a beer glass, the other flat on the surface. He knew who I was, or at least what I was and why I was here.

He looked like a predator. Not the prey.

Definitely not the prey.

This mission might need some improvisation on my part.

'Which one are you?' The voice was deep and full of contempt.

'Gabriel,' I answered.

'Don't I even merit Michael?' he taunted.

'He was busy.'

His laugh was as warm as a blizzard. It echoed in the now empty bar.

'You're here to kill me?'

'Not necessarily.'

He cocked his head. 'What alternative did you have in mind?'

'There are several.'

Silence.

'So, are you going to hover over me all evening, or are you going to take a seat while I finish my beer.'

He held up the almost full pint glass of yellow liquid. That gave me some time.

'Sit down. I'm not going anywhere.'

The chair screeched over the stone floor as I pulled it out from under the table.

My goal was not to terminate him if possible. The guy was a total soul-magnet, and he had the prospect of becoming a master-recruiter, something my father didn't want to pass up on.

'Father Ignatius,' I started. His glare stopped me mid-sentence. I raised an eyebrow.

'I am not a priest anymore,' he stated resolutely, his voice as cold as his stare.

'Fair enough. That's exactly what I want to talk to you about.'

'You're here to change my mind?' he asked incredulously.

I nodded.

'Are you serious?'

Again, I nodded.

'First your kind tries to kill me.' He cocked his head in disbelief. 'Then you want me to come back into the fold?'

I resisted the urge to nod again as he brought the glass up to his lips.

'We…' I started.

'We?' he interrupted my carefully prepared speech.

'My father…'

'God?' The venom dripped off the title.

'I guess you would call him that,' I answered slowly.

'I have another name for him,' he answered.

'Okay, allow me to rephrase. Humans call him God.'

'And he's your father?'

'He is.'

'Family business, huh?'

'Yes,' I answered. 'Family business. Isn't that what the scriptures explained?'

He huffed, not deigning to answer me.

'He wants you back,' I continued. This guy would see right through the usual lies. He was on to the whole scam. 'You're an asset.'

'An asset?' His throwing my words back as questions was starting to piss me off.

'People flock to you. You have a knack for convincing people to believe in the afterlife. We need more humans. Especially the ones you bring in.'

'The strong ones, you mean?' Another question and another sip.

I nodded yet again. This was getting tedious.

'The ones that can work. Can make you money. Keep your family's high status.' He spat out the words.

'Yes.' This time my answer was strong. Unapologetic. 'You knew the score. You were initiated into The Establishment. Kind of hypocritical that you're looking down on me now. You were all too happy to go along with our arrangement as long as you made it to the top in the church.'

'You know nothing about me.' The defiant glare was back again with a vengeance.

'I know your kind.' My turn to sneer, and now my tone became derogatory, the contempt seeping through.

He wasn't drinking. Not anymore. His eyes bore into mine. I returned the stare and the sentiment.

'You're so righteous on the outside, but deep down, you humans all want the same. You want to be king. Rule over your minions. Well, we're giving you a chance to do just that. You,' I pointed to him, 'can go all the way. You can be the first Cardinal from the islands. Isn't that what you want? Deep down, you crave recognition. I know what you were. How you lived before you joined the Church. I know the resentment you carry.'

I leant forward. 'You can fool your flock as much as you want, but I know what you are. I know you.'

'You have no idea,' he growled.

'Stop the sanctimonious crap. You're still the narcissistic killer you were in your youth. You don't fool me. You want power. You need the adoration. Well, we can give it to you. Hell, bring in the souls we believe you're capable of and we'll even make you Pope.' I couldn't keep the contempt out of my voice. The glint in his eye could mean he felt it, or I just hit the nail on the head.

He was useful now. But that would come to an end. We had to control him. If that meant promising him the moon, then that was what I would do. And finally, when he was no longer of use, then…

'That's what you want, isn't it?'

He just stared at me; the edges of his lips curled up slightly. Was that contempt or was I making progress?

Yeah, right.

'If I come back into the fold, you'll help me up the ladder? Make me a Cardinal? And eventually the Pope?'

I cocked my head and smiled conspiratorially. Another nod.

'And all I have to do is gather souls for you?'

I nodded again.

'How do I know you'll keep your end of the bargain?'

He was coming around. I'd done it again. I congratulated myself on a job well done.

I looked at the priest. He observed me intently. Waiting. On what? An answer? 'What did you say?' I asked him.

He repeated his question, now with an edge. 'How do I know you'll keep your end of the bargain?'

'You have my word. And that of my father,' I stated. What more did he want?

'Your word?' He raised an eyebrow.

A tingle started at the bottom of my spine. It moved slowly up my back towards my neck, ending in a sharp stab into my skull. Something was not right here. The way he was staring at me had changed. He was challenging me.

'Our promise,' I answered, keeping up my smug facade. Inside something warned me to be careful.

The priest moved his right hand from the glass up to the lapel of his jeans jacket and under the torn and faded material to a pocket.

My hand moved involuntarily to the hilt of one of my knives. My nerves were screaming at me now. This was definitely not right.

He took a small plastic Ziplock bag out of his pocket and placed it on the table.

'Your promise,' he repeated. 'Like this one?'

I looked at the contents of the bag and my blood ran cold. There, on the table, were the remnants of an identifier. The state it was in showed clearly that it had been triggered.

'What happened to it?' I tried innocently.

'Why don't you tell me?'

He brought the beer up to his lips and took a sip. Then another.

I didn't dare move. A stupid thought stuck in my mind; I was safe as long as he still had beer to drink.

'It happens sometimes,' I explained as I forced myself to relax. 'Not often thankfully. We're working on that issue. I'm sorry you had one of the duds. Thankfully it didn't cause any damage.'

A voice at the back of my mind tried to tell me something, but it remained just out of reach.

He drank the rest of the yellow-ochre liquid in one long

draught, emptying the glass and slamming it back on the table.

His lips curled up in a smile—not the nice kind. Pure hatred pulsated from his face. That and contemptuous amusement.

The last emotion surprised and unnerved me.

Just long enough to mask what he was doing.

The pain in my sternum pushed the air out of my lungs as the table edge hit me hard. My chair toppled over, and I landed flat on my back, my head hitting the cold stone floor with a loud crack.

Disorganised and muddled, my eyes struggled to converge on the blurred figure as he stood up from his seat. His right hand reached for the axe behind him, and he swung the massive weapon down, its edge sending up sparks as it hit the floor where my neck had been a millisecond before.

Instead of moving away from him, I turned into the man under his swing. I rolled onwards, swiping his legs out from under him. Moving back quickly, I barely avoided being caught under his bulk as he fell to the floor.

I stood up quicker than him and kicked the priest viciously in the kidney but was completely unprepared for the sharp pain in my thigh as the priest connected with a boot in turn.

We both recovered quickly and were on our feet. I had to keep him away from the big axe that lay on the ground behind me.

I reached behind my back and my hands closed over the handles of the curved knives I held in scabbards on my back.

He took in the blades and the way I wielded them, then his glance flicked to his axe.

There was little I could read from his face. No nervousness, no fear. Just amusement. He was enjoying all of this.

We had a stand-off.

He stretched his arms above his head, cracked his neck from one side to the other, took a deep breath and attacked. He feigned to the right, then pushed to the left and hit me hard on my right shoulder, almost knocking me to the ground. He ducked under my left blade. The sharp metal sliced through his t-shirt but missed the flesh.

My right arm refused to work properly from the massive impact to my shoulder. I still held on to the knife but couldn't raise my upper arm. I had no choice, I moved to my left, out of reach of his arm as it shot back, aimed at my head.

His play worked.

I was no longer between him and his axe.

I stepped back to regain control over my right arm, pushing through the pain I forced my nerves to cooperate. There was movement again, even if it wasn't up to par. It would come back; my healing was quick.

The priest took hold of his axe. A big vicious smile spilt his face. But I was by no means defeated.

We circled each other in the tight space, both focussing on the eyes. Sure enough, he blinked and swung the massive axe two-handed, aiming for my left arm. I ducked to the side easily and pushed the knife in my right hand up under the swing, cutting through more than material this time. It was just a flesh wound, but an unexpected one. The surprise on his face was priceless.

I turned quickly and went in for the kill with my left weapon, only to be blocked by the axe. He pushed his weapon hard into my blade, shattering it, and kicked out at the same time, connecting hard with my upper thigh.

With a scream of anger, I rushed him. He swung the axe one-handed, the flat side of the blade connected to my forehead and split the skin immediately. Blood poured down my face, blinding me. Before he could rebalance, I swung my knives up and rammed the remainder of my left blade into the priest's shoulder. He cried out. Hardly able to see, I followed the sound and slashed my other knife at his neck, barely missing him.

We connected body to body and pummelled each other. In the tumble we lost our weapons.

Furniture splintered below us, and I grabbed a table leg, swinging it towards his head. It connected squarely with his face knocking him back. Through my bloody vision, I rushed him again and we fell to the floor. My hands closed around his throat. He pushed his arms through mine and smashed them sideways, loosening my injured right shoulder. I felt a massive fist connect with my jaw and flew backwards from the blow.

He immediately jumped me, and his fists pummelled into my body time and time again.

He was winning. The blows were incessant. I felt panic rise, something completely new for me. I arched my body trying to dislodge him, but his bulk pinned me to the ground. My left hand groped on the floor, searching for a weapon of some kind. Nothing. I tried again, my right hand over my face in an attempt to ward off the hammering. Instead of my head, he hit me in the side. I doubled up. Even as I spasmed my hand gripped the discarded beer glass. I brought the thick stein up in a wide swing and connected to his head. There was a satisfying crunch and the pressure on my body lifted. I kicked out at him and landed a few good blows.

The world turned when I tried to stand up, and I dropped back to the floor.

I stared at the drops of blood that dripped from my forehead down to the floor. They pooled into a purple stain that would be hell to get out of the rug. Yes, purple: we bleed a different colour than you do.

I was on my hands and knees. Completely vulnerable. My head reeled from the torrent of blows and my senses were still out of sync.

Why wasn't he taking advantage of the situation? I raised my head and looked across the floor to the priest.

His beard and the top half of his shirt were bright red. A deep gash just above his left cheek-bone seeped blood. He sat with his back to the wall, his legs splayed forward. His right hand gripped the hilt of my knife. With a deep grunt he pulled the broken blade out of his left shoulder and dropped the remnants of my favourite weapon to the ground next to him. Ripped scraps of t-shirt were pushed hard into the wound to stop the bleeding.

The only sign of his pain was the crunched brow. His eyes blazed with hatred as they caught mine.

We were both floored. Neither able to push home the last winning blow. I leant back on my haunches, then sat against the column, my legs in front of me mirroring his. My anger pushed me forward. "Kill him now. He's exposed, weakened, broken-down" Yeah, well so was I.

We sat like that for more than five minutes.

'You're a lot harder to kill than I thought.' He finally broke the silence.

'Same here.'

'Surely you were warned about me by your brother.'

'He conveniently forgot to mention your size, strength and that bloody big axe.'

He laughed. This time there was real humour there.

'We have a competitive nature,' I explained.

'All trying to impress dad?'

'Yeah, something like that. Sibling rivalry. You know the drill.'

'Even in paradise?' I noticed he didn't call it Heaven.

I nodded.

The itch told me the wound on my forehead had finally closed. I wiped the last drops of blood from my face with the tail of my shirt and observed my adversary.

Despite the deep wound in his shoulder and the corresponding loss of blood, he looked remarkably vigilant.

My gaze went to our surroundings. We had done a good job of demolishing the bar. The wreckage of the table lay in the corner, three of the four legs broken off and the fourth hanging by a thread. The wooden bar-chairs were smashed, the debris used as weapons in our fight.

What impressed me most was the double-headed axe sunk deep into the oak column about a metre above my head. Gingerly, I moved my body to the left, out from under the shadow of the formidable weapon. That elicited another chuckle from across the room.

'You could have had eternity,' I said, voicing a question that had been bothering me ever since I was tasked with bringing him back into the fold.

'At what cost?' His voice was strong. Better than mine.

'No cost to you. You would have been well taken care of.'

He shook his head. 'It would cost me my integrity, my values and morals.' He sighed. 'My very soul.'

My turn to laugh. 'There is no such thing as a soul. It's a phantom your religions have dangled before you to keep you in line. It doesn't exist.'

'My soul is my life,' he continued, oblivious to my words. 'To betray it would make eternity moot.'

'What makes you think you still have a soul after what you did as a young man?' I asked. He refrained from answering.

I decided to humour him. He intrigued me, so did the conflict between his former life and the path he had chosen now.

'By all accounts you should have been the ideal candidate for us,' I continued. 'With your background and bloody history, The Establishment should be the ultimate high for you. What is it that prevents you from being our star pupil? Our ultimate partner.'

'The deceit,' he answered.

'The deceit?' Now it was my turn to answer with questions.

'My former life was violent. I murdered. I stole.' His voice lacked the menace of earlier. 'I lived as though there was no tomorrow. I was the only one that mattered. The only one who deserved to live. Everyone who got in my way was annihilated or used and pushed aside. My life was filled with debauchery and violence. I lived for me. Only me.'

He sat back and tilted his head up to look at the ceiling as though there was something there. I checked; nothing but stains and yellowish used-to-be-white paint.

'I had no use for anyone in my life. I took who and what I wanted and threw them to the curb when I was finished with them. No attachments. No emotions. No feelings.' He faced me again. 'That all changed when she came into my life. One woman changed everything.'

'How?' This was surprising.

'She made me feel.'

He stared at me. Daring me to say something. I refrained.

'She made me live. Feel. Care. Things I hadn't done since I was a small child. She made me confront my demons and gave me a new lease on life.'

'How?' I repeated my previous question.

'She was there. She never asked for anything. Didn't judge me. Didn't push me. She was just there. And she asked questions. Very persistent and deep ones.' He smiled at the memories.

'She was your girlfriend?'

He laughed. 'Hell no. She was already taken.'

I cocked my head in question, he didn't seem the kind of man who would take "no" for an answer. If he had his eye on a woman, any potential competitor would quickly be history.

He burst that bubble. 'She was a nun.' Wow. I hadn't seen that one coming. Not in a million years.

'A nun?' I asked, my surprise evident in the way I voiced my amazement.

He laughed softly. 'A nun.' We were silent.

'Must have been one hell of a nun,' I finally said. 'No pun intended'.

We both laughed at that. A distinct improvement on our earlier physical communication.

'Now what?' he asked.

'Fucked If I know.'

'Seems we are quite evenly matched.'

I nodded.

'You're not coming back to The Establishment, are you?' I concluded.

'No.'

'Nothing I can say will convince you.' It wasn't a question anymore. 'Why?'

'Because she made me care.'

'Your nun?'

'Yes. She opened my eyes. I cannot un-see what she revealed to me. It is my life now.'

'There is more.' I pushed.

He nodded, his eyes going to his hands. 'I had a new home. A meaning in life. And you took it from me.'

I urged him on.

'I believed in God. In a better life. In Heaven. Not for me, I knew my previous sins damned me, no matter how much I'd changed. But I believed I could help others achieve that which was out of my reach. I could help them gain entrance to the promised land. To a life much better than anything they could have here on Earth. These were all poor people. The ones without a prospect in this world. They didn't have a chance here, I wanted them to have one in the afterlife.'

He looked at me again. The hatred in his eyes bore into me.

'Your kind took that away. You made me part of your deceit. Instead of helping them, I doomed them to an afterlife that was far worse than anything they had here. I sentenced them to eternal slavery. Everything I held dear in my miserable life was a scam. You deceived me, and I betrayed them. In my thirst for life's meaning, I turned to the biggest scam in the world: religion. I believed. I truly believed. Like the nun before me. You and the Church betray everything that is good in humans. You enslave them with your religion here by promising them paradise. And then, when they finally die, you enslave them again. For eternity.'

I stayed silent.

'My faith was my rock. Now it is gone. There is no Heaven. No redemption. No spirituality anymore. It was all I had. What is there left than to fight you?'

'You're wrong, you know.' I shouldn't tell him this, but I figured I owed him. No idea why, I just did.

'We didn't invent your religious concepts. We just capitalised on what was already here. Made a side-step as it were.'

'What?' He raised his head and looked at me intensely.

I elaborated. 'Your religions were here long before we came. We saw an opportunity and took it. The hold religion had on humans was ideal for us. We waylaid the dead of this dimension and brought them to ours.'

'Kidnapped, you mean.' Venom dripped off his words.

'Semantics.' I shrugged, still not realising the gravity of the priest's emotions.

'No, anything but semantics,' he countered loudly. 'You wave it off so easily.'

He was silent for a while.

'Why would I believe a word of what you say? You lie so easily. There is nothing left. No higher powers. Just you and your kind.' His tone was one of resignation.

His change of demeanour was starting to irritate me. As strong as he had been during the fight, so pathetic did he look now. His faith turned out to be less than heavenly. Boehoe. 'They know what's coming.' I said annoyed. 'They know about Purgatory and that they have to spend time there before they can enter Heaven.'

'They don't.' he looked up at me, the fire back in his eyes. 'They're deceived. They're promised Heaven and go to Hell.' His voice was cold again. Dangerous.

'Religion, your religion, deceives them twice. They are

kept small and insignificant here with the promise of a better life after death and what do they get? More slavery. More exploitation.'

My brow creased and I shook my head at his dramatics. 'You make it sound like a conspiracy. It isn't, it's a business arrangement.'

The sound of his hollow laugh carried in the empty bar.

'A business arrangement, you say?' I couldn't break eye contact; he wouldn't let me. His gaze pushed deep into my mind, pushing my righteous annoyance off kilter. 'Ask your "recruits",' he continued. 'Ask them what they feel, what they were promised? What they believed?'

He pushed himself up with his right hand. 'This has nothing to do with business. The deceit makes it a conspiracy.' He stood tall, looking down on me.

I watched as he strode up to me and grabbed the hilt of the axe. Part of me wondered what he was going to do. The rest screamed at me to save myself.

I stayed put.

With almost superhuman strength, he pulled the weapon out of the column, held it up, turned and walked away. I finally let my pent-up breath loose and sank back to a more relaxed position. He wasn't going to kill me. Not just yet.

Great. Now what?

I watched him move behind the bar. He placed the axe on the old oaken counter, ripped his shirt, grabbed a bottle of something strong, pulled the stop out with his teeth and sloshed the liquid over the wound in his shoulder.

The restrained cry escaped through his clenched teeth. No wonder. The alcohol would burn like hell in the wound. But it would cleanse it. He still needed stitches though. Unlike the cuts his axe inflicted earlier on me. For a moment I reflected on how handy it was to be more than human and heal as we did.

The ex-priest turned and took a glass from the plank behind him. He poured a generous amount of the bourbon into it, then clamped the bottle under his left arm. With the glass in hand, he approached me again.

'Does your kind drink?' he asked.

'I do.' Hell, yeah. I thought. I do now.

He offered me the glass, which I accepted gingerly, then turned and walked back to where the table had initially been. He up righted one of the fallen chairs that still looked reasonably stable, propped it against the wall and sat down. His right hand grabbed the neck of the bottle and brought it up to his lips. He drank deeply of the ochre liquid.

I sipped mine carefully tasting the for me unfamiliar liquor, then threw the whole lot back into my throat. It burned a deep line down to my stomach. Not bad.

'Are we going to pick up where we left off?' The priest interrupted my thoughts. 'If so, you might need a new knife.'

'Is that what you want?'

'No,' he answered. 'I don't want to kill you. I want you to think. To feel.'

'To care?'

'If necessary, yes. I want you to find out what the truth is. Then, if you still stand by your Establishment, come back and kill me.'

He was daring me.

'Or try, at least.' He laughed again then turned his attention back to the bottle of bourbon.

I had been dismissed.

By a human.

I should be angry. But another emotion prevailed. Curiosity.

Something he said earlier stuck in my mind. "Ask the recruits." Ask them what they had been promised.

My whole life I had been brought up to believe the recruits had at least a semblance of choice in their destiny. I truly believed they knew what was awaiting them. Maybe not in detail. But they knew what we had was a temporary step in the road to their ultimate redemption. After they served their time in Purgatory, they would continue their journey to wherever they would go. Be it Heaven or Hell.

The thought crossed my mind the humans might not be the only ones with just part of the story.

I would have to find out. My rebellious curiosity compelled me.

This would not end well.

My hare-brained projects usually didn't.

I placed the glass on the floor, turned the lever on my amulet and teleported back to my own dimension.

Chapter Two

I hate teleporting. It screws up my body and mind.

I kept my eyes shut tight until I was sure my feet were completely on solid ground. The nausea rose and burned as it welled up from my stomach into my oesophagus—yes, our anatomy is much like yours—and threatened to enter my mouth. I took a deep breath and forced the vile liquid down again. I would not throw up. Not here. Not again.

I opened my eyes and concentrated on one spot in front of me while I focussed on slowing down the incessant spinning at my peripheral vision. Another unwelcome by-product of teleportation.

'Welcome back, Gabriel.' The voice was chirpy, happy, and because of that and the moment, very irritating. I compelled myself to act normal, as was expected of me.

'Thank you, Diana,' I answered as friendly as possible. It sounded synthetic to me, but her smile stayed radiant showing me she was blissfully unaware of my deceit.

'We missed you.' How to answer that? I just smiled.

I rolled my shoulders, clenched, and unclenched my

hands and took the first steps forward, still expecting my body to refuse my commands. As always, it reacted exactly as I wanted it to, at least on the outside. My stomach continued to protest. That would take a bit longer, and a glass of something strong to drink to get rid of the vile taste.

Now, to work.

I made my way from the teleportation centre out through the sliding doors into the bustle of our main city's streets. After the calm of the mountain village, the noise hit me like a sledgehammer. I zoned it out and walked onwards. I would have to report to my father sometime soon, all teleportation was registered and necessitated "paperwork". But not now. Now I wanted to get out of the city and visit one of the facilities where recruits were put to work. I would have to think of a reason, something that would allow me entry without ruffling any feathers. Once the recruits were sold, they were no longer in our charge. They had new owners, ones who were not happy with interference from anyone. I would have to pull some strings, use my family connections, after all I was "God's" son. That must account for something.

I retrieved my transport vehicle and headed out of town.

My first stop was our holding facility. This was where the recruits were housed after their reincarnation. The first few days they were disoriented and weak, as can be expected from the rather traumatic death experience. Here they recuperated and adapted to the new situation. After three days, the recruits were tagged, sorted, and sent to the holding pens where they awaited their final assignments. Okay. That's putting it nicely. They were sold to the highest bidder.

The atmosphere of the holding facility was subdued, the

colours soft and there were no loud noises or bright lights. Reincarnation wreaks havoc on the senses. Everything is exaggerated. This magnifies the sense of fear in the recruits. We needed calm, well acclimatised recruits for the sales. So, the first few days were reasonably enjoyable for them.

It was almost pleasant. Almost. The recruits were locked up—some even restrained to beds—depending on their state of mind. And it was temporary, a week at most.

I walked out to the holding pens. There the circumstances were different. Though still not bad, the comfort factor was a lot less. Twenty people of the same sex were kept in each pen. They had bunkbeds with flat mattresses and one or two blankets. All recruits were dressed in the same manner. Bright blue trousers and what you would call a sweatshirt. Sandals without socks. The temperature in our dimension was constant. There was a drop of two to three degrees during the night, but most of the time it was quite comfortable. We didn't have seasons, that was one of the things I really had to adapt to when I moved to your dimension on a more permanent basis.

I approached one of the holding pens containing the human age bracket thirty-to-forty. The occupants were spread out over the twenty-by-thirty metre block. Some sat or lay on their bunks, one or two were engaged in physical exercise like push-ups, the rest hung against the bars or sat on the floor.

I noticed that despite their shared predicament, the groups were still divided by race and skin colour. That never ceases to surprise me with you humans, that you hold on so desperately to something as shallow as the colour of someone's skin.

Even in the holding pens, there were invisible lines between the ethnic groups. All kept to their designated part of the same box. Stupid. It was also a characteristic we made use of in containing new recruits. That's why we mixed up the races. There was never one single ethnic group in a pen. That would be too dangerous for us, they might work together and then rebel against what must be dawning on them after they had been held here for a while.

Sure enough, one of the men standing at the bars gestured to me and I walked up to him. He was about six-foot-tall, reasonably well proportioned though he could use a bit more muscle on his frame. The creases in his brow and his nervous fidgeting showed his anxiety.

'You're obviously someone important here,' he started. I raised an eyebrow. 'I need to talk to someone high in the pecking order. Someone with power. Looks like you're my man.' His attempt to exude self-confidence failed miserably, it was no more than skin deep, his nervousness showing through.

He intrigued me. 'What do you want to talk about?' I humoured him.

'This.' He gestured around him at the pen and its inhabitants. 'What is this place?'

'This is a holding pen,' I answered honestly, interested in how the truth would work here.

'Holding for what?'

'What do you think?'

'I'm not sure. This place looks familiar, you all speak the same language as we do, but things are off. Where am I?'

'What was your last recollection?' I asked. 'Before you woke up in this facility?'

'It's a bit fuzzy. I remember being on the streets in Boston. I was on my way home from work. Then I felt an enormous blow to my head, and everything went black.'

'You died.' I explained harshly, closely observing his

reaction. His brow creased and hooded his nervous flitting eyes. He pulled his head back a bit while he continued to watch me. I kept my features calm and non-descriptive.

'I died?'

I nodded.

'So, what is this? Heaven?'

'Not exactly.'

'Not Hell. It can't be. I was a good Christian. I went to Church. I took care of others.' I saw sweat drops on his brow. He fidgeted with the bottom of his shirt, bundling the material in his fists, then letting it go again. He looked around at the other inhabitants of his pen, as though seeing them for the first time. His shoulders sank and he tried to be a small as possible.

'It's Purgatory.' I told him.

'Purgatory?'

'Yes. Isn't that what your priests told you? That this is a stop before you go to either Heaven or Hell.'

'I know what Purgatory is. But they said that was only for people who were on the edge. Not good enough for Heaven. A second-chance kind of place, so that you could still try to get to paradise. But I was a good man. I shouldn't be here.'

'All humans come here first.' The abject horror was visible in the tears that ran down his face.'

'It's not right. I was a good man,' he repeated. 'I shouldn't be here. I should go to Heaven. Not here. Not this.' His fidgeting increased. 'How long will I be here?'

I remained silent.

'No, no. it's not right. You must help me, please. I don't deserve this. Please.' He was crying full out now. Grasping for me through the bars of the pen. Others around him turned to see what the commotion was about.

They glanced at each other and then back to the crying man.

'Please. Please. Don't leave me here.' he cried as I turned to leave.

'No. No. You must help me. Please. I don't belong here.' His voice rose and his cries alerted the guards who came running to stop the ruckus. One of them glanced at me as I calmly walked away. I raised my eyebrow as he was about to say something. He changed his mind. He knew who I was. Here I had virtual immunity to do anything.

Handy, having an important family.

I walked onwards into the facility. The inhabitants of the holding pens all resembled each other. Most were young- and healthy-looking men. There was one holding pen with young women. But they usually didn't stay here long. Women were sold off quickly. Their futures were different. They were still put to work, but usually not the hard labour the men were destined to do until they dropped. Though whether that was an improvement was debatable.

At the last pen I saw customers walking around the cage commenting on specific recruits. The salesman jotted down which ones caught the buyer's interest, searched through his files on a handheld to offer background information and when sold, ticked the box next to the recruit's number.

Some of the recruits stared at the happenings without understanding. Others were savvier to what was going on and anger contorted their faces into scowls.

No matter, this group's destiny was the same, the mines. Most of them wouldn't last more than what corresponds to about ten years in human terms. After that they were retired.

Another nice way of saying put-down.

Exterminated.

I'd seen enough here. I wanted to move on to the mines and factories.

That was dangerous territory, even for me. The holding pens were owned by my family. The mines were not. We had no power there. Other than that, we were the major supplier of their manual labour.

The owners of the mines and factories had no reason to let me in and talk to any of the recruits, or grunts, as they called them.

I was counting on my powers of persuasion. I mean I'd convinced Father Ignatius not to kill me, hadn't I? Or had he convinced me to question what I had been brought up to believe? Whatever. I needed to talk to a recruit who had been here longer and was living the hell this place could be. I wanted to know what he had been told. And whether he still believed.

'You want to what?'

'I want to talk to one of your grunts.'

'Why?' The director of the factory was a rough looking man. Big, a full beard, barrel-chested, his feet planted squarely on the floor in front of his desk. This was clearly his domain. His small, pinched eyes locked onto mine, resulting in an uncomfortable tingle that ran up my spine. My idea looked quite rash at that moment. I'd clearly underestimated the dangers of this choice or overestimated my charm. Probably both.

'Research,' I answered in the same short arrogant tone.

'What?'

'I want to verify a new idea I have to gather even more young grunts.' I spun my carefully crafted scam. 'In my travels I've encountered a new movement in the supply dimension that could provide a rush of new exceptional quality grunts. Stronger ones that will last longer. Ultimately, this will not only benefit us, but you as well. You'll have more for your money.' I could almost see the cogs in his brain working as he processed the information.

'I didn't see a communication on that.' He was still sceptic.

'No, and you won't.' I let a small hint of irritation flow into my voice. 'Not yet. I'm investigating this myself before I involve my father and the Council. It's a water-tight plan, with enormous potential. I don't want anyone else to know about it yet. Especially my brothers. That's why I came to you. You are our most loyal customer, and I value your patronage. If you help me with this, I'll make sure you're well-rewarded for your efforts, once we bring it to my father.' I emphasised the "we" part. He picked that up. I let it stew for a few minutes. I'm very comfortable with silence, so he didn't faze me with that.

He smiled slyly. 'Ahh, the competition.' I had him, hook, line, and sinker. Everyone knew about the rivalry between me and my brothers, so a reference to that made it all sound credible. He nodded.

I slapped him on the shoulder in a show of camaraderie. He looked so smug. The bastard. I chose him not because of his trustworthiness, but because of his greed. This man was brutal, unscrupulous, totally without empathy toward anything other than his own interests, which were mainly monetary. Therefore, he was fertile ground for my plans. One thing you can always count on is someone's greed.

I followed him out of the building and into the yard. He stopped at a door to the foundry and handed me a safe-suit button. I placed it on my chest and pressed the centre. A light blue forcefield appeared and surrounded me. I looked over at the foundry owner. He was protected in the same manner.

'Just in case,' he commented. 'I wouldn't want my new partner to be damaged in any way.' That smug smile again.

So, we were partners now, were we? Hell, if he had to believe that, then okay with me. I would work out the damage control later. Everyone hated his guts, a fatal "accident" wouldn't be a stretch to anyone's imagination. He had it coming. But that was for later. Now I had to talk to at least one of his recruits.

He keyed a combination in the lock panel and the big lead door moved slowly to the left, exposing what could only be described as pure Hell. The noise hit me first. The incessant thumps and screeching of the heavy machinery assailed my ears even through the protective suit. I knew it would be much worse outside the forcefield. Slowly, my eyes adjusted to the sharp flashes of light, perpetual smoke, and fumes in the cavernous space.

The door closed behind me, and I followed the director deeper into the workplace. Everything about this place was oppressive. I'd never experienced anything like it. I was shocked. We delivered the workforce, the recruits—or slaves as Father Ignatius had called them—we never bothered ourselves with what happened to them afterwards. We were supply, not manufacturing. They left our facilities in good health. Nothing of which was visible anymore in the grunts I saw around me.

The constant hammering was occasionally broken by screams. I turned to the direction of one and could just make out a grunt-master as he swung an electric baton hard into the lower back of a half-naked human. The master was protected by the same forcefield as I was. The grunt wasn't. He wore bright red trousers and thick boots, but no upper garments or protection. The seeping welts on his back and shoulders were clear signs of the fumes' toxicity and big blisters adorned his face and hands. Still the grunt-master pushed him harder.

The director noticed my attention to what for him was normal working procedure. He cocked his head in question and raised one eyebrow. I shrugged my indifference. I had to keep up an image of coldness and push the surprise and growing aversion to the background. It would not do to show my distaste.

I turned back to him and smiled slightly, bridging the distance between us easily.

'Who can I talk to?' I pushed.

'Follow me. You wanted to talk to the young ones, right?'

I nodded. 'One of the grunts who has been here a while.'

The grunts in this hall were all about middle-aged in human terms. Somewhere between forty and fifty-five, nearing the end of their productivity. After that they were discarded. That would make the jobs here the easier work.

I felt tingles go up my spine again. This was nothing like what I had expected. The grunt-master's absolute disdain for human life angered me. Okay, call me naïve, but like you, we in our ivory towers were immune to what was needed to keep our cities running and our luxurious living standard up to par. The dirty truth of what it took to do just that was a guarded secret. One that we—as the ruling class —didn't have to bother ourselves with.

We looked the other way.

It struck me again how many similarities there were between our world and yours.

Especially the bad ones.

The feelings of apprehension and revulsion grew with every step I took deeper into the factory. The behaviour of the grunt-master in the first hall was clearly the norm here. Everywhere I looked I saw humans maltreated and abused. Most of them were covered in sores and sometimes even open wounds. Their stance was one of abject resolution to their fate. What touched me most were the eyes. They were blank. Emotionless mostly. Dead. This sent chills up my spine and a sharp pain to the rear of my head as realisation of what I was part of started to seep into my previously calm demeanour.

The director finally stopped in front of a group of younger grunts. He called out to the three grunt-masters, and they herded five men to stand in front of me. They were all young. No older than thirty, though their eyes were ancient. All except one. He looked at me with absolute disdain. The grunt-master had to prod him with the baton to stand in line.

He locked eyes with me. I saw the rebellion.

The challenge.

So, I took it.

This was someone who might tell me what I needed to know. I turned to the director, nodded to the rebellious grunt, and was rewarded with another raised eyebrow.

'The rest look dead,' I commented callously. He smiled. The bastard.

'I want to talk to him alone,' I shocked the director.

'That won't be possible. I will be there. For your protection.'

'I don't need protection. I can take care of myself. Just restrain him.' I made sure my voice portrayed strength and a clear message I would not take "no" for an answer. I stared him in the eye.

He relented and told the grunt-master to cuff the grunt and bring him to an area where we could talk.

The man was shackled hands and feet, and a restraint-collar was placed around his neck. The director gave me the remote for the collar and a baton.

'Just in case,' he sniggered.

I nodded and took the objects.

The director and the grunt-master left, turning twice to observe us as they walked away.

I waited until they were out of sight, then took the grunt by the arm and walked him thirty metres to the right into a big open space, out from under the cameras and microphones. I didn't want anyone listening in on my conversation. Especially not my new "partner."

'What's your name?' I asked him.

'I don't have a name, only a number.' His voice was deep and strong. There was an edge to it; the rebellious nature I saw earlier.

'Your name in your previous life.'

He looked at me. His stare cut deep. There was hatred there. A lot of it.

'What's yours?'

I decided to humour him. 'Gabriel.'

'Gabriel huh? You're one of the sons. An "angel".' He spat out the last word and observed me closely. 'What are you doing here? Slumming?'

My initial reaction was to lash out in anger at the lack of respect, but I deduced it wouldn't get me the answers I wanted. Besides, he had a point.

'I want to know what you were told in your previous life about what would happen when you died and came to this place.'

'Why?'

'Because I want to know the truth.'

He huffed, disbelief clear in the contempt in his eyes. I waited in silence.

'Peter Belt.' He finally answered my question. I nodded my acknowledgement. 'What do you want to know?' I guess he'd given me the benefit of the doubt.

'I want to know about your previous life.'

'Before I died?' he raised an eyebrow in distrust.

'Yes.' I nodded to encourage him.

'Anything specific?'

'What was your occupation? What were your beliefs? What was your dealings with the Church?'

He stared at me, trying to gauge my motivation. 'I was an emergency physician at the Queen Elizabeth hospital in London. It's a major trauma centre. We had a lot of stabbings and abuse victims on a daily basis. It was a violent place in a violent time.' He started his monologue.

'I was married, with two small children and lived in a modest house near the hospital. We were a Christian family. My parents brought me up to believe in God and to lead a good life helping others less fortunate. My brother was a priest. Shows you how seriously we took our faith. My wife and I continued the tradition and brought our children up within the Catholic Church. We had a good life. It was hard at times, especially because of all my extra hours, but Melissa never complained. She was proud of my commitment to help others. It was what we wanted to do.'

He observed me all the time during his speech. I didn't interrupt, just nudged him onwards with nods.

'My family went to service every Sunday. I went when I could—when I wasn't working. We did a lot for charities and gave royally when the Church needed extra funds. All because of our faith.'

'What did the Church promise you?' I asked what I really wanted to know.

'They promised us our good deeds would be weighed in our favour after our life ended. Frankly, that we would go to Heaven. We would be rewarded. That wasn't why we did it, we would have helped anyway. It was what we did.'

'How did you die?' I continued to probe.

'Ironically, I was stabbed at the hospital, while on duty. We received a red-phone alert that multiple victims with stab wounds were coming in. There had been a massive fight on the south-west side of London West-End. Two gangs in a turf war. We prepared for an influx of patients but hadn't counted on the war flaring up in the emergency ward. Nine patients were brought into A&E. All of them badly wounded. We were engrossed in stopping the bleeding on two of the worst cases when another group of gang members entered the A&E and attacked any opposing gang members they could find. They were heavily armed and just stabbed and killed everyone on the gurneys. It was diabolical. Some of us jumped up and tried to stop them. That was when they turned on us. I was stabbed by two of the killers. I felt one knife going into my chest and up to my heart. I knew I was done for.'

I remained silent. There wasn't much I could say.

'That was the last thing I remembered. Then I woke up in a hospital of sorts and ended up here.'

'You knew you died?' I asked softly.

'Yes. Clearly the wounds were fatal. More so because of the pandemonium at the A&E. It was a done deal.' He was all professional. I saw a glimpse of the doctor he had been.

'What were your thoughts when you woke up in the reincarnation facility?'

'Is that what you call it? the reincarnation facility?' I

nodded. 'Makes it sound very clinical.' His words bit deep into me. It was what I'd asked for, but that didn't make it what I wanted to hear. Part of me had hoped Father Ignatius would be proved wrong.

'What my thoughts were?' he repeated my question. 'I was confused. I remembered what happened to me, and I knew I had to be dead. But first it resembled a hospital so much, I thought I'd made it after all and was still alive. Then it slowly dawned on me that I hadn't. I had no wounds. No stitches. It was as though nothing had happened. That wasn't possible. One of the "doctors" confirmed my death and this was the beginning of my new existence.'

'I concluded I'd made it to Heaven.' He laughed. It was cold, emotionless. 'How wrong I was.'

He looked me squarely in the eye. I stopped myself from reacting, instead I asked my next question.

'Did the Church tell you about Purgatory. That there might be a holding station before you went to Heaven or Hell?'

'They did. But they also said that was only for people who hadn't believed. Not people like us. Not God-fearing Christians. We were promised Heaven. A direct one-way ticket. No other stops. Just Heaven.'

'You hadn't expected this?' I asked redundantly.

He laughed again. 'Are you kidding me?' I shook my head. He was clear.

'What's your faith now?'

'Non-existent. I know now it was all a massive scam. I was deceived. I lived my life according to lies. I strove to be a good man and follow the doctrine of what I thought was a Holy Church. Instead, I was hustled like an idiot. There is no Heaven. No reward. All of it was a pack of lies.'

'Could you have misunderstood what they promised?' I tried desperately to salvage some of my family's and our business' integrity.

He looked at me incredulously. Anger coloured his face bright red, and his fists were balled.

'Misunderstood?' He almost shouted. 'No, there was no misunderstanding. They scammed us. And I know the Church is involved in all this.' His eyes blazed and his fists clenched and unclenched. His breathing was shallow and quick. The anger threatening to overpower him, but he continued.

'When I was in the holding pens, I saw a priest come in. He wasn't one of us, not a slave. He was treated very differently. Deferentially even. He came to the pens to talk to us. Tried to get us to accept our fate. He wanted us to believe this was just another step on our way to Heaven. He urged us to tolerate what was happening to us as part of God's masterplan. Then he went off to his own home in this new world. He was rewarded for his work in recruiting us.'

He took a deep breath. 'I knew this was wrong, and then one of the grunt-masters boasted about the "business". How the Christian Church was their supplier of souls. Of slave labour. How they had to make us believe, otherwise they couldn't reincarnate us. He bragged about how well it worked and how successful this religion was. Your religion. Your family. He was proud of it. Proud of what you were doing. He didn't care what it did to us. We were just cattle to be sold to the highest bidder and used until we dropped.'

I stayed silent. My own internal rage built with his words. This was not what I had been led to believe. I came here fully expecting to be proved right and Father Ignatius wrong. I truly believed the recruits knew what they were facing before they came, and that they still came willingly. Now all that was in serious doubt.

I still couldn't accept that the lies went further than the human recruiters. If this was true, then the recruits were not the only ones who had been lied to. Our whole civilisation was built on lies. My beliefs. My values. What I did for a living. All of it.

'This is not what I signed up for,' Peter added, pulling me out of my internal reverie. 'I was a good man. I put my life in service to others and to the Church. I prayed. I raised my children to believe in God. I buried many people believing they went to a better place. To Heaven. To peace ever-after. And what did that bring me?' He gestured around him as far as the chains would allow. 'This.'

His earlier anger was replaced by deflation.

'Hell.'

We talked for another ten minutes. None of it got any better. He was clear in his accusations. Transparent in who he believed were to blame for the deceit he felt. The Church and us. My family. Our business.

I was shocked by the revelations. But mostly by the intense hatred Peter had for his former faith. He was bitter. Immensely angry. What surprised me was that his rage was focussed more on the Church than on us. They lied to him. They were the true scammers and so ultimately the ones to blame.

The intensity of his fury, coupled with the confusion of the other recruits in the holding pens, pulled at my own convictions. Were we the devils Peter portrayed us to be?

There was only one place I could really find out.

Time to visit my father.

Chapter Three

He did it again.

That annoying trait my father had where he totally ignored me.

He stood with his back to me, seemingly immersed in the documents he was reading. He knew I was there. After all, he called for me.

He cold-shouldered me. It wasn't just me, he did it with all of us. All his children, maybe occasionally with the exception of Michael.

How long would he leave me waiting?

Too long. That's for sure. My first inclination was to turn around and leave. Fuck this. But that would be a major lack of respect on my part. And besides it wasn't in my best interests right now.

My meeting with the recruits unnerved me. I didn't want to believe what stared me in the face. Surely, we weren't that shallow and callous? As children, my father told us the recruits knew about Purgatory. They knew they had to go through a stint here before they could move on to whichever paradise they believed in. They came willingly.

Maybe I was naive. But it made it more acceptable. It was easier to stick our heads in the sand than face what we truly were doing.

Okay, you're right.

It's worse than naive.

I see that now in hindsight. But not then. At that time in my life, I clung to the conviction my family was inherently good. That we—and by proxy—me, weren't doing anything wrong, even though a niggling voice at the back of my mind questioned this constantly.

Now, there was no way I could hide from what was happening. Not anymore. Not after my conversation with Peter. But old beliefs are difficult to let go, so I gave my father the benefit of the doubt. Maybe there was a perfectly good explanation. One that would allow me to continue my faith in our family.

Dad finally graced me with his attention.

'Gabriel,' he acknowledged me. 'Good to see you. I understand you came back from the twelfth dimension earlier today.' It was his way of telling me he was displeased at my tardiness. Though not an actual rule, my father expected his children to report to him immediately after their return from their allotted dimensions. I nodded but remained silent, not taking the bait. His eyes bore into me, daring me to say something that would get me into trouble. It wouldn't take much. Father was frankly a despot. His word was law. Everything—and especially the family— revolved around him and his wishes.

The edges of his lips curled up in the semblance of a smile. Secretly, I think he enjoyed my rebellious nature. It was a challenge. And my father never shied away from one of those. It might even have reminded him of himself in younger years. Father was what he called a visionary. I expected it to be a synonym for rebel.

'Are you going to make me wait?' he asked with a combination of anger and humour in his tone. 'How was it in the twelfth?'

'As it always is. A lot of strife and violence.'

'Good. That should net us more assets.' The callousness was normal for him, but it registered with me more than usual.

He drilled me about the situation on Earth, specifically on the growing unrest between races. My answers met his approval.

'What about the Islam fundamentalism?' he asked. 'We expected a surge in the Jihad violence. Did you notice that?'

'I did,' I answered, more and more uneasy with the laconic way my father spoke of the violence that was so devastating to humans. 'There have been multiple suicide attacks in the western countries. One in the UK, two in France and another in Denmark.' This wasn't new to him; Father was intimately knowledgeable about the twelfth dimension. He made sure he knew all the details. Whether that was business curiosity or because he didn't trust us, was never clear to me. Probably both. Dad never did things by half.

'And the reaction?' He was most interested in what the terrorism would fuel.

'Everyone is still in shock at the moment. Though there are some angry reactions coming from several groups.'

'What is the chance it will escalate?'

'About fifty-fifty.' I watched his reactions closely. There was no empathy there at all. Nothing. Just business interest.

A loaded silence ensued. Father eyed me carefully. I was

acting very strange in his eyes, even for me. He never had to pull information out of me. I would offer more than necessary in my childish attempt to look good in my father's eyes. All of this was lacking. As was any enthusiasm on my part.

'And the rogue priest?' he asked. 'Is he taken care of?'

'No.' I stated resolutely. He raised an eyebrow. 'The leads were incorrect. I didn't find him.' I tried to look him in the eye, but he noticed some reluctance. He knew I was lying.

'How difficult is it to find one priest?'

'More difficult than it looks.' There, my rebellious nature resurfaced. Much to his amusement.

'I was close, very close. But he slipped through the cracks. He's a master of concealment. And there are many who shield him.'

'I need him neutralised.' He said the words slowly. Emphasising every syllable. 'Should I send Michael?' The ultimate insult.

'No. I will return and take care of it.'

He put down the parchment and observed me closely as he approached. He walked around me, looking me up and down. His face close and hard. I felt tingles go up and down my spine. He finally stopped in front of me, very aware of the impact he had on my nerves.

'What else did you find out?'

'What do you mean?'

'There is something bothering you. Maybe the same thing that made you visit the holding pens this morning.' I shouldn't be surprised. Father made it his business to know everything. And of course, as his son, I was quite conspicuous.

I stayed mute, not sure how to continue. I hated the way I seemed to shrink under his gaze. He unnerved me. Always had, and probably always will. I forced myself to relax and breathe slowly and deeply.

'That bad huh?' He noticed. Of course, he did. 'Okay Gabriel. I feel some criticism coming. Out with it. What is on your mind?'

I looked at him. Not for the first time, I was astounded by the aura surrounding this man. He wasn't exceptionally tall or well built. His dark brown hair and neatly trimmed beard were nothing special, his features mediocre, forgettable. All except the eyes. They were what made him the person he was. His eyes were the window to his soul and, like them, his soul was black and putrid.

'I spoke to one of the recruits in the holding area.'

He raised an eyebrow.

'He was confused. They all were. They didn't seem to know why they were here, or even where they were. They had other expectations.' I measured every word, my nerves reeling.

He remained silent.

I took a deep breath.

'Then I went to the forge.' There. I'd said it.

'You did what?' Anger flashed over his face. I wasn't sure whether that was at my actions or the fact that I surprised him.

'I spoke with a grunt.'

'Why would you do that?' There was genuine surprise under the rage.

'I wanted to know what they were led to believe before their death. What their religious leaders told them to expect. I wanted to know if they were prepared for, well, for here.'

'Why? Why does it matter what they were told? They believed. That's the only thing that's important for us. Anything else is not our concern.'

'You always taught us they came willingly. That it was a sort of contract they signed with their faith. They would put in their years and after that they were free to continue their journey to wherever they were going.'

As I spoke the words out loud, they sounded childish, even to me. Unbelievably naive. I saw the same thought reflected in his face, in the slight upturn of his lips in contempt. I stopped talking. I knew I'd made a fool of myself. In my father's eyes, that was a major sin.

'Your strange fascination with humans is unnatural, Gabriel,' he stated after two excruciating minutes of silence. 'They are no more than a commodity to us. A product. Naturally, we need to make sure they are the best possible quality, so we take care of them. But that is the extent of our concern. We do not interfere with how they are recruited or harvested. I am astounded that you perceive them as more than an asset. It does not show good business sense. I am disappointed in you. Why did you want to know all this?'

I was surprised. He'd turned the whole situation around to me. Made it my problem, not his. I hadn't prepared myself for that question.

'It sounded wrong to me,' I blurted out.

'Be more precise. You're not talking sense.'

'That the recruits were promised Heaven, just to get them to believe.'

'We are not responsible for what the humans tell their flock. We inform the recruiters. They know what to expect. If they chose not to educate their congregation, then that is not our problem.' He turned away from me and walked back to his desk.

The ease with which he dismissed me, and my concerns, ruffled my feathers again. I felt the anger rise through my spine and stab at the back of my skull. I stood up straight, the heat in my face was a dead give-a-way of my increasing rage at my father's treatment. I had a legitimate point, and he waved it away as insignificant. Like he always did.

'Isn't that too easy?' I threw caution to the wind.

He stopped. Slowly, he turned back to face me.

The anger in his eyes registered. But I was too far gone now and determined to make my point.

'You wave away the deceit as though none of the blame rests with us. Yes, their Church leaders deceive them, but they don't do squat without your approval. You know. You have always known.'

There was no stopping me now. 'You always said our family didn't interfere with the lives of the humans in their dimension. We had no hand in when they died.'

He stared at me. I almost shivered under the intensity.

'Is that true?' I asked.

'You doubt me?' His voice was cold, each syllable crystal clear. 'Are you calling me a liar?'

He was fuming. Not at what I had discovered but at my audacity to doubt him and question his decisions.

'No. I'm not. Not if you aren't.'

He stared at me. I felt the effect in every cell in my body. My gut turned over and bile rose in my throat.

'Who do you think you are?' he almost whispered. My heart sank. I'd really done it now.

'Get out of my sight,' he ordered.

That effectively shut off any further conversation we might have.

I realised he hadn't answered my question.

Not in so many words.

But it was clear.

It occurred to me my Father was becoming more and

more comfortable in his role as "God". He extended it into our world. Here, as well as in the twelfth dimension, his word was law.

He felt elevated above everyone else and was starting to believe in some form of divinity on his part. As such, he strove to lead the company—and in its extension the family —as an autocrat. He was the only one who decided on anything important.

He was convinced he should rule. Not just your world, but ours too.

I saw it in the way he treated us, his children. In his megalomania and how he named us all after the Christian angels. He formed us to resemble what he believed your angels would look like. Though where he got the idea that we would be anything like what the Bible preaches, is an anomaly to me. It wasn't even of our world.

He ruled our family with an iron fist, showing before then unheard of tyranny over his prodigy. And now he was expanding this to the Council that effectively ruled our world. He was planning a coup. Maybe not a violent one, but a coup never-the-less.

I finally understood my father would not be content until he really was a God.

In your dimension and ours.

Chapter Four

'You're back.'

The priest continued to walk past me, unperturbed by my sudden appearance.

'Obviously.' I picked up my pace and caught up with him. We walked in silence for a few minutes. His strides were long and powerful, befitting the man, and I had to push myself to keep up.

'You expected me. You're not surprised?'

He shook his head.

This was rapidly becoming a very one-sided conversation. His short or physical answers were getting to me. I'd forgotten how irritating the man could be.

He stopped walking just as I was about to say something I would probably have regretted and turned to me. His eyes bore into mine.

'What did they say?' He knew. Somehow, he knew. So I didn't have to answer.

'I'm not convinced,' I answered.

'No, but you have doubts. You talked to one of your "recruits."'

'I did.'

His lips curled into a smile. I didn't have to tell him what the outcome of the conversation had been. He knew. I fully expected an "I told you so." But he just smiled again and continued his stroll up the mountain.

I was surprised, frustrated, and irritated at the same time.

'And I spoke to my family,' I added in an attempt to get his attention. 'They made it sound so natural. As though nothing was wrong.'

'But you know there is.'

I nodded.

'And that brought you back.' It was a statement. He had always known what I would find if I dug deep enough. He knew my discoveries would substantiate my doubts about my own actions in the service of my family. And about what The Establishment and my family were.

He'd sensed my rebellious nature and used my own curiosity against me. Kudos to him.

Part of me hated he was right and that he had so obviously manipulated me in a certain direction. Another part felt liberated.

'Where do we go from here?' I asked.

'We?' He raised an eyebrow.

'Yes. We,' I answered. 'Don't act so surprised. You know I'm part of this now. Part of whatever it is you're planning to do to bring down The Establishment. We should join forces. Our goals are the same.'

'And what makes you think I want a partner?' His stare unnerved me. The man was intense.

'Inside knowledge of your enemy is an enormous advantage. I can give you that.'

'I work alone.' He was resolute.

'Not anymore, you don't,' I stated with a calmness I didn't feel inside.

He observed me closely. 'You seem to have had a massive change of heart. What brought that on? It must be more than our tussle and your meetings with recruits?'

I thought about it for a moment. It was a question I asked myself many times in the past days.

'I have,' I answered. 'I've thought about it a lot. Not just in the past days. It has been something that bothered me for a very long time. My mother would say that it's my nature; to always back the underdog. I expect it also has something to do with my aversion to my father. It probably wouldn't be an understatement to say I hate him.'

The priest just glared at me. His stare caused goose-bumps to run up and down my arms. It also compelled me to keep talking, against my better judgement. I felt like it was as much an explanation to myself as it was to him.

'I'm the rebel in the family,' I continued. 'My father is a tyrant. He is the sole power in the clan and as such not used to being questioned, especially not by family. I am the second eldest son. Only Michael is older, and he is exactly how he should be according to my father—loyal to a fault. He will never doubt any decree father issues. He follows orders blindly. Me, I don't. I'll challenge everything, just out of principle. It's never made me popular with him or any of my family. More often than not, the whole family suffered because of my stubbornness.' He continued to stare at me. The silence was as unnerving as any answer he could have given.

'I guess I always knew something was wrong and what we did was morally repulsive. I just never wanted to acknowledge it because of the ramifications.' My admittance felt like an ice-cold hand had gripped my heart.

'And now. Have you thought this through?' he asked. 'This will have lasting implications for you. You are betraying your family. They will not take that lightly.' No sugar coating there.

'I fully expect them to try and kill me after what I'm going to do.'

He raised his eyebrows. 'And what exactly is that?'

'I'm going to expose them to your world. Show this scam for what it is. And ultimately, stop the recruitment.'

'That will not make you daddy's favourite,' he chuckled.

'Quite the opposite.' I smiled. This actually felt good. 'And the man can hold a grudge like no other.'

'Why?' He observed me closely again.

'What do you mean, why?'

'Why do you want to do this? Why will you face your father's wrath?' He genuinely seemed surprised.

I took a deep breath and voiced what had been eating away at me. 'Because I hate liars. And not only that; may father made me one too.'

'So, what do I call you?' I asked.

We were in a shack on the side of the mountain. Apparently, this was the priest's destination. The rough unshaven wood on the walls and the dirt floor emphasised the lack of comfort in this four-by-six-metre construction. The window holes—barely covered with old plastic—were hardly a deterrent to the cold wind and rain or snow depending on the seasons. I couldn't image anyone actually living here, but the bed with a thin mattress and threadbare blanket belied that. To the right of the bed stood a small table with a single mug and a bottle of water. I couldn't see any cooking utensils and the only indication of a fire had been a ring of blackened stones outside, a few metres from the cabin.

'You don't want to be called Father Ignatius anymore.' That earned me a dark look. 'What will it be? Iggy? Ig? What?'

His eyes bore into me. Quite uncomfortable. But I waited it out.

'Jonah,' he finally said.

'Your original name?'

He nodded.

'Jonah,' I echoed. 'Or maybe Joe?'

His scowl said it all. 'Or not. Jonah it is,' I declared for the moment. 'You can call me Gabriel.'

'I know.'

Okay, that was the end of that conversation. My new partner was a man of few words. I tried to keep up an exchange, get to know each other, but was constantly rewarded with short and brusque answers if any. I'm extrovert by nature, Jonah wasn't. At least not with me. We sat in silence in the small room. Me on the bed and him on the floor with his back to the wall, impervious to the rough surface. I looked around. Nothing more to see. I tried again.

'We need a plan.'

'That's exactly why I don't work with a partner,' he stated angrily.

'What?'

'Your immediate assumption I don't have a plan. How arrogant can you get? Did you seriously think I was just winging it?'

Actually, yes. But I didn't say that out loud.

'Okay. So, what's your plan?' I asked instead.

'My plan?'

'Your plan.' I urged him to enlighten me.

'Well,' he began. 'My plan is to… Well, to kill all the kingpins.'

'And do you know who they are?'

'The Cardinals and Bishops to start with.'

'All of them?'

'Yes.' His face turned bright red with anger and irritation.

'Even the ones who are not in any way involved in The Establishment?' I kept up my barrage of retorts.

'Aren't they all?' He seemed surprised.

I shook my head.

'Then only the ones who are.' He was tired of the exchange. His eyes were dark under his creased brow, and I knew I was once again on thin ice.

'And how will you know?' I pushed on.

'I'll know.'

'Yes. Well, maybe it would be better to have a more structured way of choosing your targets,' I said. 'I know where I can find out who the members of The Establishment are. And maybe more importantly, who aren't. We don't want to kill innocents. That will allow the "good" ones to continue their work.'

'I'm not convinced that there are innocents,' he said sullenly.

'There are,' I stated resolutely. 'There are genuinely good people in the Church. In all religions.'

'And you can find out who?' He didn't sound convinced, but there was curiosity there. I could work with that.

'I can. I know a good deal, because of my previous

communications with Establishment members. For the others, I'll go back home and investigate, while I still can.'

He cocked his head in puzzlement.

'When my father finds out I've switched sides, he will not be happy. Availability to any information will be closed for me. Not to mention that he will put a price on my head.'

Chapter Five

It was a short trip.

One I will never forget.

Neither will my family.

As soon as I set foot in the teleportation room, I noticed the hushed whispering of the technicians. They looked at me and then all turned back to their work in an attempt to keep up an appearance of normality. One slowly took hold of a communicator and turned his back on me.

'Welcome back, Gabriel.' The same voice that always welcomed me back came through the intercom, only this time it missed the normal warmth and happy tone. Sure, she tried to add it, but it sounded artificial. Fake enthusiasm.

I took note of it, answered as I normally would and calmly made my way out of the facility. I would not give anyone cause to doubt my commitment to the company and my family—not yet. I had to convince everyone I was still very much on board if I wanted any chance of success for my new quest. It would be a challenge, especially after my last run-in with my father. To keep up appearances I went on my happy way, greeting everyone as I normally would.

During the day, I met up with my mother, siblings, and co-workers, exchanged small talk and was constantly monitored by an intense-looking Michael. I deduced Father had shared our last conversation with my brother. The way people reacted to me, I guess just about everyone knew we parted on less than friendly terms. I had the reputation of being a rebel, a difficult son who questioned everything. You'd think they were all used to it. For the first time ever, I think I went too far. The ripples in the way family and employees alike approached me was tantamount to the impact my insubordination had caused. I would have to be very, very careful and change tactics. It was quite unconventional that anyone questioned my father, my siblings wouldn't have dared, so that was suspect, and then of course, their scepticism wasn't so far-fetched.

I attended the family dinner that evening as though nothing was wrong. I surprised Michael by joining a conversation about recruitment targets and even suggested new tactics to increase recruitment in the under-twenty group by encouraging racialism.

Later that evening I saw him speak to my father and the old man's face turned to me. I smiled and raised my glass. He acknowledged me with a slight nod of his head, but I could see he still wasn't convinced. I might have to stay longer to waylay any lingering suspicions. He knew how stubborn I could be. But did he believe I would sacrifice my family and my status for anything as trivial as humans? I don't think so. He wouldn't, so he automatically assumed I wouldn't either.

Michael took the seat next to me during dinner, quite strange as we don't get along and usually avoid each other's company like the plague. I raised an eyebrow but left it at that and turned to speak to my uncle Jacob. We had an animated discussion on the merits of teleportation.

'When was your last trip?' Michael interrupted our conversation. As though he didn't know.

'I came back this morning,' I answered happily.

'You went to the twelfth dimension again?'

I nodded and smiled.

'What for?' Finally, a real question he didn't already have answers to. 'You were there earlier this week.'

'I wanted to find out what The Establishment taught the recruits.' I decided to tell a version of the truth.

'What for?'

'I've noticed a sharp decline in young recruits for Christianity. If you compare this with the Islamic religion, then we're doing something wrong. They recently had a massive influx of fanatical young men and women. We need the same.' I had his interest, though the way he cocked his head showed me he wasn't falling for it just yet. I had to turn up the greed factor. That always worked with Michael, he was a chip off the old block in that way.

My fantasy went into overdrive.

'That is all down to the way the religion recruits their people.' I continued. 'We can hardly go out and ask Arand, he's not going to help us recruit more. I decided the best place to look was The Establishment itself. They're responsible for the supply. I wanted to know what they are doing to increase the numbers. Turns out it's hardly anything. They're too passive; waiting for the recruits to come to them, instead of actively going out and convincing young humans. This is detrimental to our business. We need more control over how they convince especially young people to believe.' He nodded slightly.

'I went to our holding pens a few days ago, to talk with recruits.' His face clouded over. Exactly like dad's had when I spoke to him.

'Anyway, they told me they were promised Heaven. Nothing about Purgatory or anything like that. They also informed me the Church hadn't actively recruited them. It was more of a family thing. The parents pass their faith on to the children.'

'That's nothing new,' contempt showed through.

'No, it isn't. But if you look at the Islamic recruits, especially the fundamentalistic ones, the recruiting is not done by the parents. Oh sure, they do the basic work enrolling them into Islam, but it's a handful of fanatical Imams that push the young men into fanaticism. They go out and search for the vulnerable and lost young men and bring them into the fold. We need to learn from that. We cannot rely on the parents. Not if we want young, strong recruits. There are more than enough young men searching for a purpose in their lives. They are distanced from their families and the goals and beliefs of their ancestors. Often, they are unemployed, have massive financial problems and low self-esteem. They need a new goal. Something to fight for. And if all goes well, something to die for. Like with the Islamic Caliphate.'

I pushed the last hook home. 'There is another major advantage to leveraging the fanatical scenario.' I gave him a few seconds to let this land. I was on a roll.

He cocked his head in question, not about to grace me with a verbal one.

'The fundamentalist not only believe more intently, but they also recruit others themselves, and they are much more violent, regularly killing their own if they are not fanatical enough in their opinion.' I paused for effect.

'So, you see, brother. It's a win-win situation all round for us. We get better recruits, and more of them, if we push The Establishment to copy the Islamic fundamentalistic tactics.'

'You've been thinking about this a lot, obviously.'

'I have.'

'Why now? You've never shown an interest in advancing the family business. What's changed? Why now?'

'Are you seriously criticising the fact that I am finally doing what you and father have been pushing me to do for centuries?' I asked exasperated.

'Not criticising.' he added, watching my indignation closely. 'Just curious, why now?'

'Why not?' I turned the question around.

'You argued with father last time you were here. About the same thing. Then you were more concerned with the human's side of the equation.'

'Yes, I was.' I answered much to his surprise. 'But what father said resonated with me, and when I returned to the twelfth, I took a better look at humanity. I observed how they treated each other. How they lied and betrayed their own.'

'Now I see that lies and deceit are part and parcel of human beings. It is inherent to the species. Not something we introduced. The responsibility does not lie with us. We were truthful in the information we gave The Establishment and their leaders. What they did with it after that is not our fault or, for that matter, our business. If the humans want to betray their own kind, then that is their prerogative. I had a childish ideology that I could save a species that doesn't want to be rescued. Compassion of any kind from my side would be redundant.'

He nodded again but refrained from comment.

I resisted the urge to keep talking. One of the biggest mistakes most people make when not being completely honest is to continue talking long past the point of persuasion. I didn't make that mistake. I shut up and observed Michael with a slight smile on my face.

He finally stopped trying to read me. 'It seems you've had a revelation.' I nodded as expected. 'As long as you have the family's best interests at heart.' He had to have the last word.

'Always,' I answered, my face stern and reverent, as he would expect.

We chatted for a while on how I thought we might be able to achieve maximal recruiting until he tired of the after-dinner conversation and left to speak to others. I turned my attention to my uncle and niece across the table and laughed at the antics of her young son.

An hour later found me still sat at the table, my hands around a glass of our local mannas—similar to your wine—staring into the pale green liquid. I was lost in thought, deciding on how I would fulfil my real goal for this visit. I would have to be careful. Even though I thought Michael was convinced of my loyalty, it was still fragile.

I felt his presence before I saw him.

The hairs on the back of my neck stood up and I turned to face my father. He stood looking down at me, his face as stern as always. I stood up from my chair, as was the custom in our family. My father was always approached with the utmost respect. It was basic self-preservation. The man was an institute. A dangerous, narcissistic, piece-of-shit kind of institute.

'Father,' I acknowledged him and even bowed my head. There wasn't much more to say. Minimal words were best where he was concerned, that way I couldn't say anything wrong. Again.

He cocked his head in reply and sat down on the chair next to me. He placed his drink on the table next to him and looked up to me, then nodded that I could sit.

I took my seat again and reached for my drink. I held up the glass and toasted my father and the company, careful not to overdo things. He smiled his agreement. At least that was what it looked like. With him, you never knew. Father kept everything close to his chest. He was an expert in silence and used it as a weapon.

As one of his elder children, I was used to his ways and copied his silent vigil.

'Michael tells me you've had a change of heart,' he finally broke the silence.

I took my time and set my drink back down on the table. 'I've reconsidered my previous rash conclusions,' I told him what he wanted to hear. There was still the edge of rebellion in my words, I didn't immediately agree with him. He wouldn't expect me to. He knew me. Complete compliance would be suspect.

'Good to hear.'

I smiled slightly.

'So, you are back on board with the company?'

'I am. I understand this is a business. Our business. What the humans do is their responsibility. They will be what they are with or without us, it is in their nature. We might as well reap the rewards of their debauchery.'

He nodded again, a small smile on his lips, then gave me a very uncommon slap on the arm and left to speak to others. I stayed exactly where I was and sipped my drink slowly, aware of the eyes on me. Perception in our family was everything and my father just repelled any concerns anyone could have about his nearly favourite rebellious son. He had forgiven me.

Inwardly, I breathed a sigh of relief. I'd pulled the wool over their eyes for now. But I had to stay alert. Complacency would get me into deep trouble, as it always did.

Sometimes I just never learned.

Next day found me in the office behind my screen. I came here for information. That was the sole reason for my visit. This masquerade was tiring, and I had to gather what I came for and get the hell out of Dodge, or Heaven in this case.

Everything I accessed was logged, which meant they would be able to track my searches if they wanted to. My father was paranoid—with reason, I guess. I had to camouflage my searches as much as possible to slow down the algorithm checking for illegal patterns in my investigation and make it correspond with the story I concocted yesterday. They would find out soon enough, but not now. Not until I was gone. Out of this dimension and untraceable.

The creative lies I spun yesterday gave me an unexpected leeway. My investigation of The Establishment was completely logical if it referenced to what I had told Michael. I was banking on it not looking suspicious.

I needed names. Names and locations of The Establishment members. I was especially keen to find the Ventus-Dei, the inner circle. These were the direct links to our dimension. These were father's business partners. If I wanted to hit the company hard, the Ventus-Dei was the ultimate goal, The Establishment would be greatly hampered if we took them out of the equation. It would take time and effort to re-populate the inner circle. But the information was hidden, deeply. There were many layers of authorisations necessary to access the date I wanted. Authorisations I didn't have. The information was on a need-to-know basis. And according to dad, I didn't.

I cross-referenced the list of supplier numbers with names and locations, added them to a list in the system to camouflage my actions and wrote the ones of interest down on a slip of paper. Electronics would show up in the scan when I left the building. The paper would be easier to hide.

Two hours later I'd compiled quite a line-up. I decided to try again for at least one of the names of the inner circle. Yeah, I know. I've never known when to stop.

The computer rejected yet another password when I became aware of someone in the room with me. I turned my head to face Michael. His face was the usual stern unreadable block of concrete. I could not determine anything from him, so I smiled.

'Hi Mike.' Trust me to use an abbreviation he absolutely hated. Wrong time for a jab, but I guess it would be in character. 'What brings you here?' I swivelled the chair around to observe him better.

'You,' he answered. 'You're trying to gain access to information that's way out of your league. Did you think we wouldn't notice? That there wouldn't be alerts?'

'No,' I answered. 'It was exactly as I expected. And how I planned.'

That stumped him for a second. I just kept on smiling.

'To what end?' He finally asked.

'Well, now that you're here, you can help me access what I need. After all, I'm sure you do have the authorisations.'

The flicker of anger and hesitation informed me that he didn't have access either. Interesting. So, information on the

Ventus-Dei was restricted to my father only. Not even his "favourite" son knew. Bummer, that basically meant I wouldn't get what I wanted.

'What makes you think I would give you that access?' he tried.

'You can't,' I laughed. 'You don't have it either. What's that about? Dad doesn't trust you? I thought you were the favourite. The heir.' I had to push it home. Silly really, but I was stalling. Desperately trying to decide how I would talk myself out of this one.

'Why were you attempting to access data on the Ventus-Dei?'

'Seemed interesting.' I shrugged.

He stared at me. His eyes bore into mine. It took all my cool not to turn away.

'It was all a lie, wasn't it?'

Now it was my turn to ask, 'what?'

'Your fantastic tale at dinner yesterday. I should have known; it was too good to be true. I don't know what you're up to, but I will find out.' He cracked his knuckles; a sure signal Michael was about to get physical. I'd seen it all through my miserable youth. Every time he beat me up. My big brother. The bane of my existence.

He rushed me, I pushed the chair to the side, making use of the wheels to propel myself away from him. He careened past me, unable to stop his momentum. I turned the chair and hit him hard in the centre of his back with both hands. His legs gave way and he fell heavily, his upper body slammed into the desk I just vacated. My hands grabbed the back of his head and hammered it onto the hard surface two, three times. He sank to the floor when I let go.

I stood up and surveyed what I had done.

Michael was on the floor, purple blood seeping out of a wound on his head. I checked his pulses. They were clear, though the left one fluttered every few beats. It wasn't anything to worry about, so I left him there and closed the door behind me, my list hidden in the lining of my jacket. I forced myself to walk in my normal tempo and to smile at security as I stood in the scan. Even God's sons had to go through the rigorous checks.

Ours is a very paranoid world. And in this case, rightly so. What I was planning would rock their world.

It was dark when I closed the door of the office behind me.

I made my way to the transporter centre, hoping against hope that no one would find Michael before I was gone. He was out cold when I left him, but I had no idea how long that would last.

My last view of my home dimension was of a shocked transporter electrician cradling the phone to his ear and staring at me with his mouth open in the realisation that he was truly screwed. He had no doubt just heard about Michael and realised he helped me escape. His future did not look bright.

Sorry, buddy.

As soon as I set foot on Earth, I pulled the amulet from my neck and smashed it. My boot made small work of the delicate electronics. Just in time. The transporter light flashed once, indicating an attempt to bring me back. That wouldn't work anymore. They couldn't force me to return, but on the other hand, I could never go back myself. It was a definite end of an era for me. I had burned all my bridges. Burnt them, blown them up and disintegrated them.

I was truly a fallen angel.

Chapter Six

'You brought a list?'

'I did,' I answered, slightly vexed at his tone.

We were in a sleepy hotel room in the outskirts of Mexico City. The place was run down. Old curtains closed out the tacky neon lights of the strip joint next door. Cracked windows and paper-thin walls did nothing to stop the sounds of arguing neighbours and drunk patrons of the bar across the street. How did he find these places?

'All of them?' he asked.

Jonah really was exasperating. 'No. Not all of them,' I explained. 'More than enough to start with.'

He turned towards me, folding his arms over his chest. His eyes locked onto mine. I resisted the urge to explain more. It was difficult.

'The Ventus-Dei?'

I sighed. 'No. I didn't get the names of the Ventus-Dei members.' I had enough self-reproach and didn't need any more from him. I steeled myself for a barrage of insults.

He just nodded.

He walked to the table. 'Where is this list of yours?' Then, when it took too long, he turned and looked back at me. He raised an eyebrow in question. I stood up, shook my head in wonder and walked over to the table. The chair screeched as I pulled it out from under the counter and sat down. I took a piece of parchment out of the lining of my jacket and unfolded it onto the table. There were hastily scribbled names and addresses.

Jonah picked up the parchment, studied it and looked at me quizzically. I didn't understand immediately, so he pointed to the writing.

'Oh, yeah,' it dawned on me what the issue was. 'That's our language.' I hastily apologised. 'I was in a hurry. Then I revert back to my native jargon.'

There was a faint smile on his lips as he put the list back on the table.

'Would you care to translate it?' he asked amused.

'Sure. You have a pen or something here?'

Instead, he pulled an I-pad out of his backpack. That was unexpected.

'I'm not completely backward,' he commented.

'Never said you were.'

He huffed.

Okay, I did think he was quite a-technical. Obviously, I was wrong. Again. Lot of that going around.

He fired up the I-pad, photographed the list for some reason. I mean he couldn't read it anyway, so what was the use? He also took a pen out of his pack and wrote numbers in the margin before every line of characters on the parchment and photographed it again. Then he opened a spread sheet application on the tablet, entered the numbers in a new sheet and pushed the tablet my way.

I turned the parchment to face me and started to type in

the letters. It was a laborious task; my English writing skills were rusty.

'Where did you learn to write in our language?' Jonah asked.

I refrained from looking up. 'It's part of our curriculum,' I explained. 'We have to be able to understand, speak, read and write your languages.'

'Languages? Plural?'

I nodded. I continued to translate the names and places on the list.

'Okay,' he said with a sigh of exasperation. 'I'll ask. How many languages do you speak? Human languages?'

That made me look up. In my mind I counted. I shrugged. 'About ten.' And went back to the task in hand.

'Ten?' Jonah exclaimed.

'Ten. Or twelve. Something like that.'

'Must come in handy.' There was a slightly cynical tone.

'It does.' I was down to the last name on the list.

I passed him the tablet. He took it gingerly and looked at the names on the spreadsheet. There were twenty-four in total. Formal church names, their birthnames and the city where they were based.

'Lot of info,' he commented.

Did I hear a reluctant snippet of praise? That couldn't be, surely? It was a chore to keep the smile off my face.

He scanned the names. Occasionally he would nod in recognition. Then suddenly his brow creased and hooded over his eyes. His lips were pulled tight, and his breath became deeper and more pronounced. He had identified a specific name. It hit a chord with him. Badly.

'Which one?' I asked.

He lifted his head to look at me, enraged by my question. I felt the anger like a wave of heat that emanated from him. His aura was almost tangible. I held my breath but stayed silent. He turned his attention back to the list.

Jonah took a deep breath. 'The last one,' he said in a deep dark tone. 'Archbishop Benedict.'

'You know him?' A redundant question.

He nodded slowly. 'I thought I did.'

I waited. He would tell me if he wanted to.

'He was my mentor.'

Yep, that would do it. Anger him. Make it personal.

'Are you sure about this?' He held up the tablet. His eyes drilled into my brain again.

'Yes,' I answered clearly. 'We get a lot of recruits through his office.'

'What do you mean?'

'We give every recruiter a rating. The list you have in your hands is the ranking of the best recruiters of the past five years. The numbers correspond with these names. If your archbishop is on this list, then he is one of the top twenty-five associates. Very important for The Establishment. There is only one way they could make this list and that's by collecting vast amounts of recruits.'

He was silent.

Slowly he placed the tablet back on the table, pushed his chair back and stood up. Without a word he walked to the door, grabbed his coat from the rack and left the hotel room. I watched him go. There was nothing I could say to him now. He had to come to terms with the impact of Archbishop Benedict's betrayal.

He stayed out all night.

I wondered for a moment whether I should go and look for him, but his last stare was still fresh in my mind. He wanted to be alone. To digest it all. I guess he also had to decide what he wanted to do.

Early next morning—around seven—while I was drinking coffee, I heard the door open, and Jonah walked into the hotel room. I watched him from the table as he threw his drenched coat on the rack, kicked off his boots and walked through the room to the bathroom without a word. He didn't even acknowledge me. No problem. I would just wait until he was ready to talk.

The sound of the shower informed me of his actions.

He stayed under the showerhead for more than ten minutes. I truly hoped the hotel had a massive hot water reserve, otherwise there would be a lot of guests waking up to a cold deluge.

Finally, the water was turned off and five minutes later he walked back into the room, dressed only in a towel knotted around his waist.

He opened his duffel bag and rummaged around for clean clothes. I watched him closely. He was a truly massive man. Hard muscles rippled over his whole body. But it was the scars that stood out for me.

His back and shoulders were crisscrossed with welts, almost whip like. Under his ribs on his right side were a trio of round puckered discolorations I identified as gunshot wounds. The calf of his right leg was dented where a blade of some kind had taken part of the muscle away. The resulting scar was ragged and lay thick on top of the skin.

The tattoos on his left arm and shoulder hid most of the burn marks, though they were more pronounced where they moved up his neck under his long hair.

He turned towards me, very aware of my scrutiny. He dared me to say something. I refrained. I didn't know how volatile he was at that moment, and I wasn't about to find out. I continued my observations, following the intricate

66

tribal tattoos over his chest and abdomen. Another knife wound, a gunshot, and more burns.

Jonah's history had clearly been a violent one.

I held up a mug. 'Coffee?' I asked.

He nodded and pulled the t-shirt over his head and down his torso as I phoned room-service and ordered more coffee and toast, still surprised this place even had such a service. Coffee was one beverage I was really starting to appreciate.

Jonah finished dressing and moved back to the bathroom to brush his teeth. In the meantime, the coffee and toast were delivered, and I set them on the table.

He took the cup with a slice of toast and sat on the bed, his back to the wall and his long legs out in front of him. He ate in silence, drank the coffee, and then looked to me.

'What you said the first time we met. In the bar?'

I cocked my head. We'd said a lot then.

'That your kind didn't invent religion?'

'Ah. That.' This was an interesting development. I'd expected him to talk about his mentor.

'Was that the truth?' he asked.

I nodded.

His eyes bore into mine, searching for validation, I suppose. I held his gaze and forced myself not to flinch at the intensity of his stare.

'When did your kind come into play?' he finally asked.

'Round about your middle-ages,' I answered.

'Tell me.'

Okay. Time for a history lesson. I took a deep breath and started.

'The abbreviated version,' he added dryly before I said a word, it brought a slight smile to my lips.

'Ours is a dominant culture and a vain one.' I started.

'We've always enslaved others to do our heavy work. First it was other tribes on our own world. Then, as we made massive technological advances, we started to look at other worlds for our resource issues.' His stare was quite unnerving, but I continued anyway.

'Resourcing became an industry. First, more or less legally—by our legal system, that is. In our world, like here, anything that has enormous financial potential attracts, shall we say, less ethical parties.'

'Your father?'

'My father.' I was going a lot deeper than I wanted to, maybe I just had to unburden myself. 'Him and a few others. I think you would call them cowboys or pirates in your world—this world.' This was my home now, but it would take some getting used to.

'Anyway. My father and his associate decided to conquer the market. Eventually they became so important in the supply chain that the authorities had to give them a semblance of legality. That, or risk a major shortage. Most of the regular resourcing business-owners had been pushed out of the market by then. My father forged the beginning of his empire that way.'

I remembered more and more. Things I'd pushed to the background. Probably to be able to validate what we—no, I —did. And why I was part of this morally repulsive business.

'He sent his children to different worlds and dimensions in search of new harvests. At that point in time all the families were caught up in a race to find the ideal workforce. Strong and longer lasting resources. Frankly, value for money. There were disgruntled customers, ones we had to keep happy. Michael was sent to this dimension we call the twelfth. He came back with fantastic stories full of potential.

Father actually joined him on the next trip, accompanied by one of his partners; Arand. It's safe to say that dad and Arand ruled the business, and still do. They joined forces a long time ago. More partners of circumstances than anything else. They hate each other's guts, as so often happens with competitors turned partners.'

I heard a deep sigh and stole a glance at Jonah. 'Too much detail?' He nodded.

'Okay. Anyway. They tried different avenues to harvest the potential workforce, without success. Until Arand found a way. He'd secretly been working on an experiment to reincarnate the souls of humans after death, something the scientists scorned as folly. Turned out it was possible. Arand wanted to keep the procedure a secret, but he and my father had a falling-out. Dad, well, he basically stole the technology and started his own version of the process. The major issue they both faced was how to waylay the souls at the precise moment of death and the soul itself had to actively participate in the reincarnation. This necessitated a lot more investigation. After a long and trying period, our scientists noticed subtle differences in some of the souls that made them stand out. It turned out that reincarnation was viable if they believed strongly in an afterlife. Then we could hijack them.'

'Arand came up with the idea to use human religions. He and dad had reinstated their status-quo by then. It was a stand-off, both were keen to get on with the harvesting, so they made a truce. Arand took the biggest human religion at that point in your history; Islam, and dad took Christianity. That was the dividing line.'

'In the years after that they perfected the harvesting procedures and fresh yields of strong workforce were guaranteed.'

'And now? Do they still work together? Or are the wars here proof of your fights?' Jonah asked.

'Quite the opposite.' His brows raised in question.

'War between the religions is quite beneficial to us,' I continued. 'It provides us with more recruits.'

He was quiet, then nodded in understanding. 'War means lots of dead young men and that generates more strong young souls for you.'

My turn to nod.

'Their current cooperation is reluctant, and very fragile, but necessary. For our—their—business.'

'The puzzle pieces are falling into place,' he said softly. 'The Establishment's views on other religions, Fundamentalism.'

'Yes. One issue we had when dad and Arand decided to use religion as a supply chain, was the apparent nonviolent doctrines of the main religions. It didn't suit our purposes, so I guess they encouraged The Establishment to promote fundamentalism.'

'You invented it?' he shot at me. I was back on thin ice with my very reluctant partner.

'Well, no. we didn't invent it as such. We just kind of helped it became more than a very small, insignificant force. Arand made massive wins with the Islamic believers, and we backed the Crusades. That increased general and violent animosity between the religions.'

'Your kind was responsible for that?' The darkness was back in his eyes. Darkness I already associated with anger and danger.

I nodded carefully. 'We weren't responsible, humans started the Crusades, we just gave subtle nudges here and there.'

'You have a lot of blood on your slate,' he concluded. I couldn't fault his thinking.

I took a deep breath. 'We do.'

We were silent while he processed the new information and I tried to come to terms with the enormity of it all. Sure, there was nothing new here for me. Not if I was honest. I'd pushed it to the back of my mind and ignored the implications. But saying it out loud brought home the magnitude of what my family had done. And this was just the tip of the iceberg. It felt as though a block of concrete had nestled in my gut.

It was my background, how I had been brought up. We didn't see humans as anything other than a commodity. There was no more empathy for them than you have for animals going to slaughter. You want your hamburgers, we want our luxuries, and to get those we need a workforce.

I guess I always had my doubts, even as a child. I was critical. I voiced my opinions, much to my family's exasperation. My mother thought I would outgrow my rebellion, prayed that I would. Obviously, I hadn't.

The significance of what we had done—still did—hit me like a brick wall. We had taken something potentially good and contaminated it. Human religions were in essence peaceful, that was still visible in the devotees of small denominations that have not been claimed by one of our families. Those people are non-violent. They live by simple rules and one of them is to take care of each other. We subdued those basic essences of religion and made it something ugly. All in our ambition for more wealth and power. And still we professed no involvement.

So much for not interfering with human religions. I was starting to feel sick to my stomach.

Chapter Seven

'We need more information than just the name and address,' I tried to convince Jonah.

'What for?'

I sighed. The guy was exasperating. 'You can't just turn up at a Bishop's house and break down the door to get at him.'

'Worked up to now.' He shrugged to show his indifference.

'What about the police? Aren't you concerned you'll be arrested before you manage to get out?' I was shocked. He actually thought it was a good idea.

'No. I've gotten away every time.'

'That's your luck. And it will run out. You'll get yourself arrested or even killed. What's the use in that?' Could he really be so callous about his own safety?

He looked at me blankly.

'Besides,' I answered. 'We need to talk to the clergymen on the list. Find out more about The Establishment before you kill them. That will require time. Some finesse is needed.' I saw in his eyes that I was fighting a losing battle. He'd decided, nothing would deter him from his goal.

'I don't do finesse,' he answered.

'No kidding.' He was trying my patience. 'Come one Jonah, even you're not so stupid you believe you can win this fight with only that axe.'

Jonah's right eyebrow raised, his nostrils flared, and his knuckles whitened around the coffee cup. Other than that, he stayed outwardly calm. His anger registered with me, but I pushed it aside and thundered onwards, disregarding any possible impact.

'You can't just keep killing everyone indiscriminately.' I paced the room in exasperation.

'I won't,' he answered. His voice was icy cold and sent shivers up my spine. 'Not now I have the list. I'll only kill the bad ones.'

The "I" registered with me. He still wasn't on board with the partnership.

'That's your plan? Barge in and kill everyone on the list?'

He stayed silent. The glare intensified.

'That is the stupidest thing we could do,' I continued, emphasising the "we" and oblivious to the danger I was putting myself in. 'The only result will be a pile of dead bodies.'

'Sounds good to me.' He crossed his arms over his chest, glared at me and dared me to disagree.

I sighed and threw up my arms in frustration. 'Don't you see?' I tried again. 'The Establishment—my family—will simply replace them. There are hundreds more waiting in the side-lines to fill the vacancies. It won't solve a single thing.'

I had to give him credit that he heard me out.

'Jonah. This is a cancer. We must rip it out by the roots. Get to the Ventus-Dei and take them out. The rest.' I brandished the list. 'These bishops. They're nothing more than expendable frontmen. Puppets. We need to get to the puppeteers.'

I saw the words register with him. But his knuckles were still troublesomely white and his muscles tense and ready to attack. I was not looking for a replay of our first meeting.

'You would know. It's your family after all.' The disdain dripped off his words.

The penny dropped. I finally understood what the issue was. It had taken me long enough. 'You don't trust me.'

'Of course, I don't.'

'Why not? I brought you the list. It cost me everything, my whole life. I can't go back. I sacrificed all that to help you. I'm committed to bringing down The Establishment. And my family.'

'So you say.' there was a vague smile on his lips. He enjoyed baiting me. That, I think, aggravated me even more.

'What?' I was astounded. 'You think I'm making all this up?' He couldn't have attacked me in a more painful way.

The smile intensified.

'I betrayed my family. Attacked my brother. I risked my life to get this.' I waved the list again.

'I have no reason to trust you,' Jonah stated, oblivious to my anger. 'You are one of them. The enemy, as far as I'm concerned. If it's true you betrayed your family, that actually makes you less trustworthy. You were quick to change your allegiance. Too quick. Two weeks ago, you were an alien soul-reaper. Your sole ambition was to impress your father and become the favourite son. According to you, that has been your goal for hundreds of years. And now, you expect me to believe you've done a full one-eighty, just because you spoke to a few of the "recruits".' His eyes pierced mine.

'You were hunting me. You tried to kill me. Now we're partners? How do I know this isn't just a ploy to set me up because you lost the fight?'

'I didn't lose the fight,' I pouted.

'Well, you sure as hell didn't win it?'

He had a point.

'Are you kidding me?' he continued. 'Is the losing part the only thing you took out of what I said?'

I shook my head.

'Of course not.' It hit a nerve with me though. 'I get you have doubts.'

'I don't have doubts. I don't believe you.' Very black and white, but also extremely clear.

'So why are we talking then?' I asked. 'If you are so sure I'm bullshitting you, maybe even setting you up, why don't you just kill me?'

It was a dangerous ploy. But I had run out of options. What the hell did he want from me? I had nothing left.

'Take your axe,' I held my hands up to show I had no weapons. 'I won't defend myself. Just get it over with. Kill me if that's your opinion.' I honestly couldn't care less at that moment.

He stared at me.

Slowly he put down the coffee mug and reached out to the axe that stood upright against the wall. He took the handle and brought the massive weapon up in a two-handed grip.

My blood turned to ice. Would he actually do it? It had been a bluff. A last resort to pull him over to my side. And now it was about to backfire on me.

We were in an impasse. He stood there with the frightening weapon in his hands ready to swing it at my head, and I remained nailed to the spot. Every cell in my body screamed at me to either fight or run. I swallowed hard and forced myself to stay exactly where and how I was.

The intensity in his eyes terrified me more than the axe.

'It wasn't that quick.' I finally broke the silence. 'You could say I was already about one-seventy turned, to use your analogy. I've always been critical of what my family does. My father calls me recalcitrant. I questioned him for the first time when I was ten. I felt his wrath then and have continued to do so my whole life. The way humans are treated in my dimension seemed wrong to me and was a constant subject of discontent between me and my family. I questioned the ethics of the business and never received satisfactory explanations.'

I took a deep breath. 'You're right. My goal was to impress my father. That kind of behaviour is ingrained in my DNA. Like my siblings, I was brought up with a desperate need to please the old man. Our youth would be what your kind calls abusive. We were continuously mistreated. Emotionally, physically, and mentally damaged by him since birth. It moulded us. It moulded me. The need to please him is one of desperation. I see that now. His approval gives us— me—acknowledgement. I guess you would say I never had any self-esteem. How I felt about myself was a direct result of how my father viewed me. He broke my spirit time and time again. Crashed everything I ever did down to the ground.'

I realised I was saying this as much to myself as to Jonah. I'd never voiced the abuse before.

'With most of my siblings, the abuse resulted in a blind commitment to whatever bull he fed us. No one ever contradicted him. No one except me. We've butted heads since longer than I can remember. I've taken the brunt of his anger for so many years that it's normal procedure for me. And yet, still I wanted his acknowledgement. Just that. I've given up on more. My father is incapable of love.'

I lowered my hands.

'If you mistreat a dog, he'll endure and try harder to please you. Until one final fatal moment. Then he'll snap.'

I took another deep breath and continued. 'I snapped. And now all the pent-up anger is coming out. I see my father for what he really is. A tyrant. An abuser. A megalo-maniac. And my family allow it. They endorse his reign of terror over them, and over our dimension. Not because they agree—though I expect Michael does—but because it's the only thing they can do. They are emotionally and mentally unable to contradict him.'

'This—The Establishment—it's the last drop. It's the one final atrocity that pushed me over the edge. So yes, to you it looks like a full one-eighty in a short time. To me it's the culmination of hundreds of years of structural abuse and debasement. Mine and my family's.'

I was empty.

'Do what you want with me,' I stared him straight in the eye. 'I don't care. I have made my decision. I've broken with my father. With my family. I have peace with that. For the first time in my life, I follow my own ethics and I refuse to be suppressed by him anymore. If this is the way I die, then so be it. At least I die a free man, as the result of my own convictions and choices.'

I sat down. Let him decide what he wanted to do.

Jonah stared at me. His visage still hard.

Slowly he lowered the axe.

'I can get information,' he finally said. 'House plans. The works.'

'Where from?' I asked, exhausted, but relieved he wasn't going to kill me. Yet.

'Not your concern,' he answered. We still had trust issues here. I suppose that was to be expected. Even after I laid my soul bare.

'If we are to work together, we will need some form of mutual trust,' I tried.

'So, trust me,' he answered.

With that, he left.

Chapter Eight

The bishop was dead.

He just didn't know it yet.

We'd judged him and found him guilty of conspiracy, fraud, membership of a criminal organisation and kidnapping souls.

Now we were here to execute the sentence.

Death.

Not just that, but also to make sure he was excluded from Heaven.

Bishop Xavier hung up the phone and turned his attention to the tall stack of documents on the right side of the massive ornate desk. He wasn't a big man, and the enormous piece of furniture dwarfed him. His crimson robes stood out starkly against the dark brown oak and the heavy black velvet drapes that covered the windows behind him. Frankly, he looked like a small child sitting at his father's desk pretending to be an important man.

The stack of papers was made up of dossiers and folders in different colours, all well organised, exactly the way Bishop Xavier wanted it. His aids called him a control freak; they weren't far off. He was obsessive. Structure was everything.

The first folder was bright red and contained the most important documents requiring his attention. A mixture of budgets, papal encyclicals, and directions.

He took the pages out of the folder, placed them on the desk in front of him in a neat stack, adjusted his platinum rimed reading glasses and browsed the text on the first page.

A sound caught his attention, and he looked up. Irritated, he lifted the glasses from his nose and scanned the office to determine where the sound came from.

I cleared my throat.

'Who's there?' he demanded.

'Judgement,' I answered quite dramatically.

His eyes opened to their max as he searched the area where he thought my voice originated from. He was off by a few metres. His face flushed with anger.

'Show yourself!' he demanded.

The slight tremor in his voice belied his projection of authoritarian self-confidence. Cracks were already appearing in the cold veneer. There would be a lot more before the end of the evening.

I decided to humour him.

I moved out of the shadow of the seven-foot-high bookcase into the subdued light of the cavernous room. If he had been surprised before, it was negligible compared to when he saw me. He sat back against the chair, and I heard an audible sigh of relief.

We knew each other from my former life. He wasn't aware of that detail, the "former" part.

'Gabriel,' he greeted me. 'I didn't know you were scheduled to visit?'

'I didn't announce it this time.'

His brow creased and he cocked his head in puzzlement.

'Is everything all right?' he asked apprehensively, the nervousness returned.

I smiled, which only compounded his anxiety. As it should, this visit would be very different from the previous ones.

I walked over to the desk, taking my time, and relishing the distress it caused him.

'Gabriel, is there something specific you are here for?' He tried to regain control over the situation. Those thoughts were dashed when he saw another shadow behind me. My smile intensified.

'Why is he here?' He gestured towards Jonah, clearly recognising my companion. 'He's a threat to us all, to everything we stand for.'

I turned my head and addressed Jonah, 'he didn't get the memo.' I said loud enough for the bishop to hear it.

'Obviously not.' Jonah smiled. Not the nice kind of smile.

The bishop paled even more. 'The memo? What memo? What do you mean?' His eyes skittled from me to Jonah and back again.

I sighed for extra drama and took a few steps closer to the desk. He recoiled visibly, convincing me he was getting the message. Finally.

'My father and I have had—how shall I put this—a falling out,' I explained as I would to a child. 'I no longer work for him, or The Establishment. I am what you in your jargon would probably call a "Fallen Angel". Maybe even THE fallen angel.' I didn't have to explain who that was.

'What do you mean?' he stammered, understanding very clear in his face, he just couldn't accept it.

'It's very simple really. My friend here and I have a new quest; to bring down The Establishment and all of you hypocrites who work for it.'

'You can't do that,' he proclaimed. I just nodded and cocked my head.

'Your father would...'

'Would what?' He was getting on my nerves. 'Excommunicate me? I just told you we had a falling out. He would probably like to kill me, but as you see, I am very much alive at the moment. This in stark contrast to what you will be before I leave.'

That silenced him. His eyes darted around the room, from Jonah to me, over the desk and back to me. I saw his right hand move towards a point just under the tabletop where I knew the panic button was located.

'That will be a waste of time,' I informed him causally. 'Your aid is unable to help you now. He has been, how shall we say this; relieved of his head.' I nodded to Jonah, who's lips pulled up in his vicious caricature of a smile.

The bishop pressed the button anyway. He had to. Just to make sure.

In the background I heard a faint buzz from the door to the antechamber. Jonah brought his bloodied axe up on to the desk, slamming home the realisation that the bishop was all alone in this now.

His eyes opened to the max and we heard a short sharp snick of terror. Then he sat back in his chair, his shoulders sagged, and his chin dropped to his chest. He resigned himself to his fate. Good idea, it was inevitable.

'Why?' he finally spoke.

'Do you really need to ask?' I was astounded. 'Are you so blind to what you're doing?'

He looked up at me, a bit of the arrogance back in the contempt of his upturned nose and lips. 'You dare to judge me?' He looked at both of us, as his shoulders squared again, and he leant forward with his elbows back on the desk. A second wind. Interesting.

'You started all this,' he addressed me. 'Your family are the real culprits here. You use these souls as slave labour.'

'Yes, my family does, and we will get round to them as well,' I answered, my voice dangerously calm and threatening. 'But you make it possible. You betray your own kind and set them up for this travesty. You lie to them.'

'They are inconsequential,' his true self was showing now. 'Why do you care about them? We give them hope, give them a reason to live.'

'Yes,' Jonah's dark tone caused Bishop Xavier to flinch again, his confidence was barely skin deep. 'You give them hope for something they can never achieve. You betray their trust. Their love. You use them for your own gains.'

'You are a fine one to judge me, murderer!' the bishop shouted.

'I am a murderer. I have taken lives. And that will haunt me for the rest of my life. But now I make amends.' he slammed the axe face down on the desktop again, emphasising his point and making it abundantly clear how he did that.

'Oh, cut the weeping heart routine, will you?' Xavier shouted. 'You're no better than any of us. Neither of you are. And if what you say is true,' he turned back to me. 'That you have fallen from your father's grace, then he will never let you do this. He will exact my revenge.'

'Do you honestly think my father cares about you and

your pathetic Establishment?' I asked incredulously. 'You are no more than puppets to him. A means to an end. A necessary clink in the chain to get what he wants—slaves, money, and status. He'll go after me, sure. But not as any misguided revenge for a minion like you.'

'I'm a bishop. A chosen one. A member of the ruling council of the Church. I demand...'

'You demand!' Jonah's booming voice muted the small man.

The silence was oppressive. The incessant ticking of the ornate clock on the mantlepiece the only sound in the room.

We waited. I don't know what for, it was a done deal.

I glanced at Jonah who shrugged and moved into position near the desk.

'You have no right to condemn me. Both of you are traitors. Traitors to the Church,' Xavier tried. There was no strength in his voice anymore.

'To The Establishment, you mean?' Jonah answered.

'The Establishment is the Church,' he turned his attention to me. 'You even betrayed your father.' Then turned back to my companion. 'You are the Judas of this age. You were in the higher echelon and betrayed everything we stand for. You broke your vows. Your holy commitment to...'

'MY holy commitment?' Jonah's voice was dangerously calm. The muscles in his body tensed ready to pounce. I took a step back. 'I'm not the one serving the false God. Unlike you and your precious Establishment.' His anger filled the air with an electricity that made the hairs on the back of my neck stand up. The bishop was oblivious to the danger.

'You are scum,' Xavier continued, his tone full of contempt. 'You are nothing more than a mindless brute.'

I put my hand on my companion's arm to stop him from silencing the bishop. It was too soon, not till after we got what we came for—information.

'Let's stop the insults, shall we?' I tried to disarm the tension. Before the inevitable, I wanted to milk everything he knew out of this man of the Church.

'You can kill me, I don't care,' he spat out the words.

'You might want to rethink that.' I answered calmly. He looked at me apprehensively. The anger was replaced with concern. I could almost see the cogs in his brain working, trying to understand what I meant.

'What do you think will happen?' I continued. The edges of my lips turned up in a mean grin. His eyes flitted from my face to Jonah, to his axe and back again. I cocked my head to emphasise my question.

He sat up straight and took a deep breath. 'You are going to kill me.' He had resigned himself to his fate.

'After that.'

'What do you mean?' He couldn't be any paler.

'After death,' I explained with another smile. He shuddered perceptively and the earlier strength in his pose dissipated.

'I have an agreement,' he stammered, the truth hitting home. 'A ticket-to-Heaven. I was promised my rewards.'

'You were promised,' I repeated, then turned to Jonah. 'He was promised Heaven.'

'Sounds familiar,' my companion commented dryly. The anger in his stance tempered for now.

We both turned back to the bishop who was trying his best to disappear in the large chair. He forced his frame hard into the back rest, his hands pushing at the edge of the desk, the tendons hard and pronounced.

'I have a contract,' he stammered, his voice without any real strength.

I laughed coldly.

'I expect your family to honour their part of the contract,' he continued. 'Like I did.'

'Yes, you did follow it to the letter, didn't you?' I stared him in the eye. 'How many recruits did you collect? Thousands? More?' He stayed silent. 'And how many new recruiters did you initiate into The Establishment?' I looked at Jonah. 'Must have been a lot, to be promised Heaven.' Jonah nodded, his features as vicious and cold as mine, the only real emotion was the fire in his eyes.

'So many even,' I continued. 'That you are about to be admitted to the Ventus-Dei. Isn't that right?'

His eyes opened even further, and his cheeks went bright red. Bingo. We hit the nail on the head.

'Now, what we want you to do, for us to even contemplate letting you keep your future paradise, is the name of your sponsor. And any other Ventus-Dei members will help your chances of cashing in your ticket.'

'Never!' he shouted. 'They will kill me.'

I looked at Jonah. He shrugged, echoing my astonishment.

'So will we,' I answered pointedly. 'And maybe we should point out that we are your most imminent danger.' Jonah slammed the axe-head flat onto the desk again. The deep thud had the intended result and the bishop jumped in his seat, his arms crossing over his upper chest as though that would save him. 'You are a dead man. The only difference you can make now is what will happen after that event in your direct future. Do you want to cash in on Heaven?

Or will you take your chances on what any real god will judge you on?'

He shrank back in his seat; his head fell to his chest in defeat. Tears even formed at the edge of his eyes and made their way silently down his face. Jonah lifted the double-headed axe from the desk and took a step back, giving us some space. Xavier's eyes were still focussed on the blood that was left behind on the desktop. That was his aide's blood, a big bright red smear over the papers now strewn haphazardly on the desk.

The silence was only broken by soft snicks. We waited. I stood to the side of the desk; my arms crossed over my chest. Jonah had both hands on the eye of the axe. The massive weapon stood upright on the knob and reached up past his waist.

The bishop took a deep breath, sniffed loudly, and brushed his tears away with the back of his right hand. He looked up, first at Jonah, then to me. 'Father Francis.' he said softly. I cocked my head. He cleared his throat again, sat upright, his hands flat on the desk in an attempt to take strength from the century old piece of furniture.

'Father Francis,' he repeated in a stronger voice.

'Archbishop Benedict's aide?' Jonah asked astonished. An aide? Not what I had expected either.

'Yes,' Xavier answered. His lips now curling in a light smile.

'An aide?' I couldn't believe what he said. How was that possible?

Xavier's voice was laced with contempt. 'You're focussed on the hierarchy so much you don't see what is in front of you.' He looked to me and then to Jonah. His scorn aimed mainly at the rogue priest. 'You didn't see that one coming, did you?' He laughed.

The axe came down and severed the bishop's arm just under the elbow. He screamed as the arterial blood pulsated out of the stump.

'Neither did you,' my companion remarked coldly.

The bishop cradled his bleeding extremity, unsuccessfully trying to stem the flow of blood, the shock of the amputation and the sharpness of the blade pushing pain away.

I looked at my companion and raised an eyebrow in a silent question whether this had been necessary.

He just shrugged. 'We have the name.' True. The bishop had outlived his value. Then the smile of Jonah's face alerted me to what he had actually done.

The left under arm held the ticket. In death, the bishop would now be delivered to his well-deserved reward. I pressed a small remote I took out of my jeans pocket and a small explosion rocked the severed limb, smashing a hole in the skin and muscle just under the wrist.

'Oeps. Now, you're not going anywhere.' I pushed the truth home. 'Well, anywhere nice.' With his arm gone and the explosion, his ticket-to-Heaven was nullified. Non-existent. The pearly gates and a plush life in the here-after disappeared like snow before the sun. I had no illusions on where he was headed now. Not with his record. Not with what he had done here on earth. If Hell existed, that was his destination.

'Nooooooo,' he screamed. The pain of his severed limb forgotten with the realisation of his predicament. Death hadn't scared this man. The loss of his future paradise hurt him more than any physical wound could.

'Bummer,' I said sarcastically. 'You'll just have to take your chances now on what's to come.'

'No. Please,' he pleaded. 'Don't kill me. Please. I beg

you. I'll change my ways. I'll help you. I can help. I can get you what you need to know.'

'Now he wants to live,' Jonah observed to me.

'Yeah. So that he can organise a new ticket. Not going to happen.'

Xavier was crying now. His voice broke and he was difficult to understand. 'Please, let me change my ways. Don't kill me. I don't deserve to die. I was following orders. You know that. It wasn't me.' He was clutching straws, and they were disintegrating.

'It was you,' my large accomplice shot back. 'You had a choice. You could have refused.'

I nodded to Jonah and the big axe swung another time. Now effectively silencing the screaming bishop.

Jonah wiped the blade of the axe on the velvet curtains leaving a bright red smear on the soft material.

'That was surprising,' he commented calmly.

Surprising didn't cover it. The archbishop's aide? Like Xavier said, we were focussing on the normal hierarchy in a church and assumed the Ventus-Dei would be organised in the same manner.

Though I still suspected Archbishop Benedict was involved, we would have to rethink our strategy,

Drastically.

Chapter Nine

Still musing over what we just learned, we failed to notice we were no longer alone until the relative silence was broken by a scream. A priest stood in the second open door to the hallway and stared at the terrible scene. The bishop's head had rolled off the table onto the floor where it faced the door and the screeching priest who could not take his eyes off what was left of his former employer.

I pulled the hood of my sweatshirt up over my head and moved back into the shadows. Jonah grabbed his axe, turned, and jumped through the window, smashing the delicate stained glass, into the manicured garden beyond. The priest continued to scream all the way back through the hallway and into whatever room was behind the second door on the right. A moment later the door was slammed shut and I heard something heavy being smashed up against it. The priest had barricaded himself in what he perceived as a safe place. I heard him shout into what I assumed was a phone.

'Bishop Xavier has been murdered! The killer is still on the grounds. Help me. Help me!'

I slipped through the hallway into the kitchen and out through the same door we used earlier to enter the mansion. The sirens in the background pushed me onwards through the gardens and over the stone wall that encircled the grounds. It was a beautiful mansion, with fantastic walled gardens, but an absolute security nightmare. With no neighbours overlooking the grounds, the entry had been easy. Lots of blind spots. We easily cut the wires of the simple ineffective security system and disarmed it. Ridiculous if you think of the artefacts that were in the building, not to mention the bishop himself. I mean, security wires on the outside of the building, really?

I pulled the hood of my sweatshirt down as I walked the still busy streets three blocks from the mansion. I had to blend in. A hooded man in this part of town would stand out like a sore thumb. My best chance was to look like everyone else. Totally unremarkable, doing what others were doing. I stopped at an all-night fast-food stall and ordered a taco. It gave me a chance to look back to see if anyone was paying special attention to me. Nothing. I breathed a sigh of relief.

Most of the people didn't pay any attention to the multiple sirens in the background. I counted five in total as I ate the super spicy taco. The salsa dripped onto my sweater and camouflaged specs of the bishop's blood.

I threw the empty paper bag into the trash and calmly walked on through the crowds, blending in completely.

It made sense to split up. It was the only thing we could have done. The two of us together would be too conspicuous. Alone we had more chance of getting out. Besides, it wasn't as though Jonah had waited for me.

I entered a bar and made my way to the counter, studiously wiping at the salsa stains and only succeeding in smearing out the sticky red smudges and further covering the blood specs.

'Just had a Taco,' I joked with the pretty blond woman behind the bar.

'Messy eater,' she laughed.

'Yeah,' I confessed and held up my shirt as proof.

'What can I get you?'

'A Dos Equis, please. To keep it in the same taste sensation.'

She smiled and turned to get me a glass and a cold bottle of the Mexican brand.'

I was half-way through the bottle when one of the patrons asked the bartender to turn up the sound of the tv hanging in the corner. It was tuned into a news channel. I turned with the rest of the clientele to watch the anchorman highlight the gruesome murder of the bishop and his aide. He reported that the police were on a manhunt for a tall man with what was probably a samurai sword or a machete.

One man. The priest hadn't seen me. Only Jonah. That was an unexpected advantage, for me. The digital rendering of the killer hardly resembled my partner, so the hysterical priest obviously hadn't recognised or been able to describe Jonah very well.

Internally, my raging nerves started to settle down. I realised I was seriously rattled by what almost happened. We could have been apprehended. Jailed. The idea was bad enough for either of us but for me it had an extra dimension. How the hell would I explain what I was. Two hearts, purple blood. That wouldn't stay secret for long.

It dawned on me what a massive risk I was taking. I felt

the anxiety return with a vengeance and had to let go of the glass and hide my trembling hands under the bar. The sound of the people in the room and the background of the now loud news bulletin felt oppressive. I wanted to run out, get away from this place. Away from humans. Away from the mess I'd gotten myself into.

I felt eyes on me.

Looking up I saw the barkeeper observing me. She had a worried look on her face.

'You okay?' she asked.

I nodded and smiled. 'It's been a tough week at work,' I explained.

'You look sick.'

'I'll be okay,' I assured her. 'A few days of rest and I'll be back to my regular bubbly self.'

To emphasise my point, I picked up my glass and toasted to her. 'Here's to holidays.'

'Yeah, I wish,' she joked with me and put a new bottle of beer in front of me. 'On the house.' I smiled my thanks. We continued small talk for a while until she was called over to the other end of the bar to serve another customer. I poured the beer into the glass and took a long haul. My nerves settled, but the voices in my head stayed.

Later that night, alone in the dark back at the hotel, I contemplated what I was doing. The police hunt brought it all home. I realised I'd grossly underestimated what I got myself into. The danger we were in hunting down The Establishment had been my only security focus, now I understood it was just one facet of what we were facing.

Jonah was still AWOL. He would turn up. The police were still looking for the wrong man and I was sure he had his ways of avoiding them. The extensive investigation we had done into the neighbourhood and possible escape routes would no doubt pay off.

I sipped the whisky. The bottle next to me was half empty. Alcohol didn't really have the same effect on me as it does on humans. At least not in what for you is a normal quantity. If I wanted any of the consciousness dulling effect, I'd have to consume vast amounts of high percentage liquor. A bottle of Whiskey just scratches the surface, but there was more in the paper bag on the kitchen table. I had a feeling I would need it tonight.

The Establishment, the police and maybe even my family. They were all out there looking for those responsible for the string of clerical murders rocking the country.

I looked at the evidence.

The Establishment knew about Jonah. He was on their radar. Not surprising, he was a rogue priest and his modus operandi with the axe was, shall we say, notable. They must have deduced his responsibility for the annihilation of their recruiters. That made him The Establishment's number-one enemy.

The police were no doubt hunting for what they viewed as a serial killer with a religious fixation.

Tonight should have been easy.

We'd researched the mansion. Chosen the best possible night when by all accounts, the bishop should have been alone. And still it had gone wrong.

We would have to be even more careful. Maybe even lay low for a while. Jonah wouldn't like that. Well, tough. Ultimately, he wanted to make a maximum impact and that would require more time and preparation.

And then there was my family.

I was still satisfied they were blissfully unaware of my

involvement in all of this. My father undoubtedly expected me to be languishing somewhere in self-pity and disgrace after my run in with Michael. But I had no doubt this was a temporary situation. All Hell would break loose once he found out I was seriously defying him.

My presence was still a benefit. There were two of us now and I was convinced I brought the common sense to the whole endeavour. Jonah would definitely have been apprehended or maybe even killed tonight without the proper preparation I insisted on.

Jonah came in halfway through the afternoon of the next day. He looked no worse for wear, holding two big carrier bags, one with his long coat stuffed inside, and a second with groceries. He seemed even cheerful, quite in contrast with my mood. A night of heavy drinking left me with a massive ache at the bottom of my skull. My first hangover. And the last, I hope.

'When did you get back?' Jonah asked while he sorted out the produce he'd bought. Mostly food, some beer, and a few newspapers.

'Last night,' I answered. The effort sending new stabs through my brain.

'Rough night?' He observed the three empty bottles of high-percentage liquor. There was a hint of admiration in his eyes. Great. The one time I get validation from him has to do with something as stupid as alcohol volume.

I nodded. He rummaged in his duffel bag and threw me a plastic container of bright yellow capsules. 'Take a few of these. They should help.'

'What are they?'

'Don't ask.' So, I didn't. I followed his advice and took

three pills, deducing their effectiveness would mirror that of alcohol in my body and that I should take more than suggested.

Something was missing. It dawned on me. 'Where's your axe?'

He upturned the carrier bag containing his long leather coat and the heft of the axe clattered to the table. I scrunched my brow, where was the rest? He observed my bewilderment and chuckled.

Jonah picked up the thick wooden heft and handed it to me. 'Take a good look,' he suggested.

I accepted the weapon and scrutinised it closely. The familiar wooden handle was much more complicated than I'd imagined. The wood only reached up to the half-way mark of the body. The shoulder and opposite sides of the body sported metal inserts culminating in a full metal eye. I noticed thick lines in the metal indicating separate components. Turning the handle upside down, I saw what seemed like a mechanism that formed the knob. Looked like it could be turned or pushed in. I tried turning, but there was no result.

After a few minutes of close investigation, I was no closer to a solution. I handed it back to a smiling Jonah. He placed his left hand on the knob of the handle and gripped the body with his right hand. There was an audible click as he turned the knob to the right. The metal sides of the handle exploded into multiple metal shards that sprung up into the form of the blades of the axe. Another loud click heralded the locking of the shards into the massive metal killing surfaces I was familiar with.

He handed it back to me.

I admired the state-of-the-art weapon. It was truly a fantastic example of technical ingenuity.

'Who made this?' I asked, truly impressed.

'A friend designed it. Others made the parts.'

'It's fantastic.'

He nodded.

A thought dawned on me. 'The same friend who supplied us with the blueprints of the bishop's house?'

He stared at me; the good mood gone. 'Need-to-know basis. And you don't,' he said curtly, turned and walked to the kitchenette, ending the subject.

I decided to let it rest. The secret helper was a massive benefit to us. I would like to keep him in the equation. Pushing Jonah wouldn't help.

'I wondered how you managed to hide it under the coat,' I continued admiring the weapon.

'Static blades are not very convenient,' he answered dryly. He came back with two cans of beer, one he offered to me.

I laughed. 'I can imagine; too sharp.'

I gingerly put the big axe back on the table. Jonah took it, pushed a mechanism and the blades effortlessly slipped back into the handle.

'How is it secured?' I asked.

'Biometric security,' he answered, the pride back again. 'It only opens for me.'

Again, I was impressed.

I took the newspapers and scanned the front-page stories. All were dedicated to the murder of Bishop Xavier and his aide. As one, they were appalled by the murder of two men of the cloth in general, and the ultimate brutality of their death, in particular. Most referred to other ecclesiastic murders, all of which had Jonah's calling card on them. He definitely was on the radar now.

'Quite a lot of attention,' I commented.

Jonah joined at the table. 'Yeah. More than I'm comfortable with.' That surprised me. I thought that was what he wanted.

'Might be an idea to lay low for a while,' I suggested. Jonah agreed to my surprise. Maybe I was getting through his thick skull after all.

'Just as well we prepared for yesterday,' he acknowledged. I guess this was as close as he would ever get to saying I was right.

We agreed to leave the next day and go back to our regular base of operations to plan our next steps.

This mission had been a wakeup call.

Chapter Ten

'Tell me about your nun,' I asked out of the blue.

As usual he answered me with a question of his own. 'Why?'

'I want to understand what makes you humans believe. Why you are all so ready to fall for the promise of Heaven.'

He just stared at me. I decided to humour him and explain further.

'You were at the top of the food chain. You had it all, the power, the money. Yet you left all that behind because you believed in what the Church fed you.'

He scowled. One day I would watch my words. But not today. If he didn't like it, then screw him. I still needed to know.

'You had it all until your nun came and made you believe in a higher power. Your newfound conviction changed your whole life.'

'Twice,' he finally spoke.

'Yes. Twice. But I'm mainly interested in your first change of sentiment.'

He approached me; his bulk blocked out the light of the overhead lamp. These moments brought back the doubt of our first meeting. Would he humour me? Or were we, once again, going to fight? I suspected he enjoyed our bouts. He was, after all, quite a physical man, predisposed to release tension with blows and kicks. Not exactly what the nun would have preached I expect. I almost chuckled at the thought.

The chair across from the fire groaned under his weight as he settled down opposite me. He put another log onto the fire and stared into the flames. I waited patiently. There was no rushing this man.

'Top of the food chain, huh?' he started, amusement in his tone. I sat back and waited.

'I suppose I was, in my own part of the world. My own, depressing, depraved part of the world.' He sat forward, his elbows rested on his knees, the fingers of his hands inter-twined as he rubbed his right palm with the thumb of his left. I heard the knuckles crack and imagined it was some-one's neck. I know, kind of macabre. But that's just me. I think he was rubbing off on me.

'The slums were my kingdom to start with. The place where no one wanted to be, and even less managed to escape from. I ruled there, not because I was the strongest, but because I was ruthless. Vicious. Without empathy. I didn't care. Not about others, not even about myself. I lived for the gratification of the moment. Tomorrow was of no concern to me.'

'How did you become that person?' I asked.

He looked at me as though he'd just noticed I was there.

Jonah sat back in the chair, his hands flat on the arm rests, his long legs stretched out in front of him, the ankles crossed.

'The person I was then started with my mother's death. She was my world as a small child. She was the balance. The empathy, where my father was the brute. I'll never understand why she loved him as she did. She was his conscience. She held him in check. And he in turn worshipped the ground on which she walked, like me. My mother installed a love of everything living in me. Nature, animals, and people. Her goal in life was to raise a kind and good family.'

'What happened?'

'Life happened. My father's vocation caught up with us. He was a criminal kingpin. The leader of a local clan. In his greed he made stupid decisions and betrayed a drug cartel. His illusions of power and invulnerability came crashing down when they attacked our headquarters in the middle of his domain and took their retribution out on my mother and sister.'

He swallowed hard and his body tensed. Jonah closed his eyes and intertwined his fingers again. I saw the struggle for control in the whites of his knuckles and the creases in this brow.

'They tortured my mother, raped her and my younger sister. Burned them, cut them, and finally killed them,' he continued barely audible. I had to concentrate to hear his whispers.

'My father and I returned to our home to find everyone dead. My mother, my sister, the guards, the housekeeper, even the dogs. They left nothing alive. The deaths had—as one—been bad. Painful. Prolonged. It was a statement to my father, the clan, and anyone who chose to oppose the new order. Betrayal was dealt with swiftly and viciously by the Cartel. They had no scruples. No restraints. Nothing was safe. The resulting war was bloody and savage. Both sides committed atrocities. No one was safe. Nothing was holy. For my father, revenge was the only goal.'

His gaze went back to the fire.

'No one wins in these situations, and no one did. Not really. My father pushed the Cartel out. He triumphed in one way; he regained the power over the island. But he lost in all others. The clan was decimated. Every family grieved for their lost sons, daughter, fathers, and mothers. All for revenge. It wasn't worth it. But it was all that fuelled my father.'

His eyes locked with mine.

'My mother's death broke him. Any smidgen of empathy he had was destroyed with her murder. He lived only to make them hurt as much as he did. It was impossible. He was consumed with blood lust.'

'He instilled the same in me. I was punished for mourning my lost family. He would beat me if I cried, pushing me to fuel my anger with my pain. He made me strong in body and hard in soul. I hated him for it then. Now I understand it was his own inadequacy to deal with his emotions and pain that pushed him to act this way. He was a broken man and the only way he could deal with his loss was to strike out. To his enemies and to those around him. I took the brunt of it, and he made me what I was to become. A mirror image of the emotionless vicious man he became after my mother's death.'

'When he died, I took over the clan and continued his reign of terror and blood.'

'Then the nun came?' I asked softly.

He looked at me and his hard features softened. A hint of a smile pulled the edges of his lips up.

'Yes. She came and changed everything.'

'How?'

'Slowly.' he answered. 'She never pushed her views, never argued. She was just there. She asked questions. Deep ones. Ones I didn't want to answer. Initially I was angry at her, but even as vicious as I was, I wouldn't raise a hand at someone from the Church.'

His smile became warmer as his thoughts returned to the woman who had such a profound impact on his life.

'She was tiny. Less than a third of me. And much older, I guess over sixty. But she was not impressed. Not by my size, my history, my reputation, or my rhetoric. She just stood there and watched me. No comments. No reproach. She just watched. That was new to me. My size and demeanour were part of my power. People feared me.'

'Understandable.' I had to add. 'Some still are.'

He chuckled.

'It flustered me. I had no idea what to do with her. So, I decided to ignore her and pretend she wasn't there. That didn't work either. She persevered. Was always just at the edge of my sight. She wasn't judgemental. Never commented on my reasons for what I did. She just asked her questions. "Why?" "What I felt?" That kind of thing. Things I didn't want to answer for myself, let alone to her.'

'She got under my skin. Her questions resonated with the person I had been before my mother and sister died. They hit a chord that was buried deep down, but not deep enough. I started to question myself. Question my reasons for what I did. My conviction to the life I led.'

'She was clever.'

'That she was. The only one who can convince me of anything has always been me. No matter what others say or do. I decide for myself. No measure of proof will convince me like I can.'

'I'll keep that in mind.' He looked up, cocked his head, then smiled.

'Slowly, very slowly, she broke down the walls of violence I erected around my pain. She exposed my anguish and torment. There was no way I could ignore it anymore. I broke down. My bravado was replaced by shame. I was not the man my mother wanted me to be. The man I wanted to be.'

He stared into the flames. The crackling of the fire was the only sound in the room. I gave him space and time. Our conversation impacted him immensely. I felt the tension and effort it took to stay calm. The air was loaded. I didn't know what to say, but anything would have been wrong anyway. The silence continued.

'I turned my back on my previous life,' he finally continued. 'I tried to change the clan, but that was not appreciated. I was the only one convinced of a new direction. I wanted to make amends for my sins. They weren't interested. Most saw my change of heart as a weakness and blamed Sister Eloise. They feared for their lives if our clan showed vulnerability. Ours was a competitive branch of work. There were more than enough groups waiting to take over our territory. My clan tried to talk me out of my newfound convictions, without success.'

'I shouldn't have put them in such danger. I should have transitioned the power to someone else, allowing them to keep the status-quo so essential to life itself in the criminal circles. But I didn't. In my stubborn and narcissistic way, I decided everyone should follow my example. The whole clan must change their ways and better their lives. It was stupid, egotistical, and dangerous. They turned against me. For survival, I see that now. For others it was finally an opportunity to get rid of me.'

His eyes went dark again. There was more to this story. His transition to a new life had been hard.

'They went after Sister Eloise. They blamed her for everything. With her gone they expected me to cave in. Either resurrect my previous self, or breakdown. I did neither.'

He raised his head just enough to lock eyes with me. The heavy brow over his fiery eyes and the hard features gave me insight into who this man was. He was dark. He was intense.

'You killed them.' It wasn't a question.

He didn't answer. I knew what had happened. It was inevitable.

The silence lasted for more than ten minutes. I stood up and walked into the kitchen, returning with two glasses and a half-full bottle of rum. He took the offered drink without a word and continued to stare into the fire. I fed another log to the flames and took my seat again.

Jonah took a long drink of the rum, emptied the glass, and held it out for a refill. The guy sure could hold his liquor. I passed him the bottle; certain I wouldn't see any more in my glass anyway. He sloshed the glass half full and drank it in another long gulp. Again, he re-filled his glass with the last remnants of the bottle. The now empty vessel was set on the ground and Jonah held the glass in both hands as though warming himself on the liquid. He was far away in his mind. In a world of his own.

'I left my home after that.' I jumped at the sound of his voice. The silence had been so complete his words resonated like a shotgun blast.

'I joined a monastery trying to close myself off from the world and to heal from my wounds. It gave me time to look deep down inside myself and contemplate what I was here for. There had to be a reason. God would not have kept me alive if he didn't have a reason. I had to find my destiny. I needed to find a reason to continue breathing.'

He drank half of the contents of his glass and looked at me. His eyes bore deep into me and, as usual, sent goose-bumps up my spine. A thick block of concrete made itself at home in my gut. This was where it got hairy.

'I never wanted to make a career in the Church. My intension was to be invisible. Do my work. Help others and find some salvation, however little that could be with my history.'

'And then we came.' I answered his unspoken reproach. He nodded.

'And then you came.' He repeated my words. I tried to gauge his state of mind, but he was a closed book right now. I picked up the story, from our perspective. "Ours" being my father's.

'Your unbelievable results with the young people in the slums was what identified you to us. You looked like the ideal candidate for the Establishment.'

'Because of my history.'

'Yes. without your pretence for violence, we wouldn't have been interested. We were convinced your new-found faith was no more than a scam. A new way for you to exhort power over others. Father saw it as a clever escape from your previous life when the contract on your head forced you to retreat. He thought it was genius of you to pretend to be reformed. You were the new talent.'

'So your minions pushed me into new roles in the Church.'

I nodded. 'You were the poster boy. A former criminal who dedicated his very life to God. You were the example.

Your presence made others turn to observe you. You have a natural superiority, a leadership. That, and the lobbying of The Establishment, hastened your journey. It made you the person to watch, and the one to affiliate with. People flock to you naturally.'

'And your lot did the rest.'

'Yes. My father was adamant you were playing everyone. He was sure your "real" character was still there and that you would easily assimilate in The Establishment. He saw you as an absolute asset.'

He raised his brow and almost smiled. 'Must have been quite the disappointment when he found out I wasn't.'

I laughed at that. 'Disappointment is quite the understatement.' He laughed along.

'My father exploded. He was that mad. Not very God-like really. But then, he isn't, is he? He invested a lot in you. Tailored you into his big plans of dominance in our industry. He was so convinced you would toe the line. Maybe even be able to bring The Establishment into the highest levels of the Church. Higher than we had ever been before. Who knows, even the ultimate position. That would have been a coup. An Establishment recruit in papal whites. Not very realistic with your background, but then, realism was never my father's strong point. Nothing could have stopped him then. He would have been able to establish complete dominance over the other families in our dimension. He planned to start new religious wars using the recruits in important political and military positions. A new Crusades that would make the previous one look like a walk in the park. It would rival what my father's biggest competitor Arand had done with the Kalifate. He had plans for you. And you made him look bad.'

'Bummer.' The smile was plastered on his face.
'Yeah. Right.' I laughed along with him.
We finished the bottle.
And another one.

Chapter Eleven

Living and working with Jonah was a challenge. The man was a walking time bomb. Every word I said was weighed and if found lacking, a row followed, often ending in blows being exchanged. It wasn't all him, I was as bad as he was. My stubbornness matched his.

More than once, I regretted my rash behaviour. I should have thought about the impact of my actions more. All my ships were burnt. I couldn't go back home. Not now, probably not ever. I didn't think my father was aware of my role in the assassinations. To tell you the truth, I doubt he was even interested in them. What the humans did to each other was completely void of interest to him. He'd made that quite clear. Profit was his first and only objective.

There was a lot more interest in Jonah. He was difficult to keep under the radar. Mainly because he didn't want to be there. He aspired the recognition he caused with the decimation of the Establishment's key figures. He wanted them to know.

I suppose the axe wounds were a dead giveaway.

His previous carefulness evaporated, and he became reckless again, sometimes going off on his own to wreak even more havoc.

We were on a collision course. He was going stir crazy and I was sick of him, his endless impatience and inability to see the big picture. He was driven by revenge. By the body count. Long-term didn't feature in his vocabulary.

If we seriously wanted to bring down The Establishment—the whole shebang—then we had to go about it in a structured and planned manner. The power behind The Establishment was enormous. It had the potential to smooth over any damage we did by just killing off individual recruiters, even if they were key players. We had to look further.

We had to get to the Ventus-Dei.

Chapter Twelve

'We move on Bishop Marx tomorrow,' Jonah announced.

'What's the plan?' I asked with an edge to my voice. 'Go in and kill everyone in sight again?'

He raised his head and looked at me. 'What's wrong with that?'

'Everything.' Were we seriously having this discussion again?

His stare gave me goosebumps 'Could you be more precise?'

'That's your answer to everything, isn't it? Swing your bloody big axe and kill whoever is within reach.'

He was silent. Generally, that was worse than when he spoke. The tingling at the base of my spine intensified, but I continued anyway.

'All that will achieve, is to get us killed. Your maniacal murder sprees attract all the wrong attention. We have the cops on our trail in three different countries. Last time, in Mexico, we narrowly missed incarceration.' He huffed his disagreement. Jonah's first reaction to criticism was always to belittle it.

'There is absolutely no finesse to anything you do. It's all just kill, kill, kill. How the hell are we supposed to take down The Establishment if all you do is swing that axe. We'll get the combined force of the police and my father's warriors after us before we can achieve anything.'

'I'm doing damage to The Establishment.' His mood was as black as mine.

'Is that what you call it? Do you even know why you're doing all this?' My voice was raised, the irritation no longer concealed. I felt my face turn red with anger.

'This is what we agreed on,' he stated resolutely. 'To take down The Establishment. For humanity. I'm doing my part to stop this scam. To prevent more souls ending up in your perpetual slavery. That's my goal.'

'That's it?' I asked. 'What you're doing? Stop kidding yourself. You're not doing this for anyone else. It has nothing to do with others. You're on a personal vendetta, murdering everyone you blame for your current situation.'

'And what if I am?' Anger coloured his face bright red in a mirror image of mine. Once again, we were headed for a confrontation. 'The Establishment, your people, took everything from me. My rock. My purpose,' he shouted.

'Get off your sanctimonious high horse will you,' I said exasperated. Jonah's endless moaning was getting on my nerves. My comment earned me a killing look. The guy had that stare down to an art form. It would turn your blood cold. But not this time. Now I was just sick and tired of his endless lamenting. So, with no thoughts to my own safety—which would have been relevant—I pressed on.

'Your faith wasn't taken from you. You abandoned it. At

the first possible moment you just let it go,' I continued. 'If it really was as important to you as you claim, you should have fought for it.' I pointed to him to emphasise my statement.

He looked at me in complete astonishment. 'What the fuck do you think I'm doing now?' I am fighting for it.'

I should have taken a hint when he picked up the axe. But no, I wanted to press my point home.

'No, you're not. You're lashing out at the perceived cause of your lack of faith. At the people on the list. At me. At my kind. But if truth be told, you are the one who was quick to lose faith in your god.'

'In your dad, you mean.' The ice dripped off the words. Along with his stare, they contributed to a temperature decline of at least ten degrees in the room.

I sighed. 'No. Your god. Your real god if there is such a thing. The one that was there before we came.' My impatience was clear in my words and their condescending tone. They didn't improve the situation at all. But I was passed that.

'All you do is whine about how you found your anchor in life and then The Establishment took it all away. Well, boo-hoo. We—they—might have tainted the idea of religion, but you were all too happy to throw away your faith at the first hurdle you faced. Your faith wasn't real to start off with. You know what? You should look in the mirror for a change and see who the real reason is for your current situation.'

His face was bright red, the hands on the axe white-knuckled. My words cut deep. His lips were pulled into a thin hard line, one I associated with the object of his anger dying a very painful death in the absolute near future. In all the altercations—or murders—I'd been party to, this was a dead giveaway. More than enough reason to stop my actions and not bait him anymore.

But this had to be done. I couldn't get through to him that his killing spree wasn't helping. Worse, it was hindering our cause. My cause. I wanted to deliver a real blow to The Establishment. Not just the loss of yet another expendable minion. If we continued on the current path, it would only result in more people hunting us.

He crossed the short distance between us and grabbed me by the throat, pushing me back to the wall with the strength of his onslaught. I felt my feet leave the ground as he pinned me to the hard wooden wall, the splinters dug into my back through the thin material of my shirt. I held on to his wrist with both hands in a futile attempt to wrest myself loose. My breath came in ragged gulps. I kicked out, my foot connecting with his shin. He was oblivious to my onslaught and brought the massive double-headed axe up above his head ready to descend in an arc that would no doubt sever my head from my body.

'You know nothing about me or my faith,' he whispered. The soft sound even more frightening than if he had shouted. I'd overstepped my boundaries. Way, way, overstepped—by a couple of miles.

His arm arced backwards. His stare bore into me.

I let go.

I dropped my hands from his wrist and just stared back into the depths of his eyes.

It felt like an eternity.

The arm with the axe slowly lowered from attack stance. My toes were still not touching the ground comfortably, but the axe was an improvement—I hoped.

Jonah pushed his face up close to mine.

'I have looked in the mirror. Many times. Deep into my own eyes. I've seen the monster.'

With that, he dropped me. I fell into a pathetic heap, gasping for breath.

Jonah looked at me one more time, then turned and left, taking the axe with him.

He stayed away for almost two days.

To date, I still have no idea where he was.

The door opened and the sun light was completely blocked out by his bulk. Jonah walked in, placed the folded axe against the wall and walked over to the kitchenette. He picked up the full coffee pot and an empty mug and walked over to the table where I sat.

'Refill?' he asked, holding up the pot.

I nodded. Not sure what else to say.

The coffee sloshed in the mugs, full to the brim. Like I said, no finesse. Nothing subtle about this man.

The chair groaned under his weight as he sat down opposite me. The silence between us felt oppressive. It had an almost physical texture. We sipped our coffee.

'Now what?' he finally asked.

'Now we get down to business.' I turned the computer so he could see what I'd spent the past day-and-a-half doing.

'You've been busy.'

I nodded. 'Had to get through the day somehow.'

'But you stayed here. Waiting for me?' his features were softer than I expected. The muscles relaxed.

Now it was my turn to nod. 'Figured you'd come back some time.' I smiled.

'Could have taken a while.'

'Yeah. But I decided I owed you. After what I said. I opened Pandora's box.'

'Why did you do it? I almost killed you.' He studied his coffee while speaking.

'It had to be done,' I answered. 'We can't go on this way, killing everyone on the list. We must step back and make a real plan. One that will bring down the whole Establishment. Not just a few of the puppets. You couldn't see further than your own pain and revenge. One way or the other, I had to get the message home. I had to chance it.'

'Quite the risk.'

'Yeah, and I'm still reeling.' He looked up; a small smile pulled at the edges of his lips. The sparkle in his eyes was a welcome sight. I mirrored his mirth.

'So, this is your master plan?' He turned the screen to fully face him.

He read in silence, occasionally cocking his head, or nodding slightly. Jonah's big hands deftly handled the computer as he scrutinised my work.

'Very thorough.' Was that a compliment? We were making progress here.

'I like your title. It's catchy. "Fall from grace."'

'I thought you might. I thought I would keep up the analogy.'

We both smiled.

'You could say I am truly a fallen angel now. THE fallen angel.'

'Do I call you Lucifer now? Or maybe Lucy?' He laughed.

'No way. Not changing my name.' That would make it all too close for comfort. It was a metaphor, a joke. No more than that.

I smiled at the thoughts that filled my head.
'I will be the devil to my father's god.'

Chapter Thirteen

'My plan is to get to the Ventus-Dei. The inner circle. Take them out and we inflict a massive blow on The Establishment.'

'Take them out? Kill them you mean?' Jonah was direct.

'No. Not necessarily.'

He cocked his head in question.

'If we kill them, they'll achieve martyrdom. That's exactly what we don't want.'

'Martyrs?'

'Look at the last one we took out. His death hasn't deterred anyone from believing the scam. Exactly the opposite. His murder is seen as the result of a terrorist attack. It's being sold as though he died for his faith. They're making this all about Islamic fundamentalism. Terrorists targeting the men of the cloth. It's making him into a saint. The direct effect is a rise in Christian zealots all aching to die for their own religion.'

'They have taken our work and turned it around to bite us.' His dark brooding mood was back again.

'Exactly.'

We were silent.

'We need to expose them for the scammers they are. Killing more of them will only backfire on us.'

'I tried that,' Jonah commented. 'When I found out what they were doing I tried to convince others about the conspiracy. They thought I was mad or laughed in my face. At least when I kill them, someone notices.'

'Yeah, but for all the wrong reasons.' Jonah reluctantly nodded his assent. I continued, 'you didn't know who was toxic and who wasn't. You thought all of them were corrupt. You have me now. We have a list of bad apples. That means at least some to of the others are good guys, or girls if you count the nuns. But they won't take our word for it. We need to get backing from people with clout. Then people will listen when we come with proof of the scam. We need to get the good part on our side so they can help us convince others about the conspiracy. With help, we can focus our combined attention on weeding out the bad apples within the religions, hopefully, without trashing everything if possible. People want to believe in a higher power. It's ingrained in your human nature to look up to a deity and to hope for something better in the afterlife.'

'But if we do that then people will still believe and still be susceptible to reincarnation and slavery after death. Won't they?' Jonah asked.

He understood where I was going to. 'They would. That's why we need to approach it differently. We can't realistically expect people not to believe anymore. It's inherent in human nature to want to have faith in something grand. And for many people it's the only hope they have. Besides the fact that we don't know if there actually is a real god. If there is, we might be robbing the faithful of an afterlife in

Heaven. We need to make sure The Establishment is wiped out but not religion itself.'

'So how do we do that?' I had his attention.

'We make sure the souls cannot be found. We hijack the supply chain.' I felt good. We were finally making some progress; Jonah had opened up to other, less violent ways of achieving our common goal. It wouldn't be easy. But this was a step in the right direction.

His brow creased in deep thought. 'How do your people know which ones believe and which don't?' he asked.

'It's quite ingenious really. It's also why my family still needs The Establishment. This is the weak point in their organisation.' I smiled. 'The believers are given a compound by the priests that makes them visible to our technology.'

Jonah cocked his head in interest. 'What compound?'

I was on a roll. 'It's a blend of chemicals and minute nanites our scientists invented. The name eludes me, but that's not important—wouldn't mean anything to you anyway.' He raised his left eyebrow. 'They're from our dimension. Can't be found here.' I added hastily. He nodded marginally, just enough to show I was off the hook.

'It's powdered and used in specific holy rites in the Christian churches. The communion, the sacraments, that kind of thing,' I explained.

'And your computers pick these up?' he sat forward with his elbows on his thighs and the fingers of his hands forming a tent under his chin.

'Yes. There's a team of analysts that monitors the frequencies twenty-four-seven, three-six-five. The chemical stays in the body and when the person dies that sets off the nanites and the computers are pinged. They home in on the signal and kidnap the soul when it leaves the body.'

'Do they distribute these nanites to everyone in the congregation?' Jonah asked.

I shook my head. 'No. Just the ones that are profitable for the family. Our customers are all in the heavy industry. They need strong and healthy young men to work in their factories. The work the recruits do is extremely taxing and often dangerous. Most don't make it longer that three or four years. Then they become worthless for their owners.' I was acutely aware of the coldness of the reasoning behind what I was saying. It sounded crass and contemptuous. I glanced at Jonah to gauge how he was digesting all of this. Outwardly, he was calm. But I saw the fire in his eyes.

I continued, 'the buyers want value for their money. So older men, or women for that matter—and I'm not being misogynistic here—are not a good commodity for my family. Reincarnation is an expensive process. My family only invests in the souls that are commercially viable for them. The first segregation is established by selective distribution of the nanites which are only given to potential recruits that fall in the profile.'

I felt uncomfortable under his gaze. His righteous anger was directed at my family, and by extension to me. I felt my earlier enthusiasm wilt.

'What about people who don't die quickly after they receive the nanites and grow old?' Jonah asked, not lingering on the atrocity that was my family.

I was pleasantly surprised at his insightful questions. 'That was a challenge for a long time. The initial nanites were long-lived. They were administered once, often when the subject was young. This resulted in the situation you mentioned. The subject lived a reasonably long life and was harvested when he died. Only he was then way too old to be of interest to my father's business. The scientists stuck their heads together and came up with a new version that has a relatively short lifespan. The host outlives the nanites and thus joins in the regular selection process.'

'So how long do the nanites last?'

'Two or three years, though the strength wanes after about sixteen months. Then the subject needs a top up.'

He nodded. 'And anyone who is potentially interesting as a recruit is subjected to nanites?' The intense look was back again.

'Yes. Unbeknownst to them.'

'Of course.' There was a clear sarcastic undertone, but I couldn't blame him.

'Do I have any in my system?'

'Undoubtably,' I answered truthfully. I let that land. 'Even without your potential as a recruiter, just your size and stature would make you an ideal candidate for sale.' This was not the time to sugar-coat anything.

He nodded again. It made sense. But that didn't decrease the invasive character of the fact that Jonah faced slavery should he die prematurely, which given our chosen quest, was quite probable.

He was quiet for a few minutes. Digesting everything.

'Quite the organisation,' he finally commented.

'Yes. It is. But it's also the weak spot in the whole process. No measure of technology will ensure success if the compound is no longer distributed to the potential recruits. No compound in the body, no nanites, no reincarnation.'

He raised an eyebrow. 'Simple as that, huh?'

'Basically, yes.'

There was a ghost of a smile. 'If we bring down The Establishment, then we stop the distribution.'

I nodded.

'Okay. Then that's the plan,' Jonah concluded.

'It's the basics.' I brought him down to earth. 'Now we need to decide how to achieve our goal.'

'How do we do that?' Jonah asked.

Chapter Fourteen

Jonah looked like he had been in a car accident when he returned from a two-day absence. There was a big lump on his forehead with a butterfly band-aid holding the edges of a tear in the skin. The eye beneath was half-closed. Dark purple and blue bruising extended from his swollen eyelid to halfway down his cheekbone. He limped slightly, pulling his left leg, and he favoured his right arm a bit. The knuckles on both hands were red where the skin was broken. All this contrasted to the enormous smile on his face.

I pitied the other guy.

Jonah walked over to the permanently filled coffee pot and poured himself a fresh cup. He held up the pot in question.

'No thanks, I'm good,' I held up my full cup.

He walked to the table where I was working, pulled the chair out and sat his bulk down with a sigh. As an afterthought he pulled a roll of bills from his jeans and put them on the table in front of me. I looked up from the money to his smiling face.

'Rent and food money,' he explained between sips of his coffee.

'Where did you get it?' I asked, my mind already computing it must have something to do with his current state.

'Where do you think?' He indicated the damage on his face. I shrugged, no idea.

'Cage fighting.' His tone was matter of fact. No indication of any anger or adrenaline, he could have been talking about a walk in the park.

'Cage Fighting?' I had no idea what he was talking about.

'Guess it's a human thing then,' he explained. 'It's underground MMA fighting. Mixed Martial Arts.' Basically, anything goes, as long as you don't intentionally kill each other.'

'You get paid for that?'

'Not so much for the fight itself, though that does bring in a few hundred bucks. I bet on myself winning. That's where the real money is.'

'And then you fight a stranger?' It sounded unbelievable to me that anyone would voluntarily take on Jonah, even if the money was good. I'd fought him many times, too many. He fought dirty, and he was immensely strong with a pain threshold that was out of this world. It was like attacking a concrete wall.

'Yep.' The smile was a mile wide.

'And by the looks of it, you won.'

He looked at me incredulously, his brow creasing in mock shock. 'Of course, I did.'

I cocked my head in recognition. 'Do you get to use the axe?' I asked.

He huffed, 'no, of course not. It's a sport. I'm not trying to kill him.'

'Well, looks as though the man you fought wasn't aware of the rules.' I pointed to his face.

'This?' His laugh was full of mirth. 'This is nothing. You should see the other guy.'

He became serious. 'We need money. If we're going to go after the Ventus-Dei, we'll need to travel. Pay for hotels. Eat. That kind of thing. And for that we need cash. Credit cards will be a liability, anyone can follow and find us. We must stay under the radar.' I nodded. He had a point. 'And your funds are running low.' Yeah, tell me about it.

We'd lived off the money I had when I came to this dimension. About twenty thousand dollars, but it was almost gone.

'There's a lot more money,' I surprised him. 'I just can't get at it without alerting my family.'

That piqued his interest. 'How much?'

'A lot. More than a million.' That raised an eyebrow.

'Where is it?'

'In accounts offshore. Bermuda and Switzerland. They have, shall we say, less than moral banking practices.' I humoured him. There was no way I could get at the funds.

'Tax havens.'

I nodded. 'We don't pay taxes.' I shrugged.

He laughed. 'No. I guess you don't.'

Serious again, Jonah sipped his coffee. 'You can't get at it?'

'No. Not without all bells going off back home. Then they'll know where to find me,' I explained.

'Not necessarily.' He grinned conspiratorially.

My turn to be surprised.

'I know someone who might be able to help.' He looked at me over the coffee mug. I nodded.

'Let me make some calls.' He stood up and walked to the back of the house and then outside into the back street as he pulled out his phone.

He came back three minutes later, his grin larger than life.

'We have an appointment at ten PM tomorrow,' he stated before he went to the bathroom for a very necessary shower.

Jonah looked marginally better the next day. The lump on his forehead was smaller though the bruises around his eye were much more colourful.

To my surprise, he steered us through the small streets of what was generally accepted as an up-and-coming side of town and parked near a former warehouse that was now the location of trendy lofts. We rode the upscaled goods-elevator to the top floor and stopped in front of one of the two formidable, grey metal doors on the small landing. It looked quite imposing. A remnant of the previous use of the building maybe.

Jonah pressed the bell and stood squarely in front of the camera. We waited for a few minutes and were rewarded with the sound of multiple bolts sliding back. The door opened. A pretty, petite twenty-something African Amer-ican woman with bright blue and green streaks in her plat-inum blonde hair and a diamond stud in her nose, stood in the massive opening. Her diminutive size was emphasised even more by Jonah's as he swept her up in his arms.

'Hey, you big lug.' Her voice was strong and clear. 'Put me down, you dope.'

He complied amidst chuckles. Her smile was as wide as his, until she looked past him and saw me.

'Who's the fashionista?' she asked nodding her head at me.

Jonah stepped to the side. 'This is Gabriel. My associate. The one I told you about.'

'Associate, huh?' She scrutinised me. Her eyes travelled from my feet all the way up to my face. I stayed put and waited until she was finished, my features neutral.

She decided I was okay, or at least Jonah's problem if I wasn't. 'Well. The two of you had better come in before the neighbours call the cops.'

Jonah entered and I brought up the rear. I passed the woman, continued after my "associate", and heard the metallic thud of the bolts sliding back into their slots behind us. She passed us and walked over to a breakfast bar in the kitchen area.

'Coffee?' she asked Jonah. 'Or something stronger?'

'I'll take the stronger,' he answered. She turned and pulled two bottles of beer from a bright red retro-style fridge along with a bottle of white wine. She capped the beers and shoved one in front of me. Guess I was drinking whatever Jonah was.

She scrutinised me as I took in the surroundings.

The loft was big and light, the four-metre ceiling-high windows on both sides of the big area let in the waning sunlight. The main area was a big living room with the open kitchen we were standing in. The walls were covered in bright comic and graffiti art in gold frames. To the right opposite the kitchen at the other end of the open space, was a construction that I guessed housed the bathroom and other facilities. The open staircase at the side of the construction led to a mezzanine bedroom. Turning back, my eyes landed on a batch of computer screens in a semi-circle frame around three keyboards on a big industrial desk. There must have been at least six or seven screens. Under and behind the desk was an array of computers and other electronic equipment surrounded by whiteboards on standards. The boards were filled with texts and images held on by magnets. One of the prints showed the design of a familiar item—Jonah's beloved axe.

'Gabriel huh?' I heard from behind me. I turned to face her. She sipped her wine and observed me over the rim of the glass.

'Yes. What do I call you?'

'You don't.' With that she turned to Jonah.

'This the guy you told me about on the phone?'

'Yeah. He's okay.'

'Is he? He looks shifty to me.' I was shocked. If anyone looked shifty or unreliable it was Jonah. How could she mean me? Jonah laughed. My indignation was compounded by his reaction.

'Can you help us?' I asked briskly, pushing my own feelings to the background.

She stared at me. 'You wouldn't be here if I couldn't.'

That shut me up.

'You bring the info?' she asked Jonah. He just pointed to me.

A large sigh. 'Where?'

I assumed she meant where the money was. 'Bermuda and Switzerland.'

'Of course.' She was not impressed. 'What kind of account?'

'Numbered.'

'No name?'

'No name.' I nodded.

'Not very secure.'

'Multiple users. It was easier,' I explained.

'Where's the info?'

I tapped my head.

'Great.' She took another sip. 'What do you want me to do?'

'The accounts are monitored,' I explained. 'I want the money to move to new accounts that only I can access.' She cocked her head as though it was hardly a challenge. 'Without leaving a trail,' I added. That got her interest.

'No tracks?'

'None.'

'How good are they in finding info?' she asked.

'Pretty good. There's a whole team.'

Now we were talking. There was an interested sparkle in her eyes. This girl liked a challenge.

She put the glass on the kitchen island and walked over to the computer screens. We followed.

My new friend sat at the desk and her fingers flew over the central keyboard, then the one on the left. Images flicked over the screens on one side and code scrolled over another.

She proceeded to drill me on the names of the banks, account numbers and passwords and worked on the computers.

We were silent. Jonah drank his beer while I just watched the young woman. She was astounding. Her chair moved from one side of the desk to the other as she alternated on the keyboards. I lost track of whatever it was she was doing. Her speed dazzled me, and I finally turned away from the screens.

Jonah indicated we go back to the kitchen to let her work in peace.

Ten minutes later she called us over.

'Where do you want the new accounts? Not the same bank I would imagine?'

'Nope.'

'Same kind of accounts?'

'Yes. Unless you have other suggestions.' She looked at me, trying to gauge my meaning. I just smiled. She was clearly the expert here.

'Same kind of accounts, it is.' She turned back to the screen.

Another ten minutes and she turned back to us again. 'You are now the proud owner of a new account in the Seychelles and one in Cyprus. Both numbered. Both password security with the latest additions. The one in the Seychelles also has an option for iris recognition security. Unless that is, you want others to be able to access your cash.'

'Iris protection is good,' I agreed.

We spent another hour on the details, at the end of which I had two new accounts with the money spread over both, the majority on the extra protected Seychelles one. Her software transferred the amounts in multiple transactions through hundreds of funds and accounts to finally end up on my new accounts. The trail didn't end there, her software continued transactions for another three hundred steps, though without the money changing hands. It would be impossible to follow and know where the money ended up, even for the computer experts in my dimension.

My family had lost the funds. Clear and simple.

It cost me though. She took five percent. I didn't argue, she was worth it. After the transactions were completed, she gave me a handwritten note with the account numbers, passwords and contact info. Nothing was saved on the computer, and she showed me how she deleted all tracks of the past few hours from her machines.

'Totally untraceable,' she stated. 'Even for me now, so don't lose the info.'

I smiled. 'Thanks.'

'You paid for it. No need for thanks.' She turned off the computers, returned to the kitchen and refilled her glass. She didn't offer us another beer, which we took for a dismissal.

Jonah leant over and kissed the top of her head. 'Thanks, Tiny.'

Her face lit up. 'You're welcome.'

'I'll come back to see you soon.' Her eyes sparkled. She softly bit her underlip and there was a decidedly sexy atmosphere in the room. Jonah raised his eyebrow and winked.

She walked us to the door, the sound of the bolts loud as we stood on the landing waiting for the elevator.

'That was interesting,' I said.

'And efficient,' Jonah answered looking very smug. 'She's the best.' I nodded. 'At everything.'

Too much information.

We had funds. Money we would need to bring down one of the mightiest organisations in the world.

Things were looking up.

Chapter Fifteen

'We need allies.' I stated resolutely. We were going over the details of the plan in our apartment. Jonah was splayed on the sofa, while I was sitting at the table facing him.

'Don't you think that's dangerous? And where would we get them?' Jonah challenged.

'I told you before, there are still good people in the Church. We need to get to them and convince them The Establishment is a real danger.'

He raised an eyebrow and the edge of his lips curled up in disdain. 'How do you propose to find out who they are?' Touché. I had no idea. 'They're not on your list.'

I tried a different angle. 'Who did you trust while you were a priest?'

'Too many people.'

Not helping. 'I get that some of them disappointed you, but what about the others?'

'I'm not sure there are any,' he answered. 'What about your list? Are those all the bad guys?'

I shook my head. 'No, it's not complete. This is the list

of the most valuable recruiters, not all humans involved in The Establishment. That would have been more helpful in hindsight. But there's no way I can get that now.' We were stuck.

I stared at the screen, trying to think of another angle.

'Would that be documented somewhere in the Ventus-Dei?' he mused, bringing me back to our discussion.

I shrugged. 'I expect so. They must know who is on their side and who isn't.'

A thought struck me. 'Your computer expert. The lady who got the money transferred. Would she be able to do a deep search for Ventus? They must have some kind of data storage somewhere.' It sounded plausible to me.

He crunched his brow. 'What if it's all on a closed off server? Something not connected to any network or Internet.'

'It can't be.' I continued. 'They would need to have access for many people, from all different places.'

Jonah sat forward and reflected on my answer. 'Could be a secure network. Or the dark web.' What was it with Jonah? He seemed reluctant to move with this idea.

I looked at him, trying to gauge why he was stalling. 'Yes, that's why we need an expert. Could she help?'

His eyes bore into me. 'Possibly. She sleeps, eats, and dreams computers. I'd be surprised if there was anything she couldn't do.' Jonah smiled at the thought, then became serious again.

'But it will cost,' he remarked.

'Of course.' I was prepared to pay for her services if it helped our cause. Frankly I had no other ideas. I was stuck.

'Negotiations will be difficult.' Jonah continued, still stonewalling.

'What about convincing her about the scam?' It was a long shot, but anything that could help had to be attempted.

'We could try. But I'm not sure she gives a shit about that kind of thing.'

'She cares about you,' I commented.

'She cares about our fun times. Not sure whether she actually has feelings for me.'

'So, go have some fun, and ask her while you're at it,' I suggested.

Jonah returned late the next day. The smile on his face was a mile wide.

'Are you going to make me ask you how it went?' I quizzed him after ten minutes of silence.

His chuckle was irritating, and he continued to sip his coffee. I turned back to my research. Fuck him.

Finally, he came over to the table and sat down. 'Quite the night,' he teased.

'I gathered.' My short terse answers only increased his amusement.

'She's really something, that girl. But hey, I already knew that' he boasted.

I turned from the computer to humour him. 'You look like the cat that ate the canary.'

'So would you if you were in my place.' He sighed to emphasise the comment.

'In your physical exuberance, did you by chance remember why you were really there?' I asked sarcastically to further chuckles.

'Who says that wasn't my main goal?' He drained the coffee. 'Of course, I remembered. That's why I'm late. She'll do it. For thirty thousand.'

'Thirty thousand?' I was aghast. 'That's daylight robbery.'

'Well, she does know your financial status, so it shouldn't be a surprise.'

'Yes, but thirty thousand!' I exclaimed.

'Don't be so petty. We need help and she can give it. Ebony's good. The best. If anything can be found, she'll uncover it.'

'For that amount, she'd better.' I had to have the last word. 'What about the scam? Did you talk to her about that?'

'I did.'

'And?' God, he was exasperating.

'She wasn't really surprised. Quite open to the idea. She's basically an atheist. The only thing she really believes in is human nature. And that's rotten. So, it sounded conceivable.'

Not what I had expected, my turn to raise an eyebrow.

'Now what?'

'She's expecting you tomorrow at ten in the morning. Make sure you're on time.' He patted me on the shoulder in an aggravatingly patronising manner.

'Aren't you coming?'

'I'll already be there.' That massive smile again.

At ten sharp I rapped my knuckles on the big metal door of the loft and was rewarded with a mostly naked Jonah who opened the door. The boxer shorts had clearly been pulled on in a hurry and were askew.

'Too early?' I asked innocently as I tapped my watch.

He laughed. 'Is it ten already?' He stepped aside and let

me into the apartment, closing and locking the door behind me.

I walked on into the central area where I encountered a slightly more clothed Ebony wearing Jonah's t-shirt that covered her down to her knees. Her bright neon hair was hastily pulled back in a big clip, stubborn tendrils escaping on all sides. She looked even smaller and more fragile than the last time I saw her.

'Hi Limey,' she called out amicably as she made her way to the kitchen.

Limey? What the hell was that? I glanced at Jonah and shook my head in puzzlement.

'It's a nickname for a British national,' he explained.

'I'm not British.'

'No, but you sound like one,' Ebony called from the kitchen.

'Where did you get your accent anyway?' Jonah asked.

I looked at him. Really? Now?

He walked to the staircase and proceeded up to the bedroom, leaving me alone with Ebony. I felt distinctly uncomfortable. Not just because I obviously interrupted something, also because of the scrutiny I was subjected to. I felt her stare burn the back of my head and turned around. Sure enough, she was observing me closely. Goosebumps ran up and down my arms. How could someone so small exhume such a strong aura?

'What will it be? Coffee, or would you rather have tea?' She was taking-the-piss out of me. Well two can play that game.

'Tea please, with a splash of milk.' I answered cheerfully. She stared back at me, trying to fathom whether I was joking or not.

'Okay, tea it is.' With that she turned and rummaged

around in the cupboards, brought out a water cooker which she filled and plugged into a socket. Tea was definitely not a regular item around here.

Jonah, dressed in jeans and another t-shirt, joined us, and was rewarded with a big mug of coffee, a plate full of eggs and bacon, and a seductive smile. My tea was set in front of me—without milk—and we all sat on the bar stools.

'Jonah already explained what we are looking for?' I asked to get the conversation going.

I almost wilted under her stare. 'He mentioned some things, but I want to hear it from you too.' She pulled a keyboard out from under the counter and flicked her fingers over the keys, linking it to her computers no doubt.

'One thing I want to get cleared up first,' she said. I cocked my head in question.

'Jonah said you weren't human. He told me you were from another dimension and your family is behind just about the biggest scam in human history.'

'That about covers it.' I glanced at Jonah. He sported a big smile as he shoved another fork full of breakfast into his mouth.

'How do I know you two aren't bullshitting me?' she continued. 'Do you have any specific alien powers?

I stared at her. What the hell was she talking about? Powers?

I was just about to answer when Jonah stabbed my hand hard with his fork. The shock of the sudden pain caused me to cry out. I grabbed my painful appendage and cradled it in front of my chest. Jonah still sported that infuriating smile, wiped his fork on his t-shirt and continued to eat.

'What the fuck did you do that for?' I shouted.

He just pointed the fork to my bleeding hand. I looked

down at the drops of blood that dropped from the punctures and pooled on the kitchen counter.

'It's purple!' Ebony exclaimed.

'Yep.' Jonah answered between bites. 'I rest my case.'

'You could have tried a different tactic,' I complained still nursing my aching appendage.

'Wouldn't have been so conclusive.'

Ebony grabbed a clean dish cloth and a first-aid kit from under the sink. 'Do you need a bandage?'

'No. It's stopped bleeding. We heal fast.' I answered.

'There you go.' Jonah remarked happily.

'Let's start again, shall we?' Ebony suggested. 'You're an alien.' I shrugged at that. It was all a matter of perspective. 'Any more talents?' she continued.

'We heal well, and I'm stronger and faster than the average human my size.'

'Just the average,' Jonah interjected. 'Nothing else?'

I shrugged. 'I never really paid any attention to what I could do here,' I answered.

'Would be handy if you had other powers, like mind reading, telepathy something like that.'

'That's all bullshit. Hollywood make-believe,' I answered. The idea of superhuman, or for humans paranormal talents, did however latch on to my brain. I would have to pay more attention to what I was capable of. Maybe there were undiscovered advantages I could exploit.

The holes in my skin were fading fast. A few more minutes and they would be nothing more than a slightly irritating memory. Ebony watched the process with obvious fascination.

'Handy,' she remarked dryly. I smiled and sipped my tea.

Ebony was serious again, 'tell me what you're looking for. Your words.'

'Okay.' I took a step away from Jonah—just in case he wanted to make another point. 'We're looking for data on an organisation called The Establishment. It's a clandestine fraternity within the Christian Church that upholds one of the biggest scams in human history.'

'Christian. So not just the Catholic Church?'

I shook my head. 'No. It's much more widespread than that. Not even restricted to Christianity. Basically, it covers all the major human religious doctrines. What we're interested in now, is the Christian side.'

'Widespread. Okay.' She mused as she typed.

'Give me some key words.' She looked at both of us expectantly.

'Key words?' I asked, not understanding her request.

'Yes. Specific words you associate with this Establishment. Words that in one way or the other describe it or are linked to it. Anything that comes to mind. Just throw it out. We're brainstorming here.'

'Religion,' Jonah started.

'Recruits. Heaven,' I added.

We continued, alternating between the two of us while Ebony typed the words into whatever software she was using to search the Internet. The constant stream of words dwindled, and we struggled to find more.

'Okay,' she said. 'That should be enough to start with. If you think of more, Jonah can text me.' We both nodded.

'What about names?' she asked.

'We might have a list of names,' I said reluctantly. She picked that up and looked up, her eyebrow raised.

'You do or you don't have a list,' she remarked coldly. 'That's the thing with lists.'

'We have a list,' Jonah answered for me, producing a written version of the list to my annoyance. He laid it on the worktop between me and Ebony. She pulled the page towards her keyboard and continued to type.

I glanced at Jonah—we'd discuss this later. He just smiled.

'These are all high-profile guys,' Ebony remarked. 'Some of them very powerful.'

We refrained from comment.

'Are we going after these guys?' she asked.

'Not necessarily. These are the front guys. Ultimately, we're looking for the ones behind them. The real inner circle of The Establishment. They're in the shadows. Could be that one or two of these might be part of the Ventus-Dei, but I don't expect it.'

'The Vents-Dei is the inner circle?' Ebony asked. Jonah nodded.

'They run The Establishment?'

'They do.'

'And what do you ultimately want to do with the information?' The question surprised me. This was just a job for her. A well-paid job if I say so myself. There was still some resentment there with me. It coloured my judgement.

'Need to know basis,' I stated resolutely.

She looked up at me, then to Jonah who shrugged, and back to me.

'I need to know,' she answered with an edge. 'It determines what kind of data I'm looking for.'

I childishly refrained from answering.

Ebony stopped typing. She moved the keyboard away from her and leant on the counter with both hands.

'Let's get somethings straight, Limey.' She stared me right in the eye. I actually felt uncomfortable. She seemed ten foot tall. The strength emanating from her stern features and blazing eyes put me on edge. I had to force myself to hold her stare. 'You came to me for help. I'll give it to you, but for that you'll have to trust me, it's a human thing. No trust. No data. I can't find what you're looking for if you give me restricted information. I need to know the details to find the one diamond in all the rocks. My first searches turned up seven million plus hits. Unless you have a few decades to spare, I need to narrow that mountain of data down to something usable. For that I need specifics.' I wilted slightly under her stare. She was a powerhouse, I understood Jonah's attraction to her.

'You choose. Either you trust me to keep your informational confidential, or I just bill you for what I've done now, and we stop wasting each other's time.' She leant back against the kitchen cupboards and waited on my decision.

I glanced at Jonah. No help there. He had his now customary smile plastered to his lips.

'You're right,' I finally conceded, quite redundantly, she knew she was. 'You need to know.'

For a tense moment, I thought I'd blown it. Then she smiled, pulled the keyboard back in front of her and we started again.

The "interview" lasted for a few hours. We moved from the kitchen to the rack of computer screens and back to the kitchen hours later to devour the pizzas Jonah ordered. Finally at four twenty-three we called it a day. Ebony shooed us out of the loft and got to work.

Jonah and I returned to our apartment where he showered and changed into new jeans and a clean t-shirt. I took my turn under the rain shower and alternated between hot and cold, my skin tingling under the deluge, my mind going over the events of the day.

It was dark by the time we walked the streets behind our apartment looking for a restaurant for dinner. Jonah announced he was starving and needed protein, so we were on the lookout for a steakhouse or Argentinian restaurant, something with lots of protein. We finally found one after a twenty-minute walk that enhanced my own hunger.

The restaurant, Los Fuegos, was a typical steak house with Argentinian touches in the furnishings and an almost cinematic ambiance, but it was the smell that hit me as we followed the maître-d to a table near the big grill not to the fire kitchen. The sizzles of the meat cooking on the open fire grill intensified the growls originating from my stomach. During my extensive stays in this dimension, I developed a definite taste for your food, especially hot and spicy meat, or fish dishes.

We ordered from the specials and the waiter brought us our bottle of Catena Alta Malbec red wine. I let the deep red liquid swish around my mouth and savoured the full-blooded liquid.

'Where did you meet Ebony?' I asked Jonah after we ordered and settled down to wait for our food.

'At the fights,' he answered to my amazement.

'She was in the audience? At one of your fights?' I could see that. She didn't seem like the kind to shy away from brutal sports.

'Not exactly,' he laughed. 'I was at one of hers.'

Well, that was unexpected. 'She was fighting?'

He nodded. 'Her opponent was head and shoulders taller than her, but she annihilated the competition. A real firecracker.'

Somehow, it seemed to fit. I thought back to the uncomfortable feelings I experienced earlier today under het scrutiny. 'Not one to take on without gloves then?'

'Un huh.' He laughed. 'Big thick fireproof gloves. At least until you really get to know her. Then she's a pussycat.'

'Like you,' I joked.

His mood changed one-hundred-eighty degrees. 'I'm no pussy cat. Not even if you've known me your whole life.'

I tried to fix the issue. 'She seems to bring out the good side of you. Make you happy.'

He sighed. 'I guess she does. At least for a short while.' We sat in silence until the food came. Big brooding Jonah was back again.

We polished off two bottles of wine with our massive dinner. It was in one word fantastic, and we left the restaurant three hours later completely full and satisfied. I suggested to go back to the hotel, but Jonah had somewhere to go to, so we split up and I walked the quite streets of Mobile on my own.

Chapter Sixteen

Jonah's phone rang.

He picked it up off the table, looked at the caller and walked to the kitchen to take it.

'Hi, Eb.' He didn't get much further. 'Yeah, he's here. Sure, I'll put you on speaker.'

Jonah moved back to the couch and placed the phone on the coffee table in front of us.

'ED, you there?'

I raised an eyebrow. ED?

'She means you,' Jonah explained.

'ED?' I couldn't stop myself from asking.

'Extra Dimensional,' Ebony beat Jonah to it. I was still puzzled.

'Extra Terrestrial, but then in dimensions?' She explained. 'Oh well, never mind. Guess you never saw the film. Anyway, turn on the TV, guys. News. CNN. I'm not sure whether this is related to what you are looking for, but it does match a lot of the keywords. And it's shocking.'

Jonah zapped until he found the right channel.

The anchor-man was clearly distraught. Looking at the images behind him, I fully understood why.

'I have to warn you for very unsettling images in the following news report concerning the terrorist attacks on three mosques.' His voice faltered.

The image switched to a full-screen view of complete destruction. The burning ruins had previously been the Amsalem Centre in Boca Raton. The only thing left standing of the monumental white clad mosque was the minaret. Fire engines and police cars were parked haphazardly on the road in front of the demolished house of prayer. Their sirens barely drowned out the screams of the wounded. Ambulances came and went in a steady stream as victims were rushed off to hospital emergency rooms. Long rows of corpses covered in sheets and blankets were clearly visible in one of the shots.

The image changed to another equally distressing scene from Chicago. What was left of the Mosque Maryam was burning fiercely. A distressed reporter with tears streaming down her cheeks shouted over the din of the sirens and wails in the background. She kept turning from the camera to the terrible scene and back again.

'More than two hundred dead. Many, many more wounded, it's… it's…' The reporter was lost for words. She looked utterly heartbroken as she slid down and sat on the sidewalk, her head in her hands.

The image changed again. Now to Columbus. A wide-angle shot showed another devastation. The Noor Islamic Cultural centre was ablaze. Angry orange, white and blue flames shot up into the sky from the roof. An explosion rocked the dome on the right side of the big building. Then another blew out the remaining windows and part of the brick wall into the small lake in front of the centre.

Jonah and I were speechless. I glanced at him, not believing my eyes. He gently shook his head in disbelief.

'No one has claimed the attacks yet,' we heard from the phone. I'd forgotten Ebony was still on the call. 'I can hack into Reuters and the Bureau of Counter Terrorism for the latest information if you want.'

'Yes.' I said in a daze. 'Please.' She hung up.

The anchor-man was back again. New images behind him showed yet another bomb site. This time in Europe. Russia had been shocked with an attack on the Heart of Chechnya Mosque in Shali. Two of the three minarets were demolished, as was the central dome. A fire raged throughout the entire complex and people frantically rushed to escape the inferno. A terrible cracking sound heralded the implosion of the roof. The screen was covered in a cloud of white smoke and dust, cloaking the destruction.

'More reports are coming in,' the distressed anchor man was barely audible. 'Italy. Spain. The Netherlands.'

'It's a coordinated attack.' Jonah remarked.

'Has to be,' I agreed. My mind was all over the place, a distinct uncomfortable feeling of recognition started to eat away at my insides.

'Your family?' Jonah put a name to it.

'Maybe.' I was dumbfounded. Surely it wasn't. I hoped against hope my family was not involved in this. But at the back of my mind a nagging voice pushed the last meetings with Michael to the foreground of my consciousness. Our conversations about fundamentalism. Surely, he hadn't taken that seriously.

'Someone will claim it. This kind of coordination has a big organisation behind it. It can't be a coincidence.' Jonah's words barely registered.

'No way. It's a synchronised attack on Islam.' I heard myself answer.

We stared at the tv screen. Jonah zapped to other stations, all with the same result. They all ran the images. The attacks dominated the news.

We watched for more than an hour. The three initial US attacks were joined by seven in Europe, Asia, and Australia. All happened within twenty minutes of the first strike.

I felt sick.

The CNN anchor man finally declared that the attacks had been claimed by the Christian Warriors of the World. A before-now unknown Christian fundamentalistic organisation. They gave no more information. Just a short video of a masked individual claiming responsibility for the biggest attack on Islam in centuries. At the end of the first hour, the tentative death count was twenty-seven hundred and seventy-six. With over five thousand wounded, many of them in critical condition. The vast majority of the victims were women and children. The bombs had intentionally been set off in the gendered areas designated specifically for them. A very specific targeting.

'Could you see if Ebony has found out any more than this?' I asked Jonah, my voice hollow and flat. My mouth was dry, and I had trouble swallowing. The extent of the destruction rocked me to my core.

Jonah nodded and dialled the number. I walked out on to the balcony. I needed air. My head was reeling. Surely, they hadn't?

This attack would have far-reaching consequences. Retaliation by extremist Islamic groups was a given. The escalation would be mind-blowing, especially if this new Christian terrorist group was backed by who I was afraid of.

Jonah joined me on the balcony. He passed me a stiff

drink. 'She's looking. Nothing to report yet, but she'll get back to us a.s.a.p.' I nodded and took the drink.

The strong whisky burned a path down my throat and into my gut. It was welcome. I had to feel alive again. Now, I was just numb.

'Nothing you could do about this,' Jonah remarked, accurately gauging my thoughts. 'Not even if it is The Establishment behind this. We couldn't have foreseen anything like this.'

'I know,' I answered. 'But I still feel responsible in some way. If my father is behind this, then I do bear some culpability. Just by association.' I couldn't bear to contemplate my responsibility could be more extensive.

'Don't kick yourself down. If it's The Establishment, we'll get them. Stamp them out once and for good. What's done is done. We can't turn back time. But we can ramp up our efforts. If there is any more info out there, Ebony will find it. That will give us a head start. Plus, they don't know we're here. They think it's just me.'

He was right.

Why didn't it make me feel any better?

Ebony called us over. There was too much to report back through the phone.

We picked up two six-packs of beer and a bottle of JD on the way and arrived at her loft just before midnight. She let us in, and we made a beeline to the ring of screens.

Each screen showed different data. One was a rerun of the CWW masked man claiming responsibility for the attacks. Another showed a para-military training camp with masked men and women in green and black garb. Three were filled with data and official forms. More showed a string of angry-looking men and one or two women, some of them holding the classic number boards I associated with a mug shot.

There was a large diversity of races and skin colours in the subjects on the screens, but the one thing they had in common was the hard fanatical glint in their eyes. Men and women alike.

Ebony had been busy.

'I dug deep,' she explained. 'The authorities and regular Internet were still clueless, so I turned to other avenues. The dark web is where most of the data comes from. The training camps and the happy looking campers are part of a recruiting video on the dark web. It's difficult to get to. Hidden behind a lot of religious trivia. I used key words from the bible after the CWW claimed the attacks. If they are as fundamental as they claim, then it stands to reason they would be well versed in the bible. Sure enough. I tried "Leviticus twenty-four". That got me into a private room with a load of weirdos. One guy led the discussions, all brimstone and hellfire. He pushed hard against Islam and other religions: Hinduism, Taoism, Buddhism. Anything not in the Christian dogma. Judaism is on the fence. Not named as an enemy, yet. I stuck it out for twenty minutes then left to research the stuff he referred to.' Ebony pulled the data from another screen to the large central terminal. She proceeded to lead us through everything she'd found.

After a taxing hour we moved back to the kitchen island to discuss what Ebony had discovered. The drinks flowed easily as we mused over the data.

'It's a very well organised alliance of multiple individual Christian groups from over the globe,' Ebony started. 'The recruitment videos rival Hollywood productions in their quality and screenplays. There is a sophisticated use of manipulation methods, including subliminal messaging.'

'What kind of images are they using for that?' I asked.

'Mostly anything we associate with Islamic terrorist actions. ISIS. 911. Beheadings. Dismemberment. All very disturbing. I even found some in the video where they claimed responsibility for the attacks.'

'The one on CNN?' I asked aghast.

'Yep. Very sneaky. They counted on the news channels airing the video without properly screening it first. Everyone wants to be the first to bring the news, right?'

'They've taken it down now,' Jonah remarked. 'Not available, even Facebook and Instagram have banned it. So, you're not the only one to have noticed that.'

'Good.'

'But it goes to show how sophisticated they are. They used the world media to clandestinely get their own message across. Very devious.' I mused.

'So not your neighbourhood bullies.' Jonah chimed in.

'No. The worst mistake we could make is not to take them seriously and underestimate them.' Ebony remarked.

'Rest assured.' I stated. 'I'm taking them as serious as cancer.' My anger was barely contained.

Jonah drained his drink and placed the glass in the sink. 'There's not much we can do at this time of night. We should get some sleep and take a new look at the data tomorrow morning.'

I nodded and took our coats from the chair where we had dumped them earlier.

'Could you stay?' Ebony asked Jonah. Her voice lacked the usual strength. 'I don't want to be alone tonight.'

He glanced at me, I nodded and replaced his coat back on the chair. 'I'll see you both tomorrow.' I said as I walked to the door. Jonah followed and locked it behind me. I heard him move back into the loft.

Standing in the lift I felt an enormous weight on my shoulders. This was at least partially on my slate. Even though Ebony hadn't found a clear link to The Establishment I knew it was them. It was just a question of time until that surfaced.

They had taken recruiting to a whole new level with the actions of the past seven hours. And I was feeling the guilt.

Chapter Seventeen

The fallout was enormous.

For two days the attacks dominated the news. CWW—formally unknown—was the single subject of every news-related show on all channels. The final death count of all attacks was three-thousand four hundred dead. A further-eight-thousand-plus injured, hundreds of them critically. Material damage was estimated at more than half-a-billion.

Internet blew up with reactions. People were outraged. Most countries expressed their sincere condolences for the families of the victims of this senseless violence. Silent marches were organised. Spontaneous peaceful vigils occurred in most large cities showing the solidarity that transcended religious borders. People held each other in their pain, shock, and sorrow.

A darker reaction followed from fundamentalist Muslim groups. Former ISIS related groups all over the world announced a new Jihad on Christianity in general—and CWW in particular—promising revenge for what had been done to Islam. A hastily set up suicide mission killed three innocent bystanders in France, wounding a further seven.

Rhetoric between the fundamentalists on both sides escalated. Threats and declarations of war dominated the news and Internet. A holy war seemed imminent.

'They're gaining ground.' Ebony stated.

'Which side?'

'Both.'

Young disillusioned Christian men and women flocked to the CWW. Their presence on the Internet grew every hour with the shared and retweeted nonsense they sprouted. Shocked and angered Muslim youth turned to ISIS for instant revenge.

It was a nightmare in the making.

It had one benefit—if you could call it that—it gave us a new avenue to find The Establishment.

We agreed they were behind the CWW. All signs pointed to them. I could feel the hand of my family in what was happening, maybe even with the cooperation of Arand and his kin, though that should be far-fetched given their animosity. A holy war would supply both sides with an abundance of strong young men's souls who in their zealot mindset rushed to die in the name of their religion. It was a dream come true for Dad and Arand.

'But doesn't your family want young men?' Jonah asked when we were once again huddled around the computers.

'They do,' I mused. 'It puzzled me initially, but if you see these attacks as a means to an end, then it all makes sense. The murder of innocent women and children impacts people much more than that of males. It incites feelings of revenge because they are perceived as the ultimate innocents. If you look at the big picture, with this as its apotheosis, then it is a calculated action. An intentional call to action.'

Whatever it was, it offered us a trail Ebony could follow.

'Be careful, Tiny,' Jonah insisted. 'We don't want them tracing your searches back to you.'

'Don't worry,' she answered to our relief. 'I'm very aware of the risks. We must assume with the level of organisation we're seeing now that they are computer savvy. I'll be very cautious and make sure any trail they might find is drowned in hundreds of proxies and jumps.'

Her fingers flew over the keys, constantly changing the contents of the screens. I had no idea how she could concentrate on anything specific with the amount of data she uncovered. But she did.

'How about you two go do something. Get out of my hair. There's nothing you can do here.' She shooed us out of the loft.

We took the hint and went back to our apartment. It was a welcome upgrade from the mostly sleazy hotels we'd stayed in at the beginning of our partnership. Money definitely has its advantages. Now we had the funds, it made no real sense to live in squalor. The police were still looking for the wrong man in relation to the earlier killings and we'd stayed off the radar since our move to Mobile.

Jonah talked me into a visit to the hotel gym. The exercise was very welcome. I'm a sporty type. Not the muscle-bound heavy-weight type like Jonah. More the cardio, long-distance kind of person. We have different sports in our dimension, but the basics are the same; do a lot of running, jumping and repeat. It helped me clear my mind. Jonah hit the weights.

After a long shower and a change of clothes we

returned to our rooms. Jonah checked his phone for the hundredth time.

'No news from Ebony?' He shook his head.

I installed myself in front of the TV while Jonah went to his bedroom for a nap. We'd worked through the night and, combined with the workout, I was beginning to feel fatigued as well. Ten minutes later I fell asleep in front of the screen.

I was woken by Jonah's phone. The TV had shut itself off after three hours and the sharp metallic tones of ACDC's Thunderstruck sounded like a megaphone in the silence of the dark room. Jonah answered it and, holding the mobile to his ear, joined me in the living room.

'Yeah, okay we'll be there in an hour,' he said. 'With lunch.' He hung up.

'Eb?'

'Yes. She's traced a lot of the chatter on Internet and the dark web to specific locations. She proposes to see if these coincide with the people on your list. Eb wants to discuss the next steps with us.'

We were making progress. Or should I say, Ebony was.

An hour later found us eating lunch at the kitchen island in Ebony's loft.

'CWW turns out to be a conglomerate of about thirty smaller groups scattered over the Christian world and even one in the middle of an Islamic strongholds. Some of the groups were already on the international terrorist radar as potentially worrying radical movements, mainly because of their violent character. Their members are generally recruited while in the prison system. The KKK is also involved though not officially, they have a strong Protestant

Christian dogma, even if it is warped.' Ebony led us through the results of her intensive research.

'Is CWW a front for White Supremacy?' Jonah asked.

'That's the strange thing. There is a big diversity in the background and ethnicity of the different groups. Their ideology ranges from Nazi's to Black power. The one defining characteristic is that they all uphold a version of Christianity. At least it's prominent in their propaganda. Whether they actually live by their dogma is another question all together.' That was surprising.

One of the things I never understood about you humans is your fascination for skin colour. You are obsessed with something as superficial as the pigment in skin. It defines you. Puts you, and everyone else in a specific clan. Characteristics that have absolutely nothing to do with skin pigment are attributed to whole races. I guess it's your unrelenting need to classify others into friend or foe. But still, based on pigment? How shallow can you be?

'There has to be a strong leadership in the CWW to house all these groups that are by nature at each other's throats,' Ebony mused.

'That's why it has to be something like The Establishment. That has the manpower and the monetary backing as well as the ideological clout, and now it's played its top card: The Establishment brought them together under one religion by identifying a bigger enemy. One they can all relate to,' I stated.

'A common enemy.' Jonah added.

'Yes. Islam. Their historical adversary. Justified by the acts of terrorism ISIS perpetrated.'

'So, we assume that it is them behind all of this?' Jonah proposed.

'It has to be.' There was no doubt in my mind.

'Okay. Now what?' Ebony asked.

'We need to follow the trail as far as possible until it shows up in a place we definitely know is linked to The Establishment.' It even sounded weak to me.

'Your list?' Jonah suggested.

'Yes. The list.'

'I checked everyone on your list,' Ebony chimed in. 'They all came up squeaky clean. That, in itself, is suspicious. No one is that angelic. There should at least have been something. Even if it was just a juvenile offence.'

'We have to assume The Establishment can doctor official data and cleanse any misdemeanours from the slate of their members,' I concluded.

'They know their way around computers,' Ebony agreed. 'There's some very sophisticated intelligence behind their sites.

'Then we must be careful. Make sure they can't find us while we search for them.' Jonah chimed in.

We all agreed.

'What if we pose as recruits?' Jonah suggested. He turned to Ebony, 'you said the CWW does a lot of recruiting online. Wouldn't that give you some room to manipulate data?'

'It could.'

'I expect somewhere along the line, there has to be a personal face-to-face moment. If they are as good at data manipulation as you say, they're probably afraid that official entities will do the same to them. After the attacks, they know they're under a magnifying glass. They will be paranoid,' I said. 'Plus, if my family is involved, then personal contact is mandatory. They want to look everyone in the eye.' I was thankful for that requirement. It seemed needless and over the top earlier, now it was an advantage.

'Then there will be an actual person in the process somewhere.' Ebony stated.

'Yes. And it will be a trusted human as well.'

She nodded. 'Okay. Then we join the CWW and see where that lead us.'

'Sounds like a plan,' Jonah added.

'I will have to make an Internet history for the candidate.' Ebony was already working on the details. 'We must assume they will check social media, that kind of thing. Probably even police records. They have to be careful.'

She grabbed the iPad and fired it up. 'I'll start off, but you need to give me hand with a profile. What kind of triggers will make them interested in the recruit? What is too much? That kind of thing.'

Jonah and I cleared up the remnants of lunch while Ebony proceeded on a basic list of characteristics. Jonah started the coffee machine, and we joined her at the computers to describe our impression of the ideal recruit for the CWW.

'Has to come from a religious background. Christian, probably easiest to make him or her white to start with,' Jonah started.

'Got that,' Ebony confirmed. 'I thought probably from the Bible Belt. Chattanooga, Tennessee. Make him a disillusioned Twelve-Tribes drop out. Parents were avid believers, he rebelled. That kind of thing.'

'Sounds good.' Jonah remarked.

I had no idea what the Twelve Tribes were, but they seemed to know, so I just went with the flow.

They discussed the details for the profile a while longer and settled on what seemed to me to be quite an extensive history. I watched them work from the kitchen. They were a good team.

Jonah came over to me while Ebony stayed behind the barrage of computers to create the persona on all official sites, not to mention social media.

'You work well together.' I commented.

'Yeah.' Jonah smiled. 'She makes it easy.'

'That's one clever lady.'

'You've just scratched the surface,' he smiled. 'She makes Einstein look like a fourth grader.'

We both smiled at that.

Less than an hour later Ebony declared she was finished. The profile was up, complete with a history sporting back-dated posts going back years, and she would start contacting the CWW as a potential recruit.

She scooted us out of the loft, and we went in search of yet another meal for my big, perpetually hungry partner.

She called us back next day in the afternoon.

'They took the bait.'

I was quite surprised at the speed. 'Isn't that a bit quick. Are we sure it's legit?'

'I had the same thought,' Ebony remarked. 'So, I set up another four profiles. Three of which already have a hit. The fourth one was a deliberate red-herring. Totally not interesting for them. I made it look like a scam. It comes back to a tabloid newspaper. They probably identified that by now. It's another potential lead I could follow.'

She really was remarkable.

'This shows us a few things,' she continued. 'One is what we expected; they have good computer people. They work quickly and do deep searches. I had some triggers on some of the deep data I concocted for the profiles. They don't do half work. Second thing is they're serious about recruiting as many psychos as possible. The tempo in which they work alarms me. All three of my "real" profiles were picked up in less than twenty-four hours, that shows a major growth goal.'

'They're interested in all three?' I was flabbergasted.

'Yes. Though the speed in which they reacted to the profiles differs.'

'What is the deciding factor for a quick reaction?' Jonah asked.

'The psycho-effect,' she answered. 'The more violent the profile—preferably with a criminal record to back it up—the quicker they react.'

We let that sink in.

'It fits the goal of maximum recruitment and maximum impact,' I said.

Ebony glanced at Jonah. 'Souls,' he explained. 'Ultimately this is all about gathering souls. Fundamentalism breeds death and destruction. That means they can harvest a lot of young strong souls.'

'What you said about the other dimension?' She was still hesitant to believe me.

Jonah nodded.

'I thought that was just a load of bull.'

'I wish it was,' he answered and laid his hand on her shoulder in support.

She turned to me. 'That's really why your blood's purple?' My turn to nod. 'And this whole thing about slavery after death is all real?'

'It is,' I answered, the impact of what this meant sinking to my gut like a block of concrete.

'That scares me.' I saw a mix of defiance and terror in her face.

'It should.'

'And this is why you're after The Establishment.' She stated. We didn't have to answer. 'Well, then let's get them.'

I had the impression this was no longer just a job for Ebony. In the past days she had become invested in our cause.

We gathered around the computer screens and Ebony showed us the communications for the three profiles. Next to the guy from Tennessee, she'd created a twenty-seven-year-old male white supremacist and a radical twenty-year-old mixed-race female MIT drop out with an IQ that rivalled Steve Hawkins.

The white supremacist had the first reply. His rap sheet was a dead giveaway. Grievous bodily harm, attempted murder—never proven— and a stint in the penitentiary where he absolutely was not released on good behaviour. The woman was next, most likely because of her intellect and the multiple run-ins she experienced with anyone of authority, not to forget her knowledge and intelligence. Our initial profile came in third.

The gist of the replies was generally the same, though most likely not automated; there was too much of the profiles in the communications. Generally, they sympathised with the hardships the profiles claimed to have experienced at the hands of the government, family or whatever Ebony had invented.

'Any mention of a face-to-face?' I asked.

'Not specific, but they are hinting at one, especially with the white supremacist. They asked whether he could travel freely. Probably because of the rap sheet.'

'Where would he have to go to?' Jonah asked.

'Miami area. That's what they mentioned.'

'Have you answered yet?'

'Naturally. I wanted to keep the profile interesting for them, so he had to look eager. I asked where and when.'

Sounded good to me.

'They said they'd get back to him a.s.a.p. with a meeting place and time. But first they wanted to do more background checks on him,' Ebony continued.

'They actually said that?'

'Yeah. I guess they want to weed out any bogus profiles before they go to the next step. Actually, meeting someone face-to-face is a much bigger risk for them than communication via the dark web.'

'Figures,' Jonah agreed. 'So now we wait?'

Ebony shrugged.

Great. Waiting was not what we did well, this would be a chore, especially for Jonah. His brooding features confirmed my conclusions.

Another thought struck me.

'How are you at repairing hardware?' I asked Ebony.

She looked at me quizzically. So did Jonah. 'Depends on the hardware,' she answered. 'I built most of my computers from scratch, so that should answer your question.'

I nodded in respect. This lady was an expert on anything technical, maybe she could help me with another job.

I walked back to my coat and rummaged in the inside pocket. I came back with a jumble of electronics in a Ziplock bag and placed the pathetic remnant of my transporter onto the table next to the computers.

Ebony was immediately interested in what would definitely be unfamiliar to her.

'What is it?' she asked as she open the bag and picked up a piece of the jumble of electrical parts.

'What was it might be more appropriate,' Jonah joked.

'It was my transporter,' I answered. 'I guess you could say it was a connection to the transportation hub in my dimension.'

'Transportation? As in "beam-me-up-Scotty"' There was clear interest in her face.

'Something like that, yes.' Even I was familiar with the old Star Trek films.

Ebony took a closer look at the multiple parts on the table. She picked up individual pieces and scrutinised them closely. She seemed especially interested in the power source.

'What happened to it?' she asked.

'I smashed it after my last transportation to this dimension.'

'Why?' Her eyes were opened wide in shock.

'It's a two-way device. I can—or could—activate a transportation from my side, but the transportation hub could also initiate one without my approval. I left my dimension in less than friendly circumstances and I didn't want to go back in a hurry.'

'Not good for your health?' She returned to the parts, scrutinising every piece in turn.

'Nope.'

'And you couldn't just turn it off?'

I shook my head. 'Not possible. It's a fallback system if anything happens to the owner, then the hub can activate an evacuation. And I guess my dad doesn't really trust anyone, so it's also an insurance. Just in case we do anything juvenile.'

'Shame you had to do such a thorough job of smashing it.' She put the piece she'd been examining back on the pile of parts. 'What do you want me to do with it?'

'I was wondering if you could replicate something like

that,' I answered. 'Without the two-way communication part.'

'Sounds like a challenge.' The smile on her face was contagious.

'Maybe,' I laughed.

'Imagine that. Me rummaging around in alien technology,' she mused as she dug back into the parts.

'If anyone can do it, it's you,' Jonah chimed in.

'Just don't plug anything into the power source yet,' I cautioned. 'We don't want to accidentally trigger anything. I expect my family is looking for me and that the hub is monitoring all traffic.'

'You want it to transport again?'

'No, that would be too much to ask,' I mused. 'The gadget needs the transportation hub to actually carry out the transportation. It's a combined technology. You need both. I don't think it will work with just this part, not unless you extend the technology, but I would imagine you would need to know the details of the hub for that.'

'You almost sound technically savvy,' she laughed.

'Well, I'm not an expert, but I can find my way around our technology. Yours—here in this dimension—is not familiar to me, but back home I was quite experienced in our mechanics.'

'And judging by a quick glance at these parts, and the fact that your dimension has cracked the transportation enigma, I would say you are light years ahead of us.'

'I don't know about that; we just took a different road.'

'I'll need you to explain the parts,' she continued, immersed in the challenge. 'What's for what. That kind of thing.'

'Yeah. Of course.' That sounded like fun. I finally had something I could excel in and make myself useful.

'Got any more gadgets like this one?' Ebony asked as she picked up another piece of for her alien technology.

'A few,' I answered. She looked up and cocked her head in question. I answered with a smile. Maybe another time.

Ebony and I spent the rest of the afternoon discussing my dimension's technology in general, and the transporter in particular. Jonah left to do some shopping, came back, and surprised us with a fantastic dinner he cooked in the loft's professional kitchen. Concentrating on something other than our quest lightened the mood for a while and we even had a good time. We all needed that.

It came to a premature halt when one of the computers pinged. The high-pitched sound cut through our conversations and Ebony reverted to work mode immediately. We left the remnants of our meal and all three moved to the bank of computers.

Her fingers flew over the keys, and she brought up what triggered the alert. There was a hit on one of the other two profiles. The female candidate, as predicted by Ebony.

'They want to meet her,' Ebony explained.

'Great,' Jonah answered. 'Looks like we're in.' He was all smiles. 'Where do they want her to go to, Eb?'

'Miami again.' I glanced at Jonah; his mood was again darkening.

'Shall I acknowledge?'

'No.' I intervened. 'Don't be too quick. Our girl is clever. She wouldn't just accept anything on face value. Maybe even be a bit paranoid. What with all the conspiracy theories going around. See if you can get them to offer any guarantees or proof that they are who they say they are.'

'You're right. She wouldn't just jump on board without scrutiny. The supremacist maybe, but not this one. She's too intelligent for that.' Ebony smiled at me then turned her attention back to the screens as she typed in her answers. She was back in the zone.

I turned back to Jonah. 'What's in Miami?' I asked. 'Can we do a cross reference on the list I gave you?'

He was distracted. 'Yeah.' He seemed reluctant to continue, his mood completely changed from a few minutes before. 'There doesn't have to be a link with anyone on the list,' he continued. 'It could just be a coincidence.'

'What's the chance of that?' I retorted angrily. 'Both of the profiles were sent to Miami. It has to be something there.'

'Okay. But it doesn't have to mean it's anyone on the list.' He was stalling.

I observed him closely. His tense shoulders, the lines on his forehead, the hooded eyes blazing. His whole stance urged me to stop my current line of questioning. Being who I am, that just made me even more curious. What was he trying to hide?

'Who's in Miami, Jonah?' I cocked my head in question.

He turned around in an attempt to avoid my questioning. Bit childish, but hey. I moved back to the kitchen island and picked up the tablet. Running through the images, I found the photo he'd made of the original list and looked through the locations.

There it was: Miami.

Archbishop Benedict.

Jonah's mentor.

Chapter Eighteen

Jonah stayed sullen for the rest of the day and far into the evening. He was a joy to be around. Not. At least not for me. Ebony took it all in her stride and ignored his behaviour. She was in her own digital world behind the rack of computer screens and seemed blissfully unaware of the change in atmosphere.

At one point Jonah grabbed his coat and left the loft without a word.

I glanced at Ebony, she just shrugged. I guess he needed some space.

I left Ebony an hour later, fully expecting Jonah to turn up at the apartment sometime in the middle of the night, but he stayed AWOL. I lay in the dark staring at the ceiling and thinking about what we were mixed up in.

Six months ago, my biggest concern was how to best my brother Michael and maybe even prank him again before he blitzed me.

I had a family. Yes, even a girlfriend of sorts. Okay, more than one. I was carefree. The son of a powerful man. Probably the most powerful man in our dimension. As long as I walked in my father's footsteps, my future looked fantastic. Not that I complied. I managed to continually push all the boundaries and aggravate the old man. It was a matter of principle to me. I was expected to rebel, and I did.

Then I threw it all away. Why? Because of a sense of morality? Or just to get back at the old man for never being a father to me.

In all its ostentatious luxury, my life had been akin to a bird in a gilded cage. There was no freedom. I jumped to my father's whims, even though reluctantly. He ruled our family in the same way he commanded his company. He's a despot. A tyrant.

The business wasn't enough. I knew that. I'd seen the signs. Dear old dad was extending his reach and his horizon. He mixed an official political push with his more familiar dark methods to gain additional influence within the Council that ruled our part of our world. With reasoning, coercion and blackmail, his power increased exponentially, almost to the point that the Council was no more than a front.

They were the puppets, my father the puppeteer.

Still, he wanted more.

He had his sights on the highest position in our dimension. The Supreme Ruler. King among kings.

I'd seen it coming and deep down inside, I knew that was what my rebellion was about. It was wrong, and I knew it. More of us did. My mother, my sister. Some of father's advisors. I saw the same questions in their eyes. The same anger at what he was doing.

And the same lethargy and inability to stand up to him. His power over us was so complete no one dared question him. Only me, and even my efforts were half-hearted.

And where did that get me? Here, on earth.

I wasn't the first to rebel. A few hundred years ago one of the council members had tried. He gathered a group of like-minded people and tried to convince the rest to curb my father's powers with legal restrictions. They proposed a governing entity to control the recruitment of souls, efficiently cutting my family's influence to almost zero.

It didn't work. The recalcitrant council member and members of his family had an accident. A very violent and public accident. One that left his children orphans. My father always denied any involvement, but it was a clear message. Stay out of my business.

This kind of brutality was unheard of in our dimension. Not that we were saints. By no means. But this was excessive. It made an impression. One my father used to further his ambitions. With his growing power in our dimension and the reverence in this one, my father was slowly starting to believe he actually was a god.

And now here I was, joining up with the most unexpected partners trying to dethrone him.

Me, a rogue priest-come-cage-fighter, and a neon-haired computer geek. Three of us against the most powerful clan in all dimensions.

The feeling of inadequacy hit me like a brick wall. I stared at the ceiling and shivered at what we were attempting and the enormity of the task. Three against the most powerful force in this dimension and the next.

We didn't have a hope in Hell.

I returned to the loft mid-morning next day. Ebony opened the door, and I followed her into the kitchen.

'Hear anything from Jonah?' I asked.

She nodded her head in the direction of the mezzanine. 'He came in around five this morning. I cleaned up his wounds and put him to bed. He's still asleep.

Wounds? I raised an eyebrow.

'His way of dealing with things,' she continued. 'He fights. It clears his mind.'

'How bad is it?'

She smiled. 'He'll live.'

I nodded, my smile echoing hers.

'Not sure about the other guy though,' she added with a grin. No. I could imagine the state of any opponent unlucky enough to run into Jonah last night.

'Jonah told me you two met at one of your fights,' I continued.

She looked at me and cocked her head determining whether to indulge me. 'Yes. We did. Quite a monumental day that,' she mused. 'I won an important match and basically put myself at the top of the ratings. Not bad for a small black girl with an attitude.'

'What got you into this sport?'

'The release really. And the fact that everyone has always underestimated me. People never took me seriously because of my size. I decided to prove them wrong.'

'It worked,' I chuckled.

'Yep. It definitely did.' She pushed a mug of coffee my way. I nodded my thanks. 'Seriously, it gives me a lot of release. My head is buried in the computers all day and my body is stagnant because of it. I've always liked physically activity because it gives a different kind of peace and relaxation.'

'Not sure cage fighting is what I would call peace,' I joked.

We laughed at that. It was good to talk to her.

'What about you? Does your kind do sports?'

'Sports is quite important where I come from. My father encouraged competitive sports between me and my siblings. He put us up against each other as soon as we could walk. I guess you would call those forms of Martial Arts. He also wanted to impart a sense of discipline in his offspring. My father demands unconditional loyalty without contradiction from his children or his employees alike. Though he is probably stricter where we are concerned. So, I learnt to fight at a very young age.'

'Jonah mentioned you two had fought.'

My mind went back to that memorable day. 'The first time we met. It was quite a battle.'

'He was surprised at your strength.' I smiled at that. He would never admit it to me himself.

'Our kind is a lot stronger that yours, kilo for kilo. And quicker. It's just a difference in the types of muscle we have. Humans generally needs a large volume of muscle tissue to be as strong as for instance Jonah. We have different fibre composition that doesn't require the volume to achieve the same result. That also allows us to be quicker and more flexible than you. We carry less weight on our frames. Not to mention we have a much more effective way to pump our oxygen-rich blood around our bodies with two hearts. It's much more efficient and gives us an edge.'

'Quite a benefit.'

'Yes, it is. We are also underestimated, like you, and use that to our advantage. Though Jonah shouldn't have been so surprised; he fought my brother Rafael.'

'Rafael was a wimp,' we heard from the mezzanine. The big man was awake.

I laughed. 'Agreed.'

He came into the kitchen wearing only jeans. There

were crude stitches on his upper right arm, a nasty bump on his forehead and his lower lip was split and swollen. The ugly bruises on his torso merged into his many tattoos and scars from earlier altercations.

He walked up to Ebony, his t-shirt in hand, and kissed her on the top of her head.

I warranted a nod.

Ebony handed him a coffee and he pulled a barstool out from under the island and sat down stiffly. I stopped myself from asking if he was all right. He wouldn't appreciate it and the answer would be the same as always. We sat in silence for a few minutes, all three dinking our coffee and lost in our own thoughts.

'There was more communication during the night,' Ebony broke the silence. 'They really want to meet our girl.

'Why about the supremacist?'

'He's still on their radar, but the girl is being pushed harder. I think they need computer expertise more than brawn and violence now. I asked more questions, on where and why. They answered that they wanted to talk to her face-to-face. How about we get our girl to ask why she should trust them? Maybe they'll give us some references we can investigate a bit more,' Ebony suggested.

'Good idea. See what they come back with.'

'Then if they do come back, give in a bit,' Jonah suggested. 'Don't be too eager but give them a bit of slack. Say she's thinking about it, but she needs a bit of time to get things organised. What with work and all. She needs to take a few days off.'

'But get them to tell us where in Miami,' I added. 'We need to pinpoint the contact a bit more before we can truly rule anyone out.' I glanced at Jonah with my last remark. He stayed calm.

'What specialities did you give our girl in her profile?' I asked.

'Mainly security expertise. And hacking prowess.'

'Wonder what they need her for? Would it be too suspicious for her to ask?'

'At the moment probably. But if we continue the communication for a few days and they get to know her a bit better, I think I can fit it in the conversations somewhere. It would make sense for her to ask. With her being paranoid and all.'

'What's our next step?' I turned to Jonah.

'We go to Miami, you and I. Ebony stays here,' he answered resolutely.

'Will you be safe without us here?' I asked her.

'No problem. My homies watch out for me.'

'You'll get them to drive by every now and then?' Jonah asker her, true concern in his voice.

'Like I said, they watch out for me. They're watching now.' I looked outside, slightly paranoid.

'They know you both as customers. And they're aware the big man stays over sometimes. I know you're here before you get within a hundred yards of the building.' She laughed at my amazement.

'Good. Because we'll be gone a while.' I turned to Jonah. 'We can either take the train or drive down. Flying is not an option. Not if you want to bring your axe.' Jonah nodded. He was just about married to that thing. We could hide it in a guitar case or something like that, but it would light up under any scrutiny at an airport. 'And we can't be sure there isn't an APB out on you after the debacle at Bishop Xavier.' That earned me a huff from my big partner.

'Not to mention the fact that I can't be scanned.' I added.

'Why not?' Jonah asked.

'My kind has two hearts. That tends to show up on a scan.'

'Wouldn't want to have to explain that' Jonah chuckled.

'No,' Ebony joined in. 'And they're in for a surprise if they want a blood sample.' I could just imagine the reaction when they saw purple in a vial instead of the expected red.

'Okay, driving or the train it is.'

'I'd prefer to drive,' Jonah opted. 'Less chance of me being identified and we can take backroads, avoid big cities.'

'You can take my car,' Ebony suggested. 'It's in the parking across the street. Big four-wheeler. Comfortable and reliable. But bring it back, please. I like that car.'

'Thanks,' I replied. Hiring a vehicle wouldn't be an option without leaving a trail and buying one on short notice would be a pain.'

'We'll leave this morning and stay over in a motel some-where on the route down. That should get us in the general vicinity around mid-afternoon tomorrow.' Jonah nodded. I turned to Ebony. 'We can touch base this evening and if you have anything just ping us then we'll get online.'

'Will do.' She took Jonah's hand in hers. 'Be careful, big man. I'm getting used to having you around.'

Jonah smiled, pulled her close and kissed the top of her head.

An hour later found us on the motorway in what can only be described as a super comfortable ride. The big four-wheel SUV coasted over the road effortlessly just inside the speed limit, the big engine purred like a kitten. The supple leather interior, wood veneer and tinted windows enhanced the comfort and had no doubt raised the price of the vehicle to astronomical levels. The biggest achievement of the car was that all the luxury was invisible on the outside. The exterior was mediocre to say the least. Quite a benefit in many crime-riddled areas. It didn't stand out. Not until you turned off the state-of-the-art security system and opened the door.

We settled down for a long ride, aiming to reach Tallahassee by early evening. I'd found a Red Roof Inn on the outskirts of the town. It was in a reasonably peaceful neighbourhood where our car shouldn't stand out too much. We wanted to blend. The Inn was frequented by many travellers on their way to Florida, we would just be two more.

Dinner was ordered off-site and delivered to the room. The less people who saw us, the better. It was a distinct downgrade from the meal Jonah cooked for us the night before, not that it bothered my big friend. He ate as though his life depended on it.

One thing I will never get used to here is what you aptly name junk food.

We Zoomed with Ebony after our meal and she filled us in on the recent developments.

'They really want her,' she explained. 'So much so that they are giving away more than I think they want to. After a reluctant start, they finally owned up to being connected to the Christian Church.'

This sounded like the link we were looking for.

'They want her to contact someone in the Church and made it look like he's high up in the hierarchy. He's supposed to convince her of their trustworthiness. He didn't actually say the Catholic Church is backing the CWW, but he did hint strongly about corresponding goals.'

'The web is tightening around our suspects,' I answered.

Jonah had gone quiet again. His mood darkened with the mention of the clergy in Miami.

'Where did they want to meet her?' I asked.

'They said somewhere neutral,' Ebony continued. 'But I refused that. I said I still didn't trust them, and it had to be on safe ground somewhere.' Pins-and-needles were moving up my spine. I had the distinct feeling we were getting very close to a breakthrough.

'They agreed to meet her day after tomorrow, at ten in the evening.' she hesitated and glanced to Jonah through the screen. He nodded encouragement. I think he already knew what she would say. 'They want her to come to the arch-bishop's offices.'

Silence fell over us. I glanced to my right at my partner. He'd closed his eyes, and his brow was creased with the effort it took to remain calm. I felt for him. This was his worst nightmare. The one thin thread he still had to his faith in humanity was slowly unravelling. It was impossible to ignore anymore. One way or the other, the archbishop—his mentor and friend— was involved in this. The outcome could only be bad for him and for Jonah.

After minutes of silence, Jonah took a deep breath and opened his eyes again. He sat up straight and attempted a smile. It got halfway to his eyes then fizzled out.

'Thanks, Eb. This is great information. We couldn't do this without you,' he said.

'Do you need the address?' She asked him.

He shook his head. 'No. I know where it is. I've been there before.'

'I'm sorry, Jonah.' She felt his pain.

He shook his head and smiled again, this time slightly more successfully. 'Don't worry about it, Tiny. No way you can change what is. If he's wound up in The Establishment, then we needed to know.'

Ebony relayed a few more details on the progress from her side and we remarked on how great her car was. Five minutes later I pardoned myself and left the room, giving them some space.

When I came back, Jonah was under the shower. I sat on my bed and turned on the TV. The majority of the news still reverberated around the fundamentalist groups and their self-proclaimed "Holy War". New—thankfully smaller —acts of terrorism over the globe pushed the total death count up every day.

The situation was escalating rapidly and there didn't seem to be a resolution on the horizon any time soon. The UN was chasing its tail running around trying to mop up the mess and a combined military effort to find and bring the perpetrators to justice resulted in a massive failure. They had no idea where to look.

But it was more than that. The way CWW avoided even the best military endeavours convinced me they had inside information. Not that it surprised me. Not if The Establishment was behind the terrorism, and for me there was no doubt about that. Their reach was immense. Greed did that.

The seemingly random attacks on both sides were choreographed. It took a big dose of paranoia and tenacity to see the links, but they were there. They were designed to be without order and that in itself was exactly the pattern Ebony found.

Surely someone else would see the similarities, we couldn't be the only ones. For now though, it was just us.

Jonah returned to the room and took two bottles of beer from the paper carrier we filled up at the supermarket before we arrived at the Red Roof Inn. With Jonah's perpetual hunger we stacked up on stores for in between meals. That, and drinks. Alcohol was a major item in our partnership.

He handed me one, turned the cap on his and took a long haul of the beer. He installed himself on his bed and watched the unfolding news on the TV screen.

'Still at it, huh?'

'Yes. It's un-relentless. They seem to be ramping it up. Something tells me a big event is on the horizon,' I suggested.

'What kind?'

'No idea. But it will be massive.'

We drank the rest of our beer in silence.

'Tomorrow,' he broke the silence.

I looked up and raised an eyebrow.

'We visit Archbishop Benedict,' he continued. I nodded.

'How are we going to handle it?' I waited for him to tell me what he had decided.

'There are still scenarios where Benedict is not corrupt.' Jonah explained his plan. I stayed silent. 'I wanted to give him a chance to explain what he knew and what his position was on The Establishment.'

'Fair enough,' I answered. 'We're not completely sure he's involved. Though everything we've found out does point in that direction. We'll give him the benefit of the doubt.'

'But you expect him to be dirty.' Jonah stated sullenly. It wasn't a question, so I didn't answer.

We left it at that.

Chapter Nineteen

Ebony sent us all the information she'd found on the archbishop.

It included articles, streams on YouTube, biographies, photos, everything. I scrutinised the material after breakfast, wanting to get a better understanding of our target.

One particular image grabbed my attention. 'The guy in the photo next to the archbishop.' I pointed to a skinny pale figure dressed in a black priest robe on the newspaper archive image. 'Who's that?'

'That's Father Francis.' Jonah answered. 'He's the archbishop's personal assistant.'

'I know him.' I stated.

'What?'

'I know him. I've met him before.' The gaunt man was well known in our company. 'His department consistently supplied a large number of recruits and so they got our attention.'

'As part of The Establishment?'

'Yes.'

'What does that mean?' The cogs in Jonah's mind were turning rapidly and coming to a new scenario.

'Could mean he's the only contact, could mean that he works for and with the archbishop on this.' I didn't want to burst the bubble my partner was creating, but I needed him with both feet on the ground.

'Does he know you?' he asked after a moment of silence.

'Yes, he does.'

'That could be an advantage?' Jonah said.

I nodded. 'Could be. If he hasn't had any recent visitors from my family. They might have tipped him off about my changed loyalties.'

'What's the chance of that?'

'I'm not sure. This department is one of the major recruiters here in the US. We try to have regular contact with them, at least once a year. No idea whether he was up for a visit or not. I guess we'll find out when we talk to him.' I shrugged. There was nothing we could do about that. It would become clear soon enough.

'How are we going to go about this?' Jonah asked.

'Carefully.'

I still don't believe the archbishop is corrupt,' he stated decisively. Did I mention Jonah was stubborn?

'You should, I answered. 'In my opinion everyone in the Church is suspect until proven otherwise.'

'I can't believe he would condone anything like The Establishment. I would have known. I know him. He was my mentor when I joined the Church. He sponsored my Rite of Ordination. The man was like a father to me.'

I observed him closely. His stubborn streak had resurfaced with a vengeance.

'The Establishment is much more widespread than you think,' I tried.

He was about to interrupt but stopped when I held my hand up. 'Please, let me finish.'

He nodded, reluctantly.

'They're con artists. They've held up this scam for centuries. They're the best actors you will ever meet. They have to be. It is in their DNA. Otherwise, the scam would have been blown a long time ago. You wouldn't know, Jonah. No matter how much knowledge of human nature you might possess. No matter how much experience you have with criminals. They will pull the wool over your eyes. That's what they're selected for. If your archbishop is a member of the Establishment's Inner Circle—and I expect he is—then he is the best of the best at deceit.'

I saw an extremely reluctant shoulder shrug. He wasn't convinced. I admired his loyalty, and I hoped he was right. But I would proceed with the assumption that the archbishop was dirty. Let him prove me wrong.

'So, again, how do we do this?' He tried to change the subject.

'We divide our attention. You take the archbishop and I'll talk to Father Francis.'

Jonah voiced his agreement.

'There could be a problem,' I continued. 'The archbishop probably won't believe you. To the outside world, you're a criminal, remember. A rogue priest. There is a big chance he'll call the police instead of talking to you.'

'He'll listen.'

'Why?' I asked. 'He has no reason to.'

'He knows me.' Anger in the tone again. Jonah was banking on his previous relationship with the archbishop. That was a lifetime ago. When he was still a valued bastion of the Church instead of a murderer killing off some of its key figures.

'He knew you. Past tense. The old you who believed. Not the man you are now. News of your recent endeavours will have reached him. If he is part of The Establishment, he will know you are the enemy. If he isn't, then there's no guarantee he will even give you a chance to explain. According to the Church, you are a murderer of innocent clergy. That's how he will perceive you.'

'He will talk to me, and I will convince him.' He was adamant.

I decided to humour him and to approach it in another way. A plan was forming. 'We need to work together on this. You just informing him about The Establishment will not convince him. He needs to hear it from someone else as well. Someone who can corroborate your story.'

'From you?' His surprise, disdain and the inherent implications stung me.

'No. Not me. He doesn't know me. It must be someone he trusts. I was thinking of his personal assistant; Father Francis.'

He cocked his head in question. 'Could work, but how do we achieve that?' He was interested.

'I convince Francis the archbishop wants to join the cause. It would be a triumph for him if he could bring in such a highly placed member of the Church. I'll promise Francis the credit. Then I'll signal you we're coming to talk to the archbishop. You will have to hide because Francis definitely knows about you. You are The Establishment's number-one enemy.' That brought a smile to his lips. 'The success of this endeavour depends on whether you can convince Benedict to play ball. He must go along with the sham. Pretend he wants to join but still be hesitant. He needs to convince Francis he's interested but needs more information. Francis will hopefully take the bait and sell The Establishment to his boss. That will convince your friend in a way nothing we say ever could.'

'This will work on two fronts. Francis will convince the archbishop we're telling the truth and inadvertently that The Establishment is a cancer that corrupts even the staunchest shepherds in the Church.'

He contemplated what I suggested. It sounded logical to me. Jonah, however, was hesitant.

'What if you're right, and Archbishop Benedict is already part of The Establishment?'

'We'll know quickly enough, and plan B goes into effect.' I answered coldly. There was no sugar-coating this.

'We kill them.' His answer was flat; emotionless. His eyes belied the sentiment.

'After we get the information we need.' I added.

'Sounds like a plan.' This time he sounded a lot less convinced.

'Father Francis.' I walked into the outer office space and approached the flabbergasted aide who sat behind the neat desk.

'Gabriel,' he stammered as he jumped to his feet. 'I did not expect you.' Fear clouded briefly over his face. Had he missed something? Was something wrong? For me it was the confirmation that he had not been visited recently from our dimension.

'This visit was unannounced. You couldn't have known.' I exonerated him with a big smile. He breathed a sigh of relief. An instant later his uncertainty came though the veneer again.

'How can I help you?' he asked apprehensively, his tone one of reverence.

Generally, there were two kinds of visits from our kind. One good, and one very, very bad. Francis obviously had no idea which way this one would go.

'Relax Francis. I am here with good news.' I smiled again. Didn't help. He was still nervous. 'Can I sit?'

'Of course,' he sputtered. 'Please take a seat.' He pointed to the formal seat in front of the desk, then to the more comfortable seats on the other side of the room. 'Whichever you prefer.'

I wanted to ease his concerns and help him relax, so I took the comfy seats.

'Can I get you something to drink?' he continued walking over to the cabinet behind the sofa. 'A wine maybe? Or whiskey?'

'Thank you. I'll have what you are having.' I answered amiably. Instead of the intended effect it confused him even more.

I lowered myself on to the extra-wide armchair, placed my arm over the back rest and made myself comfortable.

Francis placed a crystal cut glass containing two fingers of quality whisky in front of me on the salon table. The dark amber liquid was inviting. I smiled my thanks.

He took an armchair across from me and sat upright on the edge of the seat, his back stiff, his hands in his lap restlessly nursing his own drink. He waited until I took my first sip before he put his glass to his lips. The alcohol didn't have a direct effect, the anxiety was still written all over his face.

'My father and I hear good things about you, Francis.' I started my carefully practiced narrative.

He nodded slightly and attempted a smile.

'You are doing great work here recruiting new believers.

The quality of the recruits you deliver is extremely good. We want you to know we appreciate you as a major asset.' I emphasised the "we" part.

His shoulders relaxed slightly, and the smile broadened, though there was still a nervous twitch to his eyes. I continued to pile on the compliments. With every commendation he visibly relaxed more. The glass was brought to his lips again and he sipped at the liquor. Slowly he moved back into the seat and rested his body against the backrest.

I finally came to the reason I was talking to this idiot. I had to tread carefully. We were still out on how trustworthy Benedict was.

'My father and I received word that your archbishop is showing interest in our work.'

'The archbishop?' He was genuinely surprised. I nodded. Was the bewilderment because his boss wasn't involved or because he was?

'You are surprised?' I asked innocently.

'Yes. Yes,' he stammered. 'Archbishop Benedict does not seem to me to be the kind of man who would recruit for you. I didn't know he was aware The Establishment even existed.' Okay, that answered our biggest question.

'You never tried to recruit him?'

'No. It seemed impossible. He is so moralistic. His goal in life is to offer solstice to his flock. Here and in heaven.' Was that disdain I saw for Benedict? Or a chip on the gaunt man's shoulder.

He looked even leaner and paler than the last time I saw him, years ago. There was a lot behind the cold hard features. I couldn't read him any deeper than that he was terrified of me and this unannounced visit.

What I did see was a hint of fire in his eyes.

'Who recruited him?' Francis asked.

I smiled. There, that was the opening I was looking for. Greed. Had anyone else already recruited the archbishop? Who received the credit?

'No one,' I put him out of his misery. 'Not yet.'

He breathed a sigh of relief, then the addition registered.

'What do you mean; not yet?'

'I want you to take the credit.'

The surprise lit up his face. The realisation of what I suggested landed.

'My father was told the archbishop was testing the waters. He has been approached by some of The Establishment's esteemed members. Never directly of course, in case you are right, and his morals and ethics would not allow him to stand behind our directives. They report interest, but he is hesitant. I believe he does not trust them. We need to groom him, to get him to commit to our cause. His commitment would be a major achievement. That is where you come in.'

'Me?'

'Yes. You. You're his personal assistant, have been for more than a decade. He trusts you, trusts your advice. You could bring him around to our cause. He will believe you.'

My words had their intended effect. I first saw confusion, then excitement, and finally greed in his face. He knew he would profit greatly from any assistance he gave us in this, especially if his actions were the determining factors in recruiting his boss. And to top it all off, he would be doing my father and I a personal favour. One he would no doubt reap the reward of in this life and the next. He was falling for the scam. It's so predictable. Greed is the one emotion that decisively brings humans around to any venture.

'And we, my father and I,' I laid on the charm again,

using dad in as many sentences as possible. 'We want you to profit from this recruitment. You should have the glory for this. No one else.'

His face shone with pride as well as greed.

'Are you on board?' I asked innocently.

'Yes. Of course. I will do whatever you want me to do.'

I had him where I wanted him.

'We need you to talk to the archbishop. Convince him of the validity of our goals. Bring him around to our way of thinking. He is almost there. We just need that one voice of reason from the person he trusts most of all. That will bring him over to us.'

'I will. Of course. Yes. Thank you for considering me. I am honoured.' He fell over himself in his need to become part of this.

'No need,' I complimented him. 'You're a valuable asset for us. We want to reward you for your great work and loyalty.' This excessive outpour of appreciation was making me sick. Anymore and I would start retching.

I drank the last sip of the excellent whisky and held up the glass for a refill. 'This calls for a drink,' I said.

He jumped up out of his chair, took my glass and made his way to the bar where he took the bottle of eighteen-year-old quality whisky and poured another generous amount of the liquid into my glass. He poured a similar measure into his own. The excitement was getting to him, and he probably needed something strong to calm his nerves. He didn't look like a drinking man to me, but I wasn't complaining. Alcohol would most likely loosen his lips and hopefully numb any misgivings. Ultimately it would help us.

While his back was to me, I quickly pressed the send button on my phone. It sent the prepared WhatsApp message, signalling Jonah we would come to the archbishop's office within ten minutes. The silent reply was almost immediate. I glanced at the phone. It read "A". I breathed a sigh of relief. The archbishop was one of the good guys. No need for our more radical and bloodier plan "B".

Francis was back and offered me the refill. I took it, clinked the glasses in a toast, and drowned most of the amber liquid in one haul. I looked over at the aide. He mirrored my example, his face contorting as the whisky burned a way down to his stomach. His face went bright red —definitely not a drinker.

'Let's go see the archbishop, shall we?' I suggested. He nodded. The nervousness was back.

I stood up and invited him to lead the way. He turned and headed off uncertainly in the direction of the archbishop's office, his posture unsure. I put my glass on the table and followed my somewhat intoxicated new friend.

Francis knocked on the door and waited for permission to continue.

A deep voice came from the other side of the ornate door. 'Enter.'

He opened the door, and we made our way into the large office space.

Where the aide's office had been simple though classy, this one was warm, homely, and filled with religious artefacts. It looked like a cross between a countryside church, a museum, and a cosy living room. The lights were subdued and there were dark shadowed parts where it didn't penetrate. I felt Jonah was in one of those. Francis was completely unaware of his presence. I wanted to keep it that way and walked up to the big desk and the slightly rotund man sitting behind it.

The archbishop looked up, first at his aide, then his gaze

moved to me. 'We have a guest?' he asked Francis. He raised an eyebrow.

The aide turned sideways so that he could see both the archbishop and me. He held his hand up in my direction. 'Your Grace, may I introduce Gabriel.'

The archbishop held out his hand and I took it. He had a strong grip and a firm handshake. He looked me in the eye and smiled warmly. Underneath the friendliness I saw a strong personality. A man to take notice of.

'Nice to meet you, Gabriel,' he said.

'Your Grace, the honour is all mine,' I answered with a small nod that could be confused for a bow.

'Gabriel,' he continued, looking at me intently. 'A biblical name.'

'Yes. My father named us all from the bible.' I explained.

'A god-fearing man?'

'Something like that.' He raised an eyebrow in question. I just left it at that. No doubt Jonah had explained who I was. Otherwise, we would get round to it soon enough.

He turned his attention to Father Francis. 'What can I help you with, Father?' he addressed the aide.

'I think we need to sit down, your Grace. I have something to tell you.'

'And this has to do with Gabriel?'

'It does.'

'Okay,' Archbishop Benedict pointed to the two chairs in front of the desk. 'Please, take a seat, both of you.'

I rested my frame in the comfortable armchair. This would be interesting.

Benedict cocked his head at the aide indicating he could begin.

'Your Grace,' the thin man began. 'What I am going to

tell you will sound very strange, unbelievable maybe even. But please bear with me and let me explain.'

The archbishop nodded.

Francis looked flustered. How to begin?

He took a deep breath and started.

'In the holy bible mention is made of Purgatory.'

Good place to start, I thought, admiring his opening.

'It is positioned as the condition, process or place of purification or temporary punishment where souls of those who die in a state of grace are made ready for Heaven.'

'I am aware of the contents of the bible,' Benedict said casually. There was a hint of impatience.

Francis was flustered. 'Of course. Please excuse me, your grace. I did not wish to imply…' his speech floundered, insecurity surfacing.

Benedict nodded him onwards. 'This is about Purgatory?' he asked.

'Yes. Yes, Your Grace,' Francis stammered, grabbing on to the olive branch his boss handed him.

'This is all about Purgatory. I know this will sound very strange, but please humour me.' He took another deep breath. 'Gabriel.' He turned to me. 'He's from there.'

Benedict raised an eyebrow. He looked from Francis to me and back again. Francis stayed mute, so the archbishop turned back to me again. I just smiled my acknowledgement.

'You are from Purgatory?'

I cocked my head. 'You could say that.' I smiled again.

He turned back to Francis, 'please continue.' The required scepticism was apparent.

'I know how it sounds, Your Grace. But please keep an open mind. There are things going on here that will test our faith, but please be assured that what I am going to tell you falls within our beliefs and our dogma.'

This would be interesting.

Archbishop Benedict nodded and Francis continued.

'Purgatory is a necessary step in the ascension to Heaven. We know this. Our flock knows this.' He took another deep breath and glanced at me for assistance. I let him swim.

'What they do not know is how they come there.'

Benedict kept his eyes on his aide. He was totally unreadable. Made me wonder what Jonah had told him.

'There is an organisation within the Church that takes care of, shall we say, the logistics.' The earlier good opening was waning quickly.

'The logistics?'

'Yes, Your Grace. There must be a way for the afterlife to distinguish between those who go directly to their end destination, be it Heaven or Hell, and those who need Purgatory first. This is when The Establishment comes into the picture.'

He was starting to falter. I wasn't sure whether it was the nerves, the difficult subject or the booze that unnerved him, but whatever, it would take forever this way. I decided to intervene.

'Where would you imagine Heaven is? Or Hell, for that matter?' I asked the archbishop directly.

He turned to me. 'I don't know. Typically, we think of Heaven above and Hell below.' The archbishop watched me intently.

'Above you. So somewhere in space?'

'Maybe. I wouldn't know, not that it matters.'

'How about in another dimension?' I suggested.

'Another dimension?' his brow creased; Jonah hadn't explained that part then.

'Yes. There are many dimensions, all with their own worlds and many with civilisations that resemble yours,' I continued.

'And one of them is where you come from?' Benedict asked. I nodded and smiled.

'What does that have to do with the Church?'

'Could you imagine that the afterlife is in another dimension too? And that the soul of someone in this world transfers to another dimension on death.'

'To be born again there?' His gaze was intensive and probing.

'Not exactly born again, as in that life starts all over again. They souls are reincarnated into the same age and body structure they had when they died. If they die young, they will be that age when they awaken in the new world.'

'Continue.'

'Keep that in mind please, while we tell you about something else.'

Benedict sat back in his chair and stared at me and Francis. The latter wilted under the glare. I returned the smile.

'The organisation the good Father mentioned, The Establishment is instrumental in the process of reincarnation. They make it possible for my father's technicians to intercept the soul of the deceased in time to be reincarnated in one of our facilities.'

'Yes, your grace,' Father Francis had found his voice and enthusiasm again. 'That's exactly what it is.'

Benedict turned to me in a wordless question.

'Something like that,' I answered with a smile.

He looked confused. 'What do you mean, something like that?' I stayed silent.

'You're telling me this Establishment is a company that recruits souls for reincarnation after death?'

'Yes, Your Grace. Exactly.'

'And where are they reincarnated? In your dimension.' He pointed to me. I nodded. Benedict glanced at his aide who smiled his reply.

'And that isn't Heaven?'

His aide answered. 'Not exactly. At least not for all of them. It is more a stepping off point before they go to their designated eternal resting place.' The nerves were back again. Francis's voice faltered. I think it was the imposing figure of the archbishop. Though not a large man, he had a powerful aura.

He turned back to me. 'And your father heads a company that reincarnates the souls of believers?' the archbishop continued.

'Exactly. He has developed a procedure to revive the souls of those who believe in the afterlife here and reincarnate them in our dimension.'

I let it sink in. The archbishop was on the right track.

'Do you reincarnate all the believers?' he asked.

'No.' I answered honestly. 'Mainly men between the age of eighteen and fifty-five.'

This registered with Archbishop Benedict. He looked at the aide, then back to me. Francis nodded his agreement with my narrative. His enthusiasm at his boss's interest was so extensive that he failed to see the barely concealed scepticism and abhorrence in the archbishop's features.

Benedict stared at me. His eyes hard and condemning. 'Why do you target only that group?'

'The recruits, as we call them, work for us before they

continue their journey,' I said circumventing the real answer. I wanted that to come from Francis.

'They work in your dimension?'

'Yes, Your Grace. They do.' Francis quickly answered.

'And they get paid for that?' The question sounded so innocent at first glance.

'Not exactly. Though they do get food and board, they are taken care of.' Francis was struggling.

'And this Establishment that you are part of recruits souls for this reincarnation.'

'Exactly, Your Grace,' he answered again enthusiastically, happy the archbishop hadn't continued the previous train of thought.

'And The Establishment would very much like to welcome you to their cause,' he rambled on, oblivious of the impact on his boss.

'Tell me why I would want to do that.'

'The Establishment promotes our faith, Your Grace. It gathers true believers and helps them achieve the paradise after they move from this world. That surely is what our ultimate goal is. Are we not shepherds that bring our flock to the pearly gates?'

'With a detour in this other dimension.'

Francis nodded. Certain the understanding Benedict portrayed was born of agreement and shared values.

'We, the recruiters for The Establishment, are rewarded for our good work. In this world and the next,' he continued.

Now this was what I was waiting for.

I let it all sink in. I could almost see the thoughts as they took hold in the archbishop's mind. Whatever Jonah had told him was now substantiated by the aide; the one person he'd trusted without fail. The skin in his neck reddened until it slowly blended with his crimson garbs. Anger was rising in our archbishop.

'Let me get this completely clear,' he said. His warm voice now had a very hard edge. Again, it completely eluded Francis. 'You want me to join you in this Establishment and gather new souls that will become recruits in Gabriel's dimension to work there for his company.'

Francis nodded energetically.

'Not exactly,' I interrupted. 'They don't all work for my father's company. We are more a recruiting organisation. The middleman, as it were.'

He turned back to me. 'The recruits work for other companies in your dimension?'

'Yes.'

'They contract the recruits from your company.'

I cocked my head to the side. 'Well, no. Not really "contract" them.'

'Then how?'

'They purchase them.' My words were intentionally cold and void of any emotion. It brought the harshness of reality home.

Father Francis finally noticed the abhorrence in the archbishop and quickly tried to smooth things over. 'It isn't as bad as it sounds, Your Grace. It isn't slavery.'

'Yes, it is.' The voice came from the shadows behind us. A smile adorned my face. Father Francis jumped up from his seat in shock. He'd been completely oblivious to another presence in the room.

Jonah stepped out from the shadow and slowly walked over to our small group.

Francis's eyes opened to their maximum. He recognised Jonah immediately and almost fell over his chair as he tried to move backwards from the apparition that approached him.

'It is slavery.' Jonah's strong voice echoed in the silence. 'They are sold to the highest bidder and work until they drop in mines and foundries.'

Francis's eyes flitted from Jonah to the archbishop to me.

I was still in my seat, the cynical smile plastered on my face.

'This goes on for centuries. If they last that long. Most don't.' Jonah turned to me. 'Right? Gabriel.'

'Right.' I answered coldly. 'Usually no more than max ten years. Then they are exterminated.'

'This is what The Establishment is all about,' Jonah continued as he placed his frame squarely in front of the desk.

'But it gets worse.' He surprised the archbishop.

'Even worse than slavery?'

'Yes. The Establishment needs their recruits young and strong. That means young believers must die.' He paused to let that sink in. 'The Establishment makes sure they do.'

'No. No,' Francis cried. 'They do not interfere with the lives of the believers. They only reincarnate them after they die. The company does not intervene with the living.'

Jonah turned his imposing physique towards the aide who pushed even further back as though physically struck. 'Then how do you explain that you are actively recruiting young men and women for the CWW?' Jonah dropped the bomb.

Francis stared at Jonah. Then he turned to Benedict, his eyes pleading.

'Is this true?' Benedict asked. His voice hard.

Francis was silent. His lips moved but no sound escaped his throat.

'It is,' I joined in the conversation.

'What is he doing here?' Francis found his voice again and pointed to Jonah. 'He is a murderer. A monster. A fallen priest.' His voice broke on the words, scrambling to change the focus to someone else.

'Oh, I forgot to mention.' I said in a friendly voice, my eyes hard and the smile vicious. 'Jonah and I work together.'

'Impossible. He is a traitor. He is an enemy of The Establishment and your family.'

'So am I.'

That shut him up.

He sank down into the chair. All fight gone.

'You tricked me,' he whispered.

'Yes, and no,' I answered. 'We did need you to convince the archbishop. That aspect was completely correct. And thank you for playing your part. I bent the truth a bit about him being interested in The Establishment. Up till today, he'd never heard of it.'

'You tricked me,' he repeated.

Jonah answered. 'No more than you do with your recruits.'

Francis was deflated. His shoulders sagged and his frame seemed to fall in on itself in the big chair. He looked defeated.

'Why did you do it?' Benedict asked his aide. 'How could you go along with something as abhorrent as this.'

Francis looked at him. There was defiance and a measure of disdain in his face. 'Why?' He scoffed. 'Because I was on a dead end.' Anger fuelled his voice that now sound stronger. 'You, you've made it big. Archbishop before your sixtieth and your career is still in the lift. You are an important man in the Church. People bow to you. Listen to your every word. One day you may even become Pope, though you deny that is your aspiration.' We stayed mute, the guy was doing our work for us, and digging his own grave at the same time.

'What about me?' He slapped his chest. 'I'm the aide. Permanently in the shadow of your greatness.' His tone was cynical, sarcastic even. 'Where is my career going? I have ambitions you know. I wanted to rise in the Church. Be a bastion for the masses. Instead, I am stuck in the shadows like a glorified secretary. Always in the dark. Never appreciated. You keep me there. You and all the others. The Establishment offered me what you would not. They promised me status, validation, appreciation. And when I die, they will reincarnate me to live in their dimension forever in wealth and power as a reward for my work and dedication here. Of course, I jumped at that offer. Who wouldn't?'

The archbishop was silent. The shock apparent on his face. I guess Jonah hadn't told him details about the reward part yet.

'Why didn't you come to me?' he addressed his aide. 'If I had known, I would have helped you advance your career.'

Francis laughed. A hollow sound, maniacal. 'You would help me?' he shouted. 'Why would you? Don't lie to me. I'm not a charismatic man. I don't work well in teams. I know that. No one wants me in any position of power. You would have given it a perfunctory attempt, then stopped before it marred your perfect scores. Don't make me laugh. You hypocrite. You are no different from all the others in the Church who are addicted to the adoration of your flock. And now you damn me. I can see it in your face. You. Look at yourself in the mirror before you condemn me. Before you cast the first stone Archbishop Benedict, make sure your slate is clean.'

'And you.' He turned to me. 'You are a traitor to your family.'

'That about covers it, yes,' I answered to his surprise. 'I finally came round to what The Establishment and my family are doing. It is not something I can condone. Definitely not what I want to be associated with. My goal,' I pointed to Jonah. 'Our goal; is to bring down The Establishment, and with that my family's company. We are going to rid this religion of the cancer that corrupts it.'

Francis laughed hysterically. The sharp, shrill tone cut through the silence.

'You really expect us to believe you?' he stammered between his frenzied howls. The three of us stayed silent and waited him out. We were deadly serious.

'You,' he continued. 'You betrayed your family. Your father. A man who should be a god to you, like he is to us.'

'A god?' Benedict interjected. 'Do you compare Gabriel's father with God?' he was astounded.

Francis turned from me to the archbishop. He sat up straight in his chair, a massive scorn on his face. Disdain and contempt gave him an extra strength that was missing minutes ago.

'Yes.' He stated resolutely. 'He is my God. He gave me a purpose. A goal. One that will benefit me. Not the masses. Not your precious flock of needy arrogant humans. Me. Your whole religion is centred around a precious few reaping the rewards of the work of the majority. We simple priests are the ones that face the rabble while you, in your crimson robes, are safe and comfortable in your ivory towers. And when my life is finally done, what will happen to me? I may go to somewhere that is better. But somewhere that your kind will also be. So, what difference will it be?'

He was rambling. Jonah and I refrained from interfer-

ing; he was substantiating our cause with every word. Benedict was rooted to his seat in a combination of astonishment
and overwhelming anger at his ward.

'Heaven as you know it, is a pipe dream. No one knows
if it's real. No one knows whether the righteous really are
rewarded for their sober and selfless lifestyle. This. The
Establishment delivers. They reward their loyal soldiers.
When I die, I will transfer to their dimension where a life of
luxury awaits me. I am a valued member of the organisation; they appreciate me and my work. When has the
Church ever done that? Never.' His eyes blazed with his
conviction.

'I finally chose something real. I have a guaranteed
place in paradise because I chose a new God. The real one.
The only one I am concerned about.'

He focussed on the archbishop. 'You can condemn me.
You and your hypocritical faith that is no better than what
The Establishment offers to the masses. Your flock. They
are the basis of my salvation. I will use them as you do. No,
don't contradict me. Your kind uses the masses in much the
same way. You keep them small and weak. They are
promised eternal paradise if they comply to the powerful
here. It's all about power. I chose to use them for me. For
my salvation.'

He held up his arm as he ranted onwards.

I watched the archbishop. He was outraged. At what I
wasn't sure. Could be the betrayal by his aide, but it could
just as well be the audacity of the man to throw accusations
his way.

'I will have my paradise. My heaven,' Francis shouted,
spittle dripping from the edge of his mouth. His face
showed the hard, sharp image of perceived righteousness.

I pulled a small remote from my pocket and pressed the

top button. A small explosion shattered Francis's right underarm, spraying blood in all directions.

'Oeps,' I said. 'There goes the guarantee.'

Francis cradled his bleeding extremity. Realisation of what had happened crept into his face and pain was replaced by anger. His eyes opened to their maximum and a scream escaped his lips. With his left hand he pushed himself up off the chair to attack me.

He was stopped by Jonah's axe. The massive weapon struck the priest squarely in the chest and impaled him on the back of the chair.

The silence was complete. Jonah and I waited for a reaction from the archbishop. This would be the decisive moment.

I was relieved Francis's arm was the only one to have exploded when I pressed the remote. If the archbishop had been dirty, his would have gone off as well. It was a risk I had to take. Not only would a negative result have exposed Benedict, but it would also have convinced my big friend.

Now, the archbishop had the benefit of the doubt.

I still wasn't convinced.

'Did you have to kill him?' Benedict asked.

'Regrettably, yes. We did,' Jonah answered for the both of us. 'He would have ratted us out to The Establishment. And to Gabriel's family.'

'And the explosion in his arm. Was that necessary?'

'There is a transponder in his arm,' I commented. 'It registers when he dies so that his soul can be reincarnated. He would remember everything as a new reincarnation. We could not allow that. Our greatest asset is secrecy. The Establishment and my family have no idea Jonah and I work together. We need to keep it that way as long as possible.'

'And they must never know you are aware,' Jonah chimed in.

It was silent for a few minutes.

'What are you going to do now?' I finally addressed the elephant in the room, assuming Jonah had already asked the archbishop to join our cause.

Benedict looked at me over his crossed hands.

'You want me to help you bring down this Establishment?'

'We do,' Jonah answered. I let him take over the conversation.

'Go undercover as it were?'

Jonah nodded. 'We need someone on the inside. We need access to the secrets of the Inner Circle.'

'And you expect me to be able to get them?'

'Yes.' I picked up the narrative. 'Your standing and importance will almost certainly guarantee you a seat on the Ventus-Dei, the Inner Circle. But for that you need to become one of them and outwardly embrace their ideals. It will be dangerous. If they discover you work with us, they will not hesitate to kill you. There is a lot at stake here.'

'Why do you trust me? I could join them and double-cross you.' He stared at me pointedly, reading my mind.

'You could. But you won't.' Help came from Jonah.

He cocked his head in question.

'You won't because this sickens you as much as it does us.' Jonah answered. 'Your morals and ethics cannot condone The Establishment's actions any more than ours can. This is an abomination to Christianity, to every religion, and it needs to be eradicated.'

'We will take the people's faith from them.' Benedict prompted, concern pulling deep ridges in his brow.

'No. We won't,' I assured him. 'We will uncover the

scam my family perpetuates for what it is. A travesty. One that uses your religion but does not have a connection with the real faith.'

'Is there a real faith?'

'When my father and his accomplices started harvesting souls, they did not invent the religions. They saw an opportunity to capitalise on what was already there. Your human faith goes back much further that the conspiracy my family imposed on it. When The Establishment is gone, whatever is real will still be there.' I stayed vague. Benedict picked up on that.

'Is there a real god?' he asked. 'A true religion?'

I had wanted to avoid this question, especially because of the impact any answer may have on this fragile collaboration with the archbishop and Jonah.

'I don't know,' I answered truthfully. 'As I said, your religion was there before we came. Either there is a god, a real one, or someone else scammed you before we did.' I couldn't sugar-coat it; they would have to make up their own minds.

'Thank you for your candour,' Benedict replied. 'I chose to believe what was there was genuine. That there is a real faith.'

Jonah elaborated. 'True faith will receive a blow. That is inevitable. How much depends on how we unveil the scam. That is why we need all the information we can get. Then we can expose The Establishment for what it is and distinguish between the true Church and the deceit.'

I added, 'We need convincing proof that The Establishment is not what it portrays itself to be. My father is not your god. We, my brothers, and I, are not angels. What was here before my kind came, that was pure. That was your religion and for very many people, it is still what they believe in.'

'What do you mean?'

'The Establishment waylaid the faith of only those it deems profitable for them. They have no interest in old people, the sick, or many of the women and children. These souls cannot be reincarnated to anything profitable.' The archbishop flinched at my crude words.

'I'm sorry to be so blunt, Your Grace. But I need to make the situation clear.'

He nodded for me to continue.

'The true faith is strong in these people. It is the men we must convince that their leaders have misguided them. Your Christian faith is not in the fundamentalism of the CWW. Just like Islam is not in ISIS. These are travesties that have been perpetuated by The Establishment. True believers, true religion could never condone what these terrorists propagate. These young men are brainwashed by The Establishment and their ignorant allies. The majority of the CWW and ISIS alike are not aware of The Establishment's hand in their actions and cause. It is all clandestine. But be assured my father and his cronies are behind all the fundamentalistic religious groups and their terroristic activities. The current rise in violence and counter violence has their mark on it. My father and Arand— the patriarch of the family that controls the Islamic recruitment—have concocted this together. They both stand to profit from a holy war where many young and strong men die.'

I couldn't read Archbishop Benedict. His face was a closed book. The only give-away were the eyes. They blazed with the fire of indignation.

The silence was complete. Jonah and I glanced at each other and waited for Benedict to decide what he wanted to do. He could still refuse to join our cause and call the police. We had, after all, killed his aide.

'You want me to help you expose The Establishment?' He stated more than asked.

'Yes.'

'Know that I do not do this for your revenge against your father.' He aimed this at me. 'Nor for your peace of mind, Jonah.' My partner nodded his agreement. 'I do this for the faith. For the people. As you said. This travesty must end.' We both breathed a sigh of relief.

'But understand this,' he continued. 'I will help you as long as your and my actions align with that goal, and as long as it benefits the Church. My intention is to destroy this cancer before it pulls the real church down with it. To achieve that I will go undercover. I will work with you.' He turned to Jonah. 'There are conditions. You will reign in your violent actions. No more killing.'

'I can't promise that' Jonah answered. 'But I will strive to keep it to the barest minimum.'

'We are being hunted,' I added. 'We may need to retaliate to stay alive.'

'No more attacks. Only as self-defence.' He pushed.

We reluctantly agreed.

'Francis's death will serve another purpose,' I stated. 'When we're gone you must call the police. Tell them your aide was attacked by an intruder. A misguided fundamentalist screaming about some kind of organisation.'

'Gather Francis's confidants together. People he saw on a regular basis. Interrogate them on what Francis was involved in. Pretend not to know any details. Show interest in what secrets your aide was keeping from you. I guarantee you will be approached by one or more of his associates. Let them recruit you into The Establishment. Do not seem too enthusiastic. Let them work for it. Be reluctant at first. Critical. Otherwise, they will not believe you.'

'Why not?'

'Francis was your aide for a long time. He would have tried to recruit you if he believed it possible. It would be a major coup for him. He no doubt already reported you were unwavering in your faith and therefore not a potential candidate. If you seem too eager, they will doubt the validity of your resolve. That will result in an extremely dangerous situation for you. They will not hesitate to engineer an accident.'

Benedict nodded his understanding. 'How do I contact you?'

Jonah pulled a small box out of his coat pocket. It contained a burner phone. No names were connected to it, it was untraceable back to us or anyone else.

'You use this,' he explained. 'There is only one number in the contacts. It connects to another burner phone. You leave a message on the voice mail, and Gabriel or I will get back to you.'

The archbishop picked up the box and opened it. The small simple cheap phone and a charger were the only contents. He took them out of the box and placed them in a hidden pocket in his robe.

'When the investigation into Francis's death dies down, we will contact you to discuss more details. By then they will have approached you. We cannot rush this. It will be a lengthy mission.'

'You had better leave,' the archbishop suggested. 'I have to call the police before the time of death no longer corroborates the story.'

'Yes. We'll be in touch.'

We turned to leave.

'Jonah,' Archbishop Benedict called out.

We faced him again.

'The Establishment will know our history.' He took a deep breath. 'I will have to give you up to them. Tell them I know you.'

Jonah nodded. 'Don't tell anyone about Gabriel.'

'What would I tell them? That I just met the son of God?' his stare bore deep into me. He trusted me as little as I did him. Jonah was the one who bonded this strange and irregular collaboration together.

We took our leave.

Chapter Twenty

'Do you trust him?' I asked completely redundantly. I knew what Jonah was going to say.

'Yes. I do.' He stared at me. 'You obviously don't.'

'No. I don't.' There was still a niggling feeling in my gut that all was not as it seemed.

'Why not?'

'His whole attitude. The lack of any reaction to Francis's demise. Francis was his aide. They worked together for years. I can't believe Benedict was so abhorred by what Francis said that he threw their history away in the blink of an eye. Either the man has no empathy, or he wasn't surprised.'

'You're wrong on both accounts.' Jonah stated, irritated at my attitude.

'How can you be so sure?' I wouldn't let it go so easily.

'I know the man.' Oh, hell, not that again.

'You think you do.' Why wouldn't he see what I did?

'I know him.' He was uncompromising.

It was the end of the afternoon on the day after we

visited the archbishop. We were holed up in a sleepy motel more than two-hundred miles from Miami. The small room was claustrophobic, and I was already going stir crazy. Jonah's demeanour wasn't helping either. We were both moody and looking for a fight.

'He didn't even flinch when you killed Francis,' I stated, fully expecting us to come to blows in our argument. Maybe even welcoming it.

'Benedict is no stranger to death,' Jonah surprised me, he stayed remarkably calm, not reacting to my baiting. 'As a younger man his postings brought him to rough places. Sometimes even war zones. He's seen it all.'

'When he found me, he'd just returned from central Africa. What we did yesterday to Francis pales by the atrocities he witnessed there. And still he kept his faith in humanity.'

'Then he is either a saint or an idiot.' I couldn't leave it alone.

Jonah observed me intently. His arms were crossed over his chest, and he leant back against the dresser. 'It's not going to work, you know.'

I looked up. 'What?'

'What you're doing here.' He waved his hand in the air between him and me.

'And prey, what am I doing?' I demanded sarcastically.

He smiled. A sparkle in his eyes. He pushed himself off the dresser and walked to the door.

'If you want a fight, you'll have to find someone else,' he astounded me. 'I'm not going to indulge you today. We can agree to disagree where the archbishop is concerned. I'll get some groceries.'

'Yeah,' I wouldn't let him off that easily. 'Go out and get

yourself arrested. They're looking for you, remember? They have your name now, and your description.'

He turned to me. 'You're right,' he said, flustering me again. There was no way I could gaud him into a fight today. I'd have to work off my frustration some other way. I wasn't mad at him specifically. There was no real reason. Well, other than that we disagreed on Benedict. But that was nothing new. We disagreed on a lot of things. What was it that was pissing me off?

Jonah came back into the room and sat on his bed.

'Then you'll have to go out,' he suggested happily.

'Me?'

'There's no one else, and as you so eloquently pointed out; I'm a wanted man. You, in contrast, can easily walk into any supermarket you want in broad daylight.' The smile aggravated me even more, but he had a point. It would have to be me. It might even help me to order my thoughts. I would have the last word though.

'You're going to have to cut and dye your hair. Oh, and shave off that beard.' I said offhandedly.

His eyebrows lifted and he stared at me, caught between anger and laughter. 'Say what?' The humour won.

'Your photo is all over the news. Benedict gave a perfect description and true to his word, he named you. They pulled up some old mug shots, adapted them to ten years older and plastered them over everything. There's no way you can stay like this.' I waved my hand up and down to emphasise my point.

'Oh. And we need to get some Dermablend,' I added.

'Some what?' He was truly confused.

'Dermablend. Isn't that what it's called?' I looked at him. 'Tattoo camouflage.' Did I really have to spell it out? I was enjoying this.

'What?'

I sighed. 'Your tattoos. They need to be covered. They're specific to you. As unique as a fingerprint and much easier to identify from a distance. Even if you had surgery on your face, the tattoos would still be a dead give-away. From now on, every time you go out in public they must be covered. At least the ones that are visible and not completely covered by clothes. The same applies for the scars.'

Reluctantly, he nodded.

'And we leave here at midnight,' I added before I opened the door to get our supplies.

'Where do we go?'

'Somewhere no one knows you. Maybe New Mexico or California, somewhere like that. Name a place. You know where you've been better than I do.'

Then I added as an afterthought, 'somewhere on the western coast. We need to find a new way into The Establishment. Let Benedict do his thing here.'

'How do we travel?'

'By car, for now. Tickets need registration. A car is inconspicuous most of the time.'

'Not really, they can track a car from one side of the country to the other with all the traffic- and security cams everywhere. There's a camera on every street corner, not to mention every store front and home.'

I sighed. 'True.' I looked at him. 'What do you suggest?'

'What about a train?' Jonah asked. 'It will be a lot quicker if you want to put a big distance between us and here. Plus, it's less tiring.'

'Can we pay for tickets with cash?'

'No problem.'

It sounded like a good idea. We would have to bring the car back to Ebony, then hop on a train somewhere.'

'So, where do you want to go to?'

'I've always liked the sun and the sea,' Jonah answered with a big smile. 'California it is.'

I left him in the motel and went off to find something to camouflage the big man.

Chapter Twenty-One

'They have to be working together,' I said as we drove on the back roads between Panama City and Pensacola. We'd agreed to drive back to our home base, then hop on the train to California.

'Who?' Jonah looked up from the documents he was reading.

'My father and Arand.' I stated.

'Who's Arand?'

'He's the patriarch of the Islamic family. The fake Allah, if you like.' I thought I'd mentioned him before. Jonah wasn't good with names, especially if they didn't interest him.

'Does every religion have a separate family?' He asked out of the blue.

'Just the big ones. The size of the religion is what makes it financially interesting.'

'And this Arand's family harvests the souls of the Muslims?'

'They do.' I wondered where he was going with this line of questioning.

'How did that work? Did all the families sit down and decide who would get what?'

'More or less. Arand was the first to claim a religion. The whole reincarnation process was his invention after all. He took what at that time was the biggest: Islam. Dad was second, so he took Christianity. After they made their fortune, others followed. There are seven families now covering the major religions on earth.'

'What makes you think they are working together?'

'The escalation,' I replied.

'Don't you think that's just the reaction to the Christian fundamentalist?'

'No. It's just too convenient.'

He cocked his head in question.

'Think about it. The reactions are very swift and calculated. Almost as though the attacks were expected. I suppose the reaction by the Christian groups to the Islamic attacks were. Even a moron could anticipate that. But I'm talking about the Islamic reaction to the CWW. No one knew they even existed before the first attack. How were the Islamic fundamentalists prepared for something like that? How did they know? Unless it was all a coordinated plan to start off with.'

'Really?' Jonah exclaimed. 'Are you suggesting the two extremist groups got together and decided to launch a war? They'd kill each other rather than talk.'

'No, of course not.' I answered. 'Not them. They are just the puppets. I mean the puppet masters. My father and Arand got together and planned the whole thing. A Holy War to eclipse any previous one in history. It would positively rain souls for both families.' My gut felt as though a massive block of concrete had taken up residence there.

'Would they work together?' He asked. 'I thought they were competitors.'

'They are. But they are also businessmen. Both would see the benefits. I can't see it lasting though, it would probably be a short, temporary partnership. My father doesn't share well. And they need to make sure the market isn't flooded with new workers, that would push the price down again.'

'All a question of supply and demand.' The edge was back in his voice.

'Exactly.'

'It makes its sound so clinical you'd almost forget we're talking about humans here.' The words were hard and cold.

'I'm sorry Jonah. I can't sugar-coat it. This is what it is. For them it's business. Humans are a commodity. My father called them cattle. For him there would be no difference. Okay, we don't eat humans, so I guess it's not exactly the same.'

'Nowhere near.'

I suppose that depends on your perspective. I kept that to myself. But it did make me think. I was so immersed in human life, I thought I'd assimilated fully and that my perception would be the same. Obviously not.

'If they are working together, that means there is a plan.' Jonah remarked deep in thought.

'That's what I just said.'

'No. I mean the attacks are all planned.'

He was right.

'So somewhere there's a detailed plan. One that we could use to expose the Establishment.'

Now that was a thought.

'Yes. You're right. Only issue is that I expect the plan to be in my dimension. Not here.'

'But some of the inner circle should have at least the outline. I mean they're recruiting with a purpose. And they need to steer their recruits in a specific violent direction.'

'Possible.'

'I'd say probable.'

Chapter Twenty-Two

'They're on to me.' The concern was audible in a slight tremor in her voice on speaker phone.

Jonah and I looked at each other. Our worst fear had come true. Ebony's searches led The Establishment back to her.

'Get the hell out of there. Now!' Jonah said.

'Way ahead of you, big man. I'm clearing out, erasing the data, and bundling up my valuables. My homies will be here within twenty minutes to take me away.'

'How far behind are they?'

'Couple of days probably. They haven't found me yet, not exactly. But they know someone's digging around and they're attempting to trace the searches back to the source. I put up a couple of hundred swaps but it's just a question of time before they find the address.'

'We'll be over in ten.' Jonah hung up the phone before she could protest.

We were back in Mobile for a short visit before we left

for California. We arrived yesterday late and hadn't been to see Ebony yet.

Ten minutes later we were let into the loft.

On the way there, an idea started to form in my brain.

'What if we use this as an ambush?' I asked when we were gathered around the kitchen island.

Jonah reacted immediately. 'What do you mean? We are not putting Eb in more danger.'

'No,' I was quick to answer. 'Not for Ebony. Us. We sit here and wait for them to come to us. Ebony needs to leave, go underground and we will deal with The Establishment when they come to find her,' I explained.

Ebony picked up on the idea instantly. 'That would mean one of the computers would still have to be online and searching, as though I hadn't found their trail yet.'

'Exactly.'

She continued to run with the scenario. 'I can program it to search automatically. Use more AI to extend the searches depending on the data recovered. That way you can still get more info and they can follow the trail here without it being too obvious.'

I nodded.

'What about you?' Jonah was clearly worried for Ebony. So was I.

She smiled at him and placed her hand over his. 'I'll disappear. I always expected this to happen one way or the other. I thought it would be the government after my ass, or the Cartels, but I made my provisions years ago.'

Clever girl.

'Besides, none of my clients know what I look like. Hell, they all think I'm a thirty-eight-year-old single white man. No one will be looking for me. As far as anyone knows, I'm just another successful Rap producer.' There was no nervousness at all.

'Do you need money?' I asked.

She laughed. 'Hell no. I'm set for life. Multi millions stacked away. Half a big one. I can live in luxury forever on what I've amassed.'

She never ceased to surprise me.

'How do we contact you?' Jonah asked, reluctant to break off all contact.

Ebony pulled two new burner phones from a drawer containing at least ten in their original boxes. She gave one to Jonah and one to me. 'They're programmed with my new number. It's under "Mom". The number will be active in two days and stay that way for five. After that, if things haven't calmed down and we still need to talk, I'll give you another number. We'll do that for as long as necessary.' She gave us the phones. 'Enter a password straight away, be careful and don't lose them.'

We opened the boxes and took the phones out. They were fully charged and ready to go. In the contacts I saw more than a hundred names that meant absolutely nothing to me. I located "mum". Then navigated to the security, entered a six-digit code, closed the phone and put it in my jacket pocket.

There was a knock at the door and Ebony went to open it, accompanied by an anxious Jonah. They returned with two big dark-skinned gangster-type guys, both rivalling Jonah in size and intensity. Introductions were not made. Ebony showed them a pile of boxes that needed to disappear. They picked up two, Jonah took the third one and all three went out of the loft to what I expected was a waiting car.

Ebony came up to me. 'Gabriel.'

What, no ED?

She smiled. 'Do something for me, will you?'

I nodded. She took my hands in hers and locked eyes with me.

'Take care of the big lug, please. Make sure he doesn't do anything dumb, nothing more stupid than normal.'

I nodded and smiled, internally wondering how I was supposed to achieve that.

'He's reckless. Thinks he's ten foot tall.'

'He is, almost.' I joked.

'He's grown on me. Big man has a special spot in my heart.' Her face had softened.

'It's mutual,' I answered, knowing Jonah's feelings.

She smiled. 'Yeah. But it's also temporary. He's not the settling-down family type.'

'You'd be surprised.' I laughed with her.

She chuckled. 'Maybe. But not until he finishes this quest. And then maybe the next one after that.' She had a point.

'I want to believe I will see him again—alive—someday. Please watch out for him.' The tear in the corner of her eye slowly made its way down her cheek.

I wiped it away with the back of my fingers. 'I will. Don't worry.'

Her smile was hesitant. She knew Jonah. Knew what he would be like when The Establishment finally came to discover who was investigating them. Her fears were pertinent, especially because of their bond. I didn't know how much influence I had on my partner, but I would sure as hell try.

'I have his back.' I answered.

'I know.' She nodded and smiled again, now slightly

more at ease. 'Thanks.' She stood on her toes and kissed me softly on the cheek.

'Sorry I got you into all this, Eb.'

Her smile was deeper now. 'Hey, it was fun. I like a challenge.' We both laughed at that.

She became serious again. 'Get them, Gabe. Make them pay for everything they're doing.'

'I will.'

She nodded.

She knew I would.

Chapter Twenty-Three

We moved into the loft an hour after Ebony left. The blinds were kept closed most of the time with the lights on, and we made sure my shadow on the material was the only one anyone could observe from outside. It would be difficult to spy on the loft anyway; it was higher than any of the neighbouring buildings. Anyone trying to peer into the apartment would be looking up at an angle.

Jonah stayed out of sight. His bulk was a lot more difficult to disguise.

Anyone following the trail would be looking for a man. My presence would only confirm that. Being a lot smaller than my partner was finally a benefit, I fit the profile. Well, at first glance.

We sat and waited. Jonah checked the computer every now and then to make sure it was still running and to keep tabs on the clickers Ebony installed. They would alert us when The Establishment got closer.

After breakfast on the second day the computer let off a piercing signal. Jonah dropped what he was doing and raced to the terminal. He pressed some keys and read the data on the scene. The screen showed a map of the US, a red line originating from over the ocean crept closer to our location with every beep.

'How long?'

'Couple of hours.' Jonah answered.

'Then they'll have to mobilise and case the area.' I posed.

'I'm thinking they'll wait until dark before they try anything.'

I agreed. We would be under surveillance in a few hours and had to convince whoever was watching us that only one person was home. The deed and all the utilities were in the name of William. B. Mackay. Any background checks would only substantiate the scam that a geeky white dude lived in this apartment. We wanted them to believe that. It would give us the advantage. They wouldn't be prepared for us.

We would be ready for them.

'How many will they send?' Jonah drilled me.

'Four or five, more would be too conspicuous. Seasoned soldiers, most likely. Depending on whether The Establishment alerted my family, there might be one or two of my kind as well.'

'Is that good or bad?' He hadn't entertained that scenario.

'Depends on who. But it will blow my cover. They'll know we're working together. My family probably believes I've gone underground to avoid going back. Our partnership will mean betrayal, I don't think they would expect that. Not even from me.'

'It could cost us our edge,' he surmised.

I nodded.

'Not much we can do about it. And only if one of mine is there. If they are all human, and none leave here alive, then my cover will stay intact.'

The silence said it all.

Whatever happened today could change everything.

They came at four AM, in the darkest part of the night. There were four of them, big beefy men, all in black camouflage. Balaclavas hid their faces.

The first indication was an almost negligible scraping at the door. The lock turned slowly as someone painstakingly worked the mechanism is near silence. A siren outside camouflaged the last click as the catch slid free and the door opened. We'd left the bolts open and the alarm off.

Soft footfalls were muffled on the carpet of the hallway.

I stayed where I was in the shadow of the fridge in the kitchen. Jonah sat in one of the big recliners facing the hallway, his axe next to him propped against the side of the chair. His hands were folded in front of his chest, the elbows on the armrests.

They moved into the room, fanning out in a semi-circle as soon as they left the hallway.

Jonah pressed the switch. The standing lamp illuminated him, the axe, and a circle around him. It left the rest of the loft in darkness. The advance stopped. All attention was on Jonah.

He observed them over his folded hands. From my perch I saw the effect his dark countenance had on the invaders. Some clearly flinched. But not all. One stayed cool and collected. As I knew he would.

'Well, if it isn't the rogue priest.' The familiar voice

raised the hairs on the back of my neck. 'Father Ignatius if I'm not mistaken.'

'I used to be.' Jonah's tone was a mixture of cold viciousness and amusement.

'Ah yes. You've distanced yourself from the Holy Church, have you not?'

Jonah didn't answer. He just stared at the man who was obviously the leader of the attack force.

'Happy to make your acquaintance, even if it is just briefly. You've taken us on quite the journey in the past months.'

The figure lowered his sword, and his left hand went up to the mask covering his head and face. He pulled it off and dropped it to the ground.

'You have caused us a lot of bother,' he continued. 'And killed some of our best recruiters.' He stepped forward a metre, the sword still hanging by his side. Jonah stayed put. His hands still completely in full sight. It lulled the speaker into complacency. A dangerous trait I recognised so well.

'God wanted to keep you in the fold,' he laughed. 'He even sent his pathetic excuse for a son to persuade you to pick up the cloak again. And now Gabriel's missing. I don't expect you killed him. Did you?'

'No.'

'Shame. It would be nice to get rid of that fucker. But I digress.' The condescending tone mirrored that of my father.

They were all so engrossed with Jonah no one looked behind them. I stayed put, waiting for the right time to show myself. Sure enough, it came soon enough.

The pompous prick continued his monologue.

'You really have overrated yourself; you know. There are four of us, and just one of you.' Jonah refrained from answering. The attacker continued, 'what did you expect? That I would come alone? How stupid can you get? I'm really very disappointed. With all the stories about how dangerous you are, I expected more.'

'You going to talk me to death?' Jonah reacted. A massive smile pulled his lips wide.

'See, there you go. Ignoring the odds. You have no chance. It's four against one.'

Jonah cocked his head in thought, then the smile changed to one of disdain. 'Nah. Not exactly.'

'You're on your own,' the leader taunted.

'Wrong again.'

'Hello, Michael.' I stepped out of the shadows.

My brother's surprise couldn't have been bigger. His eyes opened to the max and his mouth gaped in shock. He stared at me, not believing what he saw.

I walked around his henchmen and stood in front of him, about a metre-and-a-half to the side of the chair where Jonah sat.

'I would say it's nice to see you, Michael. But I imagine this is not a social call.' I calmly addressed him.

'What the hell are you doing here?' he finally found his voice.

'Surely even you could figure that out,' I taunted him. 'It's not that difficult.' I easily reverted back to the hateful relationship that had so characterised my life back home.

Michael looked at me, then to Jonah and back to me. It was dawning on him. Finally.

'You two are working together?' he asked incredulously.

'See, Jonah.' I teased. 'I told you he was the brainy one in the family,' The sarcasm dripped off my words, all aimed at riling my older brother.

Jonah laughed, this incensed Michael even more.

'You can't be.' Michael stated in disbelief. I shrugged and smiled.

'You would betray your own family? Your father?'

'Looks like it,' I answered, the smile ever widening. I was enjoying this.

'How could you?'

'Not so difficult really.' I turned deadly serious. 'I just opened my eyes to all the bullshit dear old dad constantly vomited over us. I finally got my head out of my ass and looked at what our family is really doing. What the old man stands for. And it made me puke.'

He couldn't even speak.

'I refuse to be part of this scam any longer,' I continued. 'You can kiss dad's ass as much as you like, I'm out.

'You can't,' he shouted. 'It's not possible.'

He was genuinely astounded. 'How can you turn your back on father? After everything he had done for you.'

'That's exactly why I can,' I retorted. 'What did he ever do for me? For you? For any of our siblings? Dad only thinks of dad. No one else. His ambitions are the only thing that counts. He uses us—used me—as a tool to achieve his goals.' My anger rose against my earlier resolve. I had to push it down. I needed to stay focussed.

'I don't own him anything, except my contempt.'

That pushed Michael's buttons. He flipped.

'You ungrateful bastard.' His face almost glowed with indignation. Spittle flew from his mouth as he spewed his rage at me. I wasn't impressed.

It occurred to me Michael no longer had the same impact on me as the last time we met. My victory in our last meeting, and everything that happened to me since, including my self-reflection, made me stronger and I saw my older brother for what he was—a bully. An insecure, vicious bully.

'Whatever,' I answered indifferently.

I didn't think he could become any madder; I was wrong. He exploded.

Michael came at me, his sword up over his head, ready to arc down on me. His swing came down and was stopped by Jonah's axe. The blades clashed and my brother's sword shattered. He jumped back in shock.

I glanced at my partner standing next to me, and nodded my thanks, my own sword in my hand. I could have handled it, but this made even more of an impression on my brother and his henchmen.

I deduced they were all from my dimension. Michael hadn't seen fit to add any humans. He wanted the glory for himself. Bummer. It was not working out as he had planned.

Michael looked at the remnants of his sword, then back to us. His anger was tempered by the shock, but it was still there.

'You're so desperate to kill me,' I stated.

'I am,' he answered totally disgusted at me. 'You have disgraced our family. You have shamed your heritage. Not only did you attack me back home, but you have joined forces with this… this human.' He spat out the words. 'You betrayed your own, chose humans above your kin. Your own kind. You…'

'Yes, yes. I know. Bla bla bla. Cut to the chase, will you? You sanctimonious git.' The hatred dripped of my words.

Michael's eyes opened wide in shock; his mouth stuck in the last words as he took in a big breath in astonishment. I'd never dared speak to him like that. Well, get used to it. This was the new me.

'How dare you?' he began. 'You will award me the

respect I am due as your elder and the designated heir.' He was rambling.

'Come on brother, you can do better than that.'

'Don't call me brother, you are no longer family.' He literally spat at that.

'Oh, I don't know, we share the same father, that's usually a defining characteristic of a sibling tie and you have to admit the resemblance is striking.' Sarcasm is one of my better traits and I was on a role.

'I do not resemble you other than on the exterior.' He tried to sound commanding, it came out petty and weak.

'We're not really as different as you'd like to believe,' I continued. 'Except of course that you're a pompous prick and I'm quite a nice guy.' Oh, the joys of baiting my brother. I'd missed that.

'You butter up to these creatures as though they are your equal. You are the son of God. Not a lowly human. You degrade yourself. Degrade your ancestry.'

'Son of God? Don't tell me you're starting to believe that crap now, are you? Dad is no more a god than you are an angel.' I laughed to emphasise my disdain.

'He is the symbol of this religion. That makes him God in my books.' His face turned bright red.

'Yada yada.'

'You're such a hypocrite,' he shouted. 'You embraced your mission in this dimension with open arms, intent on cementing your position as father's favourite.' He tried to rile me. Not going to work. This was the new me.

'Ah, now we're getting to the real reason for all this animosity. You're still jealous of my bond with him.'

'The bond you had—if there was any. The one you threw away when you denounced him: your father, our family. Our business.'

I pretended to consider his words. 'I never actually denounced Father, now that I think about it. It's the family business I disagree with. I will not partake in that anymore. Mind you, I have no love for the old man. So, I guess you're right there.' I nodded and shrugged my shoulders.

'You never complained when you were growing up. When you had all the benefits of a god's son. You basked in the wealth and the power. Now who's sanctimonious? Now who's the hypocrite?' he still tried to rile me.

I laughed again. 'You forget my rebellious nature. It continuously brought me into conflict with the old man. We never got along. And that was even when I didn't realise what we were doing. I do now.'

'What does it matter? Why do you have empathy for these lowly creatures?' There was a hint of true curiosity there.

'It's not the humans. Sure, they have endearing traits.' I glanced at Jonah. 'Well, some do.' Jonah chuckled.

'Then what?' Michael truly had no idea. Our conversation hadn't registered anything with him.

'The deceit. The lies. The Hypocrisy. That's what got to me.' I was deadly serious.

He laughed. A shrill cold laugh.

'The lies? You really disapprove of the lies?'

'I do.' I didn't expect him to understand what I was talking about. He was a mirror image of my father, without the brains or the brawn.

From the corner of my eye, I saw my partner was starting to fidget. Never a patient man, this verbal rally between siblings was irritating him.

We were at a stale mate. What to do now? I knew what Jonah preferred and believe me it was tempting to kill all of them. It had benefits. It would save my cover and make life a lot easier, but we were talking about my brother here. Even if he was a dick. I wasn't sure I was ready to go that far.

'I should thank you really.' Michael's smile was cruel. He looked from me to Jonah and back again.

'That you're back in dad's graces?' I answered, dismissing the comment. 'You're welcome.'

He laughed. 'No, nothing as trivial as that.' His amusement sent alarm bells up and down my spine. Something was very wrong here. He was gloating. Why? The odds were not in his favour, and his favourite weapon had just been demolished. He should be mad. Instead, he looked like the cat that ate the canary.

He stared me directly in the eye. 'No, your idea.'

I took the bait. I couldn't stop myself. 'What idea?' My heart sank.

'About the Cristian Caliphate. It was your idea to copy Islam and fanaticise young men. Foster a fundamentalist movement within Christianity. The CWW.'

My blood ran cold. I felt Jonah's eyes bore into the back of my head.

'Was it?' he asked as he moved forward and took up a position next to me.

'Let's talk about this later, shall we? I answered without taking my eyes of my sibling. The bastard was enjoying this. He'd expertly identified Jonah's main shortcoming: his temper.

'Was it?' Jonah asked again with more force.

'Don't be so humble brother,' Michael pushed the distrust deeper. 'Remember the last time you were home? At the dinner. You elaborated on the basic idea, I just went with it and brought it to fruition.'

Jonah didn't have to ask again. The way he held his axe was enough to illustrate his thoughts.

There was a block of concrete in my gut. 'I might have mentioned a hair-brained idea remotely like that,' I answered the unspoken question carefully. Keeping both him and Michael in my line of sight.

'Don't do this, Jonah.' I addressed him directly. 'It's what Michael does. He's trying to get inside your head.'

'It's working.'

Michael's laugh was cold, completely without mirth. He enjoyed my discomfort, and the possibility Jonah just might do his job for him and kill me. The revelation would sow dissent, not what I needed now. It had been difficult enough these past months to gain even a semblance of trust from the big lug. With one comment, Michael smashed that to smithereens. Once again, I felt the hatred for my sibling rise and threaten to engulf me.

I had to diffuse the situation before it spiralled entirely out of hand. We now had proof The Establishment was behind the CWW, that was what we hoped. I realised I should have spoken to Jonah before about my last visit home, especially after the initial CWW attacks. I'd hoped against my better judgement that the Holy War had nothing to do with my stupid suggestions. They weren't viable options. I needed to get out of a tight spot. That was the only thing I could come up with at the time. And now they'd come back to haunt me and landed me in deep shit. Fuck, fuck, fuck.

My brother's voice brought me back to the current situation. 'You're soft. Being here, amongst your pets has made you squeamish and weak. You are no longer a warrior. You even need your pet to fight for you.' His taunts were irritating. I had more important things to do.

'I guess we'll see, won't we?' I countered. 'Unless you want to talk me to death. Brother.'

That last word did it. I saw the hatred flash in his eyes again. Then his gaze went past me, and the right edge of his lips turned up almost imperceptibly.

I ducked down and to the right, bringing my knife up in an arc behind me. The blade made contact, first with steel, then with flesh and bone. It sliced easily though all of them.

The first soldier fell to the ground, mortally wounded. From the corner of my eye, I saw Jonah dispatch the last two attackers with a mighty swing of the axe. At least he was focussing his attention on our initial enemy.

I was already on my feet and facing my brother. His smile transformed to a scowl. I guess he hadn't expected us to vanquish his best so quickly. He was the only one left.

'Still the cheater, Michael. Nothing changes. You still don't dare face me alone. No guts.'

The venom shot from his face, but he stayed where he was. Anger alternated with fear. I suddenly realised my big brother feared me. Now that was a new development. Maybe the result of our last tussle back home.

'I'll be back,' he scowled.

'Oh, get some new cliches, will you? You're boring.' I said.

He smiled, keeping an eye on both the approaching Jonah and me. 'Much as I'd like to stay, I have more important things to do. It was good seeing you, brother, even if it will be the last time I see you alive. At least I can tell father what has become of you.' I heard him say just as he transported out of sight. Back to dear old dad, I suppose.

The other bodies disappeared as well. They did know how to tidy up. Just as well, a body leaking purple blood would be hard to explain here.

I turned and focussed on Jonah. I had to diffuse the situation but was at a loss on how to do exactly that. The silence was heavy. Almost tangible.

'Well, it proved one thing.' I tried.

'What's that.'

'My family is behind it all.' Jonah huffed. He wasn't impressed. Nor distracted from the main issue. My idea. My culpability, and probably more, the fact that I had failed to share it with him.

The silence could be cut with a knife.

Jonah's voice made me jump involuntarily. 'So, it was your idea?' The venom was back in his tone.

'It wasn't like that,' I tried.

'What was it like?' He moved in front of me and locked eyes. My first inclination was to lower mine, anything to avoid the hatred emanating from my partner. I took a deep breath and held his gaze, trying desperately to ignore the butterflies in my gut and the nagging voice in my brain screaming at me to get the hell out of here while I could. Maybe.

'Michael hates me.' I started. Jonah didn't react. 'It's mutual.' Still nothing.

'He will do anything to keep me out of my father's good graces and into as much trouble as possible. Last time I was home, well, they suspected something was wrong. That I might be more rebellious than I usually am. Michael was hell-bent on exposing me. He prevented me from leaving, I had to stay the night and that meant attending the family dinner. It wasn't in the plan, but I had no choice. He cornered me after the meal, and I had to think of something to convince him I was still loyal to the company and to the family. I spun a yarn about copying our biggest competitor: Islam. I fantasised that they started the Caliphate, the whole thing with ISIS. It was all orchestrated by Arand, the family Patriarch to generate more young souls.'

I watched his eyes while I tried hard to ignore the axe he'd planted between his feet. His whole demeanour was one of tense aggression. The anger resonated off him in waves. His shoulders were rigid. The big arms taut and ready to swing the weapon.

'It was the first thing that came to mind. It seemed so far-fetched and stupid I didn't think he would take it seriously. He never did with any of my other hair-brained ideas. I never meant it to be a real option. It was pure survival at that time. I had to buy time to get the list. Be realistic, I had to get out, so I just said the first thing that came to mind.'

His eyes bore into my head. It felt like an intense heat that sent a wave of pain into my skull.

'I'm sorry,' I said. 'I know that doesn't mean anything. Not in the scale of what's going on now. But I am. I never imagined they would do this. Never.' He remained silent.

'And I should have told you.'

The weight of the silence rested heavily on my shoulders. It took all my strength to stay silent and hold eye contact, and to keep breathing for that matter.

For the first time in our shared endeavour, I started to doubt myself and what I was doing here. If it was my fault —and all arrows pointed that way at the moment—then I was responsible for the destruction of innocent souls. It wasn't something I thought I could live with. And to boot, it would cost me the only allies I had. It might even mean I would have to kill Jonah before he terminated me.

I waited for whatever would come next. Internally I weighed my options. I still had the knives, one in my hand and the other on my back, and this time there was a gun within reach. Jonah had the double headed axe. I wasn't so sure I had the advantage. Not even with the firepower.

My nerves were flayed. It took all my concentration to keep still and wait. Jonah would make a move. I was sure of it. And I would react. I wasn't looking forward to this fight. It would not end well.

Michael had done it again.

Jonah stood silent. His hands still resting on the pommel of the axe. His eyes were fixed on me.

There was a subtle difference. I wasn't quite sure what it was, but there was something different. My gut churned. Was it good? No idea. I still couldn't read this man.

He broke the silence.

'How fast can they work?' The previous edge to his tone was absent.

'What do you mean?' I creased my brow in question. What was going on? Wasn't he going to fight?

'The Establishment, your family. How fast can they set something up?' he continued.

'That depends on what it is.'

'The Christian Caliphate? How long would that take to set up and get it to the phase it's in now?'

I understood where he was going. I felt my eyes open in astonishment and at the same time heat rise in my face as I understood what he was getting at.

'A long time,' I answered slowly. 'Years probably. They would have to groom the fanatics, recruit many more. Arm them. Get them information on where to strike. Build up the fear.'

'Exactly.'

I looked at my partner, the smile that touched the edges of his lips lacked the menace of earlier.

'You were back home, when? About five months ago?' he asked.

'Yes. Way too short to get things organised to the point where they are now.'

He nodded.

'The fucker,' I shouted,

'Whose head was he in now?' Jonah was enjoying this.

'Point taken. I'm obviously still susceptible to my brother's manipulations. I—we—will have to do something about that.'

'Anything particular in mind?'

'Other than killing him, no, not yet. Though that is very tempting.' I pictured Michael with one of my knives in his chest. It made me smile. He would re-incarnated anyway, so it wasn't actually permanent if I did take his life here on earth. Dad would no doubt order the reincarnation, though he might let Michael wait in limbo for a while as a punishment.

'We have to watch our back. They will try to manipulate us into breaking this fragile partnership.' Jonah added.

'Is it fragile?' I asked, a bit surprised he would call it that after all we had been though together.

'It's a partnership that suits me now. No more than that. So yes, it's fragile.'

'Then we will have to make it stronger and more of a threat to them.' I stated resolutely. I wasn't about to give up on our quest yet.

'How?'

'We need to separate the wheat from the chaff. Get more ally's and kick some ass.' That brought another smile to his lips. One that did touch his eyes. 'We need to find out how high up it goes.' He nodded. 'It's time to go up in the world.'

Chapter Twenty-Four

'Something has been bugging me for a long time,' Jonah stated out of the blue.

We'd just finished our dinner and tidied up. I sat at the table working on the information Ebony sent us and Jonah was watching a news channel on the tv. He switched off the station and turned towards me, his face looked deadly serious. I closed the laptop and moved to the comfortable seat opposite him.

I raised an eyebrow. 'Okay, shoot.'

He sat forward on the sofa, his elbows on his knees. 'Technology wise, your dimension is much further than we are.' I nodded. 'You have these transporters. You've got the whole "beam-me-up-Scotty" thing worked out. You can reincarnate souls. Everything.'

I nodded again. Where was this going?

He looked me straight in the eye.

'So, why do you need slaves?' He dared me to convince him. I could see it in his whole stance and attitude.

'We don't,' I answered much to his surprise. He sat up, curious.

'We have the technology to do most of the work the slaves do. Some things still need a person's hand, but even that doesn't necessitate slavery from a technological perspective.'

'So, there's no reason,' he concluded prematurely.

'It's not that simple. You're right that we don't need slaves from a technology perspective. But there are more sides to this equation. We can replace manual labour with machines. The technology is there. However, it's more expensive. Human labour is relatively cheap. Sure, there are the costs of the reincarnation, but that is now minimal as it has been automated as much as possible. Machines cost a lot more in core materials that we don't have in our dimension. They would have to be imported from other dimensions, like this one.' He opened his mouth to protest; I stopped him with a raised hand. He started this, now he had to give me room to explain.

'Expense pays a big role in the validation of slavery for our kind. Whether that is legitimate is another question. I'm not voicing my opinion here. You asked why there was slavery, these are the argumentations used in my world.'

He nodded, urging me onwards.

'There is more. There is the power perspective that plays a large role in the whole package. Slavery, and the dependency it secures, is a mighty tool in our world. Supplying the right manpower to guarantee the comfort our people are used to, is a pre-requisite and therefore a very powerful tool for social status and ultimately domination. Like here, there are power-hungry people in my dimension. My father is one of them, and slavery is his ticket to achieve that. Another reason why we could not—I should say would not—live without slavery is because our civilisation and culture are centred around comfort. My people do not do the dirty work necessary in any civilisation. We do not pollute our pampered lives with menial tasks. Basically, there is no one who would do the work that remained after automation was complete. We would still need to import others to do it.'

He continued to stare at me.

'So, if you look at the whole picture, slavery is an economic and social thing in my dimension. Not a technological necessity,' I concluded.

'You agree with it?'

'If I did, I wouldn't be here.' He didn't look very convinced.

'Do you believe what you just said validates the use of slavery?' he rephrased.

'No, I don't. That should be clear to you by now. I believe slavery, in any form, is morally despicable and should be abolished.' He was irritating me. I could feel my face becoming warm and the red anger-blush started to creep up from my neck.

'Then we agree.'

'Do we?' The simplicity with which he pushed his convictions on me riled me. He was so quick to judge me and my family. What did he know about my life? Our dimension? Talk about prejudice.

Jonah was confused. His brow creased and he cocked his head in question. 'What do you mean? You just said you were against this slavery.'

'I said I was against any kind of slavery.' I stated resolutely.

'Same thing.' He shrugged.

'No. It isn't,' I continued. 'What my family does is repulsive. But at least they're honest about it. They know it's slavery by any name.'

'You called it recruiting. How does that fit in with your statement?'

'That is solely for the peace of mind of the human Establishment members. They coined that phrase. To make them feel lees guilt maybe or to make it more accept-able. Anyway, we know it's slavery and own that. You humans clothe slavery in other terms, economical depen-dency, communism, even democracy, in the full knowledge they are barely veiled forms of the same thing; enslavement.'

He was riled. Well, bummer, if he couldn't take the truth. 'How do you come to that ridiculous conclusion.' Oh, how he hated being contradicted.

'What is slavery?' I asked, switching the roles.

He looked at me incredulously. I returned the stare and waited him out.

'Slavery is when one person owns the other and has the power to determine his or her whole life.' He humoured me, certain he had me beaten.

'Agreed,' I surprised him. 'But it's all down to your defi-nition of ownership.'

He cocked his head in question, now more curious than angry.

'In this dimension ownership is less obvious than in ours. Here people are owned not because of a payment that was made to a previous owner, but by religion, finances and dogma.'

I had his attention. 'Your versions of slavery are concealed but none the less debilitating to those who cannot escape the boundaries set on their lives. Religion confines the freedom of its believers with a myriad of laws and restrictions. People must do the Church's bidding and are punished when they question why. How is that not slavery?'

He declined to answer, but I could see the questions boring their way into his mind.

'Consumerism is another slave driver. Status, and comfort all depend on how affluent a person is. Life is marketed as a constant stream of purchase, some necessary, the majority ludicrous and redundant. To count in life, you need to have the next iPhone, brand-name clothes, a German car. Is life really better with a Rolex? I think not. But your kind have become dependent on the acceptance money brings. You hunker for belonging. To be part of a group, not just any group. No, the popular one. It's the high school conundrum that lasts for a lifetime. And that is a form of slavery to money if you have it. What about the humans who don't? They are pressed into what can only be called oppression to find enough cash to survive. They, and their families are held hostage to the success of their owners. Yes, owners. The ones who determine who live, and who dies. Maybe not directly, but they have the power, and they mandate the outcome.'

I realised I was ranting. But his sanctimonious done-me-wrong mentality got to me.

'The exploitation of man by his own kind is nothing new. It is as old as mankind itself, maybe even older as your animals show the same tendencies. We didn't invent it. My father just saw the opportunities and embraced them.'

He stayed mute. 'You can call my people immoral and unethical, and you would be right. In some respects. But, by all means, look in the mirror before you judge.'

He was silent.

I realised everything I said referred to both his people and mine.

'My turn,' I stated. He nodded, knowing what I meant; my turn to ask a question.

'Why did you become a priest?' I asked Jonah.

'None of your business,' he tried.

I wouldn't let him off that easily. 'Actually, it is. We're partners in this, whether you like it or not. And that means sharing information that is—or could be—relevant for our cause.'

He was silent again and moped like a small child. It didn't help. I was used to his tantrums by now.

'What happened after the nun was killed?' I pushed. 'When you joined the monastery.'

He sighed and took another swig of his drink. His shoulders sagged and he sat back in the sofa.

'After she died and I completed my revenge rampage, I left my home. I travelled. With no specific destination, I went from one cesspit to another. My life was filled with violence and pain. Mine and other's. I had no empathy for anyone. All compassion was eradicated with Sister Eloise's death. Once the rage dissipated, there was nothing left. I was empty and lost. After a fight went particularly bad, I was badly banged up and lying in my own blood and vomit. A good Samaritan picked me up off the street and brought me to the monastery. There the monks took care of my physical wounds. They nursed my body back to health, but my mind remained desolate. Slowly I descended into a massive depression.'

There were sweat drops on his brow. This was not an easy tale to tell. I nodded to urge him onwards.

'I broke down and cried, I couldn't stop. I never left my cell and stopped taking care of myself. I ignored the food the monks brought me and barely drank any of the water. I slid into an even deeper state of despair. The monks and the abbot continued to bring me food and water and clean me and my cell. They never forced me to do anything. Just put the food where I could reach it and left me alone.'

'My mind fell in on itself and I entered a void. There was nothing. No light, no darkness. Nothing. I've never seen anything like that before or since. I was at absolute rock-bottom.'

I filled the glass in his outstretched hand from the bottle of Vodka on the table.

'My eyes were closed, I was silent. Didn't eat. I just lay on the cot in a foetal position. The monks took up position opposite me in the cell. They kept a constant vigilance on me, day, and night, gave me water and cleaned me when I soiled myself. I was catatonic. Dead to the world. In a place without sound, or smell or sight.'

'What brought you out of it?'

He looked up at me. 'I don't know. Not really. To this day.' He shook his head. 'One day sounds penetrated my emptiness: the monks praying and singing in mass. Slowly, over the course of days, I became aware of a monk sitting with me. He prayed out loud, reading from the scriptures and the gospels. His words didn't mean anything to me to start with. But the sounds were a lifeline. One that I hesitatingly took hold of. He noticed and brought me water. Later someone brought some kind of porridge. It took a long time to bring me out of the state I was in. There were relapses, many of them. But they never took me to the absolute pits I had been in before. Every time the monks brought me back simply by being there and talking to me. I started to eat again and slowly regained some strength. I was a wraith. Skin and bones.'

'The abbot came to my cell and spoke to me. What he said didn't mean much to me to start with, but that didn't hinder him. He continued to visit and speak to me about the power of prayer and meditation. His words started to come through the haze that filled my mind. I responded. Asked questions. He didn't have all the answers, but he was patient and together we searched for what I needed to know.'

'I finally left the cell and went outside. The light hurt my eyes. I'd been in my self-imposed isolation for more than five months. I sat on the ground in the sun and cried. The tears flowed down my cheeks and wouldn't stop. It was the first emotion I experienced after the void.'

'It felt good. To be able to feel something again. Even if it was loss. Not just for sister Eloise, but for me, for my humanity.'

'In the course of the next year I became stronger in mind and body. The abbot and the monks taught me how to pray. It was my form of meditation and gave me the peace I so desperately needed. I despised myself for what I was and what I had done in my life. The Abbot taught me my history was not what made me. My humanity was. And if I embraced it, I could start again. Rebalance myself. Make up for some of the atrocities I'd perpetrated. I longed to be human again.'

He turned to me. 'I found that humanity in the Church. In the revelation I encountered in the monastery and the peace I felt. That was all taken from me once I found out it was part of a scam. I have nothing left. No faith. No emotions. Nothing.'

'I disagree,' I answered his unspoken question. 'Sure, my father is responsible for the scam that is The Establishment.

But he had nothing to do with the emergence of your faith in the monastery or how the monks helped you. You brought yourself back from the brink. That was what the monks understood. They couldn't do that, only you could. Whatever you found there is yours. It's not something my father or anyone could give to or take from you.'

'There is something you need to understand,' I continued. 'The worst atrocity I get from you about the whole Establishment scam is that it destroyed the foundations of your beliefs. That makes it extremely personal to you.' He was about to disagree, but I cut him off.

'I understand that. It's logical, if you assume my people consciously targeted your religions to undermine and contaminate them. But that is not how it happened. My world is void of gods and religion. We didn't even know the concept until we came to this dimension. It is something so unique to Earth we didn't recognise what it could mean to you. We saw it as a means to an end. As a manner in which the powers were controlling the population, no different from wealth or politics. We observed the subjugation your churches placed on their believers and the exploitation it ensued. We learned by your example.'

He was still fuming. But held his tongue. For now.

'You are responsible for your own humanity. Not a higher being, or my father. You. You are accountable for what humanity means to you and how you act. That was what you found in the monastery. Your own morals and ethics, that is what made you what you were then. And that is what makes you what you are now. The responsibility for what you make of your life and your humanity lies with you alone. Laying that with another—be that a god or a con man—is no more than a cowardly way to avoid culpability.'

I was on a roll. I stood up and advanced towards my surprised partner.

'And you know what the worst thing is?' I was shouting by then, standing over him. 'It's not even a human thing.' My mouth vomited what I didn't want to hear, but I was unable to stop myself. The voices in the back of my mind screamed at me to stop. Not to dredge up what was about to erupt into the light.

'I did the same. For hundreds of years, I waived any culpability because it was our family business. It was my father's decision. Not mine. Bullshit! By reneging on my responsibility to stop him, I perpetuated what I knew was despicable and morally wrong in any dimension.'

'I am just as guilty as he is. Just as accountable. Not by my actions maybe, but by the lack thereof. We are much alike, Jonah. No matter how much you try to contradict that. We both fold to powerful entities. To the comfort of not having to decide. To not being accountable. And to the fear of someday being called to answer for our actions.'

I was shaking. The impact of my words dug deep into my soul.

Taking a deep breath, I looked down at Jonah. He appeared in shock. I wasn't sure whether that was because of my revelations or because I dared to go up against him. Maybe it was even my overpowering conviction that kept him in his seat.

On shaky legs I turned and walked to the apartment door. I pulled it open and stumbled out into the dark streets.

I walked, and walked, and walked. I had no idea where I was, and I was way past being lost. It didn't matter. I needed distance. Not so much from Jonah as from what had really happened. I wanted to make a point to him and ended up ripping myself apart.

It hit me like a brick wall. My role in what my family did. How my own actions were as despicable as what my father stood for. Sure, I had turned a corner. I was attempting to change what was happening. But if I was completely honest it was still with a feeling of trepidation, and half hearted. It was more than going through the motions, but the actual scale of what I was guilty of had been pushed to the background and shrouded in a self-imposed mist.

I was kidding myself that my father was the culprit. My rebellion was no more than a vague and inferior attempt to exonerate any guilt I might have. It was a sham. Like everything else I did in my lifetime. I was trying to buy my own absolution. Or I thought I was. But it was no more than another scam. One I was perpetuating on myself.

My previous pathetic attempts at rebellion now seemed childish and inept. He never took them seriously, never took me seriously. And why should he? I was so incompetent. He knew I was never a real threat. Not as long as I didn't take responsibility for my actions. I would always, always, be in search of his sanction or approval, even of my defiance. I ultimately wanted him to be proud of me. If not because of my contribution to what he held dear, then for my defiance of that same thing.

And what did that make me? What more than a scared, lonely child with daddy issues?

I was so pathetic, it was ridiculous.

It was also sobering.

…And scary.

I returned when the sun was up. How I found the apartment was a complete mystery to me but find it I did.

Jonah still sat in the exact same spot on the sofa where I left him hours before. The only difference was the empty Vodka bottle next to him. He looked up when I came through the door, walked to the table and pulled a chair out.

'You okay?' he asked.

'Maybe,' I responded, truthfully not knowing how to answer his question. 'I'm not sure.'

'It's a lot to take in.'

'Yes. It is.'

Jonah stood up and walked to the kitchen where he started a pot of coffee. We waited in silence until the machine finished the job. Jonah poured two big mugs full and brought them over to the table. He handed me one and leant back against the back of the seat opposite the sofa, both hands around his own mug.

'You're right,' he broke the silence. I sipped the coffee; the strong black liquid burned a welcome heat down my throat. It warmed me.

'I have been hiding behind the concept of God and a higher being that determined my destiny. It was an escape from the terrible things I've done. Even of the things I'm still doing. Like you said, I concluded if it's not my decision, then I wasn't responsible. Knowing it is hurts. It slapped me in the face and opened my eyes. I am the one responsible for what I do or don't do. I still have to answer to another, but the decisions are mine.'

I nodded. We had both come to the same conclusion.

'I guess I should thank you. Part of me feels like hitting you in the face, but the other part, the less primal side,' he chuckled a bit. 'That part knows you're right. I hate to acknowledge that. But I must.'

'You don't have to thank me,' I answered. 'Or hit me, for that matter. Nothing you could do to me now compares to the brick wall I ran into when I held up the mirror to you. It backfired big time.'

'Maybe we both needed a reality check?'

'Maybe we did.'

'Well, we sure as hell got one.'

Chapter Twenty-Five

'Now what?'

I shrugged. No idea. Now my family knew I was involved, our chances of finding anything truly incriminatory on The Establishment, were melting like snow in the bright spring sun.

'Michael will have reported to dear old dad, and they'll be putting new defences and security up. I don't expect any of the little access I had will be available anymore. They will also fortify the security for key recruiters and warn them of my involvement. We'll have to find a different way to get to The Establishment.'

We sat in silence. Jonah and I in the apartment, and Ebony via the computer stream.

'Any bright ideas, guys?' she asked cheerfully. We didn't know where she was, or at least I didn't, she might have told Jonah. But wherever it was, it looked comfortable. Bright sunlight streamed in through big windows behind her. The sky was blue, not a cloud to be seen. The ambiance of the room she was in looked fresh and bright. Friendly and inviting.

A bit like where we were.

Jonah and I had made our way to California, San Francisco to be exact. We'd rented a short stay apartment near the harbour. It was spacious enough, a living room with an open kitchen and balcony, three bedrooms, two baths, use of the communal swimming pool and a reserved parking space. Not bad really. The price was astronomical, but it offered us privacy and no questions were asked, not to mention adequate security. We paid cash for three months in advance and moved the few things we had into the apartment. The view—though not waterfront—was nice. It offered us a good outlook over the bars and delis in the street below and, more important, both sides of the one-way street in front of the block.

Back to the meeting with Ebony. Did we have a plan? I shook my head. Nothing.

'We still have some addresses on the list,' Jonah tried.

'Yes,' I answered despondently. 'But by now they will have linked what I downloaded with the killings. Anyone left on the list will be protected.'

I still wasn't used to Jonah's new look. Clean shaven, the hair on top of his head just millimetres long and blond. The tattoos were covered, and his dress sense had radically improved. Instead of the compulsory jeans and t-shirt he now wore camel-coloured chinos and a tailored silk shirt. He looked good, just not like Jonah, which, though strange, was the point.

He was even getting used to the new look. His initial discomfort was ebbing, and he enjoyed the impact his new look had on the fairer sex. The Bad Boy was replaced by a more sophisticated version.

His cover named him a business consultant for offshore oil companies, courtesy of Ebony of course.

'A while ago when you explained this whole Establishment to me,' Ebony started, 'you said the Establishment was for all major religions. Not just Christianity.'

'Yes. That's correct.'

'And the families in your dimension heading these religions are competitors. Right?'

I nodded.

'But they work together as well?'

I wondered where she was going to with this line of thinking. 'Like most businesses they can put their arguments side when there is mutual benefit to be achieved.'

'As with this Holy War?'

'Yes.'

'So why don't we look into one of the others?' she concluded.

'What do you mean?' I asked surprised.

'If they work together, wouldn't we be able to find some proof of that in one of the other religions? For instance, Islam.'

'You might be on to something.' I acknowledged. A tingle of excitement started at the base of my stomach.

'And they are part of The Establishment itself. That means any damage we could do to them would ultimately be damage to The Establishment in general.' Jonah chimed in eagerly.

The pieces were falling into place. But there was a big risk here. 'Yes, but we do need to be careful. The families are not exactly on speaking terms. If anything, they are partners of circumstance.'

'So do you have any suggestions on where and how to

start?' Ebony asked me. I thought about it for a few minutes as the idea started to take hold in my brain.

'Any agreements between the rival families would be very clandestine. Officially, like with the fundamentalists in the religions, we are competitors, enemies even. But they could put that aside for a good cause, which in this case is mutual wealth. Maybe we could try to find out who would benefit most.'

'Follow the money?' Jonah concluded.

'In a manner of speaking, yes,' I agreed. 'But I think we need to go back a step. The "money" is in the harvesting of the souls. That means revisiting the recruitments. Only this time the enlistment of the Islamic fundamentalists.'

'ISIS?' Ebony asked?

'Yes, and any other zealots.'

Johan chimed in, 'wouldn't it be very dangerous to go after ISIS itself?'

'That's what I was thinking,' Ebony added. 'ISIS is technically savvy. They have state-of-the-art equipment and the ability to use it. I'm not entirely sure they wouldn't be able to find us.'

She had a point. I absolutely didn't want to bring the fight to Ebony and put her in any kind of danger, especially after our earlier run in with Michael. She was a massive asset to our cause, and she was a friend. Quite a new concept for me.

'Then they are a definite "No."'

'Agreed.' Jonah's face relaxed slightly, and I thought I heard a sigh of relief from Ebony. There were some groups even we didn't want to mess with. There was no guarantee The Establishment actually controlled ISIS. Maybe they didn't have to. They were a means to an end to fan the flame of the Holy War. And frankly, they were doing that job very well.

'I'll look into the splinter groups,' Ebony offered. 'See what I can find there.'

'Yes. But any direct links to ISIS and you back off, okay?' Jonah stated resolutely.

'Don't worry, big man. I'm not suicidal. I know when I get in over my head.' Ebony smiled at his concern.

'I'll get back to you guys.'

'Take care, Tiny.'

With another radiating smile, she signed off.

'An interesting development.' Jonah said.

'It's a good idea. The Christian angle is way too hot for us now, so we need a new one.'

Two days later Ebony called us again.

'I found a small splinter group actively recruiting young men for the Jihad against the Christian faith.'

We were once again glued in front of the computer screen. I still had no idea where she was. We'd agreed that was on a need-to-know basis and we didn't need to know. It was safer that way. The video link was heavily encrypted and bounced off countless bogey addresses before it got to us. There was even a hardly discernible delay in the connection. She was somewhere warm and exotic, judging by the background, but even that could be a hoax. Probably was.

'They don't have any obvious links with ISIS, but a lot of what they stand for corresponds,' she continued. 'The Imams are zealots, and they promote the Sharia with very extreme interpretations. They call themselves "The Sons and Daughters of Islam". They have clandestine connections to a small mosque in San Francisco. Nothing very notable. But they do get a regular influx of new zealots attending service there. Mostly young men. That was what sent up the red flag for me.'

Ebony took control of the screen and presented a slide deck with the more detailed information on the mosque, the Imams and the services offered by the community.

'This is the head Imam. Abdul Ibn Musa.'

The picture on the screen showed a friendly looking African American man of about forty with the familiar, grey-streaked black beard and dark robes. He didn't look especially angry or violent. His eyes were soft and amicable. Hard to believe he was the man behind a fundamentalistic organisation.

'He doesn't look the part,' Jonah commented.

'No. I thought the same,' Ebony answered. 'Then I looked him up. He had quite a violent adolescence in Chicago and ended up in prison, like so many young poor black men. He was convicted of a multitude of violent transgressions. An indictment for manslaughter didn't stick and he was exonerated on that count due to contradicting witness statements. In prison he converted to Islam and studied law. After he was released, he set up a mission in San Francisco to help underprivileged youths.'

'Did he have any run-ins with the law after that?'

'No. Not for him personally. His work with young men and women did bring him in contact with the prosecution and law system, but more as a consultant than as a lawyer. He passed the bar exam in prison, but never applied for a licence to practice law. He stated he preferred to work with the youths from a religious perspective.'

'He sounds like the poster boy for a rehabilitated ex-con,' Jonah chimed in. I detected a hesitancy in the statement.

'My thoughts exactly, big man,' Ebony continued. 'He sounds too good to be true. But I couldn't even find a parking ticket, nothing after his release fifteen years ago.'

'And still he came up on your radar?' I asked.

'Yes. Well, the mosque did. It's contradictory. Unless he has nothing to do with the recruiting, and it's the other Imams at the mosque.'

'Could be. We'll have to find out.' That sounded more probable.

'There are two other imams. Both young men, both converted to Islam by our main man. It's feasible one of them has developed fanatic tendencies. My money is on Ibrahim.' She showed us two photos of the same man. One a mug shot, and one from the mosque's website. They could have been completely different men, except for the eyes. In both photos, the eyes were cold and dark. This man may have changed his colours, but the anger was still there.

'Sounds like a good place to start,' I commented.

'We need someone on the inside,' Ebony suggested. 'There's just so much I can find out on Internet.'

'You're right, we need to get a feel of the atmosphere in the mosque. Maybe get to know all three of the Imams.' Jonah agreed.

'Is this community restricted to African American Muslims?' I asked.

'No. There are people of all origins in the congregation. All races, all ethnicities and all backgrounds.'

'How big is it?'

Ebony brought other documents up on the screen before she continued her narrative. 'He started off with a small mission out of a disused factory. They moved to the new-build mosque last year. The official numbers state the congregation to be several hundred. There must be some opulent people amongst them because they paid for the whole construction without outside money. Or so they claim.'

More photos of the exterior of the mosque. 'It's still a reasonably small flock by general standards. But growing rapidly.'

'We need to get in there,' I stated, the excitement growing now that we had a way forward.

'I think you would be the best choice, ED,' Ebony proposed. 'With your olive complexion and dark hair, you could pass for someone with mixed Arabian heritage. The big man is too conspicuous, even the way he looks now.'

'True.' I agreed. 'I would need to read up on Islam before I show up there. Maybe be a lost soul, searching for the missing goal in life, disillusioned by the mainstream Islam.'

'Sounds good.' Jonah chimed in, the excitement was contagious, and we were all three sitting forward in our seats.

'I'll send you all the information I found, plus background information on Islam dogma and law. Oh, and let your beard grow. It's compulsory for men in Sharia.'

'Great. Thanks again, Ebony.'

'You're welcome. This quest of yours is growing on me. Besides, it's interesting, and life here is quite boring now I'm underground.' She smiled and laughed.

Jonah raised his eyebrow at me and nodded to the door. I took that as a massive hint that I was no longer needed in the conversation and should go.

I took the not-so-subtle push and went out to the store in search of ingredients for our next meal.

As I closed the door behind me, I heard them talking and laughing in the background.

The next two weeks were filled with study. I had to cultivate a good understanding of Islam to be able to pull off any kind of undercover operation. I knew the basics, but that was the extent of it.

Truthfully, it was making me nervous. Even though I had hundreds of years of experience in pretending I was someone else, this particular role was still new.

I blended in the Christian world, now I had to switch to something very foreign for me. A completely different dogma. My whole life revolved around the Christian faith. Not as a believer, naturally. But my family lived and breathed the Christian faith. From a young age, we were bombarded with everything Christian. My previous stays in this dimension were immersed in that one religion. I was here during the Crusades, rode with the Templar's into Jerusalem and erected their headquarters on the Templar Mount. Then later I was a spectator to the inquisition. My last posting was in the Irish troubles. Sure, I'd been exposed to Islam, but more in a bystander role. Now I had to be in the thick of it all, and make it look natural.

Arabic was no issue. It was one of the languages I was familiar with. I spoke and read it proficiently. It was the dogma I was worried about. My cover was that of a formerly devote Muslim who had begun to lose his faith. Devote meant I had to have an intimate knowledge of the holy books of Islam.

Ebony sent me everything I needed: the laws in the Tawrat, Psalms of the Zubar, the gospel in the Injil and the final revelation of God; the Quran. It was a lot. Just reading it wasn't enough. I had to understand what was written. Feel the dogma.

Jonah wasn't any help; his knowledge of Islam was as shallow as mine. And he was getting on my nerves. We'd been holed up in the apartment now without any real progress for more than a month. He was going stir-crazy and pulling me along with him. Not that he was ever an easy man to get on with, but now he was downright impossible. I finally kicked him out after yet another argument. Told him to go get whatever was bugging him out of his system.

He returned two days later, bloodied, and bruised, but with a faint smile on his face. I guess they had a fight scene here too. At least he'd let off some steam. That made him marginally easier to live with.

After that he spent most of the day either in the gym or surfing while I studied. Finally, I felt ready, and Jonah contacted Ebony to go through the profile she set up for me. I was a businessman in IT, owner of a small consultancy firm specialising in security software for international banks. Born in Lebanon, I came to the UK with my family as a child refugee. That grounded my credentials of an Arabic background, and my accent. I emigrated to the US five years ago with my company and recently moved here from Boca Raton where I attended the Assalam Centre before it was blown up by the CWW.

I entered the mosque for the Maghreb prayer and followed the rest of the male congregation. It was all very serene. The atmosphere was friendly and warm. The stark white building gave off an aura of tranquillity compounded by the soft murmuring of almost a hundred voices. An Imam welcomed me as soon as I came through the door and showed me where I could perform my absolutions. I thanked him and joined the others in a beautiful room where I unrolled my prayer mat and took up my positions.

I went through the motions.

It felt strange. As an atheist, here I was in a mosque pretending to be one of the faithful. I was afraid my acting was sub-par. With no real experience in any religion, and no concept of a heavenly entity, I was winging it. My only fall-back were the hours of studying I had done. To make up for my lack of experience and bad acting, I'd decided to do my prayers in Arabic. Hopefully that would make it all look more authentic.

The peace and the consistent repetition of the sing-song words calmed me, and I found myself immersed in what was quickly becoming a meditation. I was even enjoying the moment.

An hour later I rolled up my prayer mat and made my way back to the entrance of the mosque.

I followed the others out into the sunshine where people stopped to talk to each other. They exchanged pleasantries and there was a general sense of belonging. I made my way through the laughing and chatting groups and walked back to the apartment I rented earlier that week. I couldn't be seen with Jonah, it wouldn't be explainable in my current persona, so I moved out and found a small one-bed studio. It wasn't much, but it was clean and close to the mosque, right in the middle of the affluent Arabian quarter in the South Bay.

I visited the mosque every other day for a week, then more often, staying longer each time. I wanted to give the impression that I was gradually finding my place here. I shopped at the local stores, ate in the neighbourhood restaurants, and slowly started to greet and exchange small talk with the area's residents.

This was the affluent part of the Muslim community. It surprised me really that the mosque we were investigating was here. I would have expected the influx of new fundamentalism to be rife in the poorer, more traditional Muslim communities of the landlocked areas. But all Ebony's research pointed to this one mosque. She suggested maybe this was where the fundamentalists recruited their tech wizards. After all it was Silicon Valley.

That determined my disguise. My business was IT. State-of-the-art IT security targeting banks and high-tech companies. My company protected secrets, and we expected that would be too good to pass up on for the recruiters, if they were here. The longer I spent with the congregation, the less convinced I was that we were in the right place.

'I'm new in the area,' I answered Imam Ibrahim. He accosted me on my way out of the mosque and we exchanged small talk.

'What brings you here?' His tone was friendly.

'What I expect brings most people to this part of San Francisco; work.' I answered with a smile. 'I work in IT, so this is the place to be.'

He smiled. 'You will find many of our congregation work in the same field as you,' he continued. 'They even help us with our own IT solutions.'

'My area is IT-Security,' I offered. 'Often in the financial or high-tech sector. We make sure our companies cannot be hacked.'

'I'm afraid I am completely computer illiterate,' he stated, I wasn't sure I believed him, but that was moot.

'That is exactly why we are here,' I joked. The Imam smiled. Ibrahim seemed to be a friendly man; the opposite of the image Ebony portrayed earlier thanks to her research. The dark, hard eyes and stern visage of the photos I had seen, were very different from the man standing in front of me.

We talked for about ten minutes, mainly me expressing my gratitude for the warm welcome I experienced at the mosque. At the end of the conversation, he thanked me and once again emphasised how welcome I was in the community.

I left the mosque and went back to my studio apartment. Nothing I had seen or experienced up to now corroborated our earlier findings. The friendly reception even contradicted them, but it was still early in the process. I was three weeks into the cover and had to be patient.

Not my best trait.

Infrequent calls and the occasional trips out of town to meet Jonah were the only moments I could step out of the role I was playing. The whole escapade was extremely exhausting and quite frustrating.

For the first time, I found myself questioning Ebony's research.

Chapter Twenty-Six

Five weeks into the undercover project things finally started to turn a corner. Just as well, I was about to throw in the towel. Cracks appeared in the mosque's carefully constructed facade.

By then, I was there at least four times a week and staying much longer than before. After prayers, I mingled with the men standing outside the beautiful white building. Initially, the conversations were centred around the community and how we could help each other. The longer I stayed, the more serious the topics became, until finally, the CWW came up.

The conversations became heated with most of the men condemning the terrorist attacks that continued to reign down on the Islamic communities world-wide. There was pain in the faces of those who had chosen to stay after prayers. Pain and anger.

'It is travesty,' one of the elders stated. We all agreed. It was. There was no doubt about it. Since the first mass attacks on the mosques five months ago, many more followed leaving the death count at a staggering thirteen thousand and counting.

'And what is the government doing about it?' Another asked. 'Nothing. Absolutely nothing.'

'Why would they?' A young man interposed. 'The CWW is solving the American problem. Getting rid of their enemy, Islam.'

'That is too much, Mustapha,' the elder tried.

'Is it?' The young man was not to be pacified. 'Why then do they do nothing? Absolutely nothing. The attacks intensify every day. They kill women, children. Peaceful young men. These victims are all completely innocent. They are all assimilated into the American society. They are upstanding citizens. Yet still they are murdered.'

There were nods all around.

'You are right. The government does nothing to protect our people. None of the countries take any extra precautions to keep Muslims safe.' Ibrahim joined in the heated conversation. His earlier friendly countenance was gone. The dark eyes glinted under his creased brow. His thin lips were pulled in a scowl.

'They will continue to slaughter our people,' he continued. 'Death will come to us here in San Francisco. It is only a question of time before our families die. Our mother's, our sisters, our children.'

He let that sink in. There was total silence. No one knew what to say.

I observed the group around us. There were some who clearly felt uncomfortable with the direction the conversation was going. Others were becoming more and more agitated and mirrored Ibrahim's anger.

I made sure I nodded along with the younger angry men, staying in my role. The hairs on the back of my neck stood on end and I was sure someone was scrutinising me as I was them, but I still chose to show some reluctance. Every move I made now would determine the success of the whole undercover operation, I had to look sympathetic but still reserved. I would need more convincing. To jump at the first opportunity would look suspicious.

'We must pray,' The Imam suggested. 'All our voices will call on Allah to help our people and stop this senseless violence.'

The men nodded and averted their eyes, conscious that they had been close to violent thoughts. I experienced a feeling of disappointment that the moment of zealotry had passed, but realised I needed to be more patient.

I returned to the mosque the next day, and the day after that. Imam Ibrahim noticed and praised my dedication. I explained that his request to pray had really touched me and that it was the least I could do. He looked at me intently and touched my shoulder in recognition.

After a week of daily prayer, and sometimes heated discussions afterwards in the communal area outside the mosque, I started to feel part of an inner community. Every day the conversation came back to the CWW and the terrible horrors they perpetrated. The same group of men congregated every evening, and I was an accepted member. Every time it was the same, there was frustration and a call for action, but it fizzled out and everyone went home.

Until that one night.

'No one is doing anything,' Mustapha lamented yet again.

'Someone is.' We all turned to the new voice that joined our group. 'We may not agree with their methods, but there are groups that push back on this genocide.'

We all reverently made room for the head Imam. He

smiled his thanks. It seemed out of place given the setting we were in and the subject of the discussion.

'I am not condoning the violence,' he continued. 'Not on either side.' Agreement all around, well, except for Ibrahim maybe.

'But the group known as CWW has passed the point of peaceful intervention. We cannot count on regular law enforcement or the government to solve this. The CWW is out of control even for their Christian masters. I don't believe they work for the US government, but they are not hindered by it either. There are like-minded people in high circles within the law enforcement, within politics. Most likely also within the military.'

We were all quiet. Most of the men hung on to the revered Imam's every word. Others looked apprehensive. There was a big difference between ranting over a lack of action and actually doing something about it. For many, it would be a step too far. Some, like me, were simply astounded this line of reasoning came from the highly esteemed Head Imam.

'Do you men ISIS?' I asked, breaking the silence.

'No,' Musa answered, his answer evoking a sigh of relief from most of the congregation. 'ISIS is too extreme. They have no boundaries; they are as bad in their way as the CWW. I am talking about "The Sons and Daughters of Islam".'

A shiver of thrill ran up my spine. This was the first time the "Sons and Daughters" had come up in any conversation, we were finally making headway. It was unexpected though, coming from Musa. The man had seemed a bastion of leniency in his khutbahs. Nothing pointed in his direction for any form of extremism. Quite the opposite. In his sermons he preached leniency and love for his fellow man.

It was my turn to nod.

'You have heard of them?' Ibrahim asked, disbelief in his tone. I would have to watch this one. He was still reserved about me.

'I have seen posts online that mention them,' I answered.

'You have been searching?' Ibrahim wasn't appeased.

I nodded. 'I have. I want to do more than pray. But I have no idea what, so I started to search the internet to find any mention of retaliation.' I looked his straight in the eye. His dark countenance made lesser men shake. Not me. I was used to worse; I'd lived with Jonah.

'And you found that on the Internet?' He stared at me from under his thick brows. From the corner of my eye, I saw Musa observing me intently.

'Not the normal internet. The dark web,' I answered clearly.

Musa and Ibrahim exchanged glances.

'Why were you on the dark web?' Musa asked.

'It is my work,' I explained. 'I am in cyber security. The main danger to my customers comes from hackers and cyber criminality. I go where they are to find out what they are doing and stay one step ahead.'

Again, they exchanged glances. Goosebumps were prolific on my arms and an irritating electrical current went up and down my spine. This was the defining moment. Either they would accept me now, or I would have to make a very hasty exit. I had no reservations that Ibrahim would happily do away with me. Or at least try.

'Your company,' Musa asked. 'They are situated here in Silicon Valley?'

'Yes, they are.' I cocked my head in question, but he refrained from explaining.

'What can we do?' One of the others asked, changing the subject, and defusing the tension between the two Imams and me.

'We can investigate what the Sons and Daughters of Islam need.' Musa proposed.

One of the men seemed hesitant. 'The police call them terrorists?'

'That is a matter of perception,' the head Imam continued. 'They are zealots. That is for sure. In normal circumstances I believe they would not revert to violence. However, these are not normal circumstances. We live in a time where the violence against Islam is escalating to the point that something must be done to stop it. The polarisation is escalating to unknown proportions. Former friends are becoming enemies. We cannot turn to the government or the police. They will not help us. The power of the Islam haters is too great. They control public opinion. They escalate the hatred for our kind.' He let his words sink in. I glanced to the others from the corner of my eye, making sure it wasn't obvious. There were many nods, red faces from anger, and a lot of fidgeting. 'So where else can we turn to?' Musa continued.

He looked at each man individually. His gaze boring into their very souls. When he came to me, I held his glare, then lowered my eyes and my head, as expected.

He was a very intense man. Nothing of the friendly grandfather type of earlier was visible in his features anymore. His countenance and demeanour edged more to the hard stares of the ISIS spokesmen in their propaganda streams. I had the distinct feeling I was seeing the real man now. The one who had been incarcerated multiple times for violent crimes. The whole persona of a changed man was an elaborate scam. One that rivalled The Establishment.

A thought crossed my mind that even this devout pretence was a deeper layer of the deceit this man was capable of. He was like an onion. Every layer hiding more and different lies until you got to the core of the man. I suspected that core was pure greed and he had correctly identified this current persona as a good way to achieve just that.

Ibrahim, with all his posturing, was in my opinion a real zealot. He truly believed in Islam. In the cause. Musa didn't. His role playing was commendable. But I had the impression that was exactly what it was. I wasn't the only one acting here. I just hoped he didn't see through my facade as I did his.

We all left the mosque that day reeling from the words of the two Imams. I returned to my studio and continued my elaborate role playing. I felt eyes on me all the time. The way Musa had stared into what he envisioned was my soul, gave me the creeps and I was sure I had to stick to my profile with a vengeance. Just in case they were observing me.

I was sure they were.

That meant radio silence. I couldn't contact either Ebony or Jonah. There was just too much at stake.

Musa accosted me the next day as I walked into the mosque. 'I would like to speak with you.' His friendly demeanour was back again. It would have been very convincing if yesterday hadn't happened.

'Yes, of course, Imam Musa.' I bowed slightly to emphasise my respect.

'Please join me in my office after your prayers,' he asked amicably. Not that I could have declined.

'I will.' I bowed again.

He smiled—a deep sociable friendly act, no trace

apparent anymore of the radical hard features he had the day before—and left to talk to the other believers. I continued to the prayer room and went through the motions. During the repetitive actions my mind wandered to the coming meeting with the head Imam.

Chapter Twenty-Seven

'Great work, ED.'

'Thanks. But it's just scratching the surface.' I had finally contacted Ebony and Jonah. I was on a two-day trip to San Diego for an authentic consultancy job. In the hotel I linked up with my partners through a VPN. Ebony made sure it was all untraceable.

'Will he let you in to the computers?' Jonah asked in the three-way video call.

'No. I suggested I secure their systems. After all, it is my cover. But they kindly refused. They have their own system administrators to do that. Ibrahim also explained they were not concerned about hackers as their system is not linked to the internet. It's a single on-prem system. No interfaces outside the in-house landscape. Nothing. At least that's what they said.'

'Did you get a good look at the computers?' Ebony tried.

'Not really. Plus, I'm not exactly sure what I would be looking for.'

She explained. 'Some kind of cable other than the regular wall outlet or the screen. I expect they do have a connection outside of the premises, but that it is via a dedicated line.'

I shook my head. 'They still don't trust me completely. I don't think they will let me rummage around behind the computers.'

'No probably not.' Ebony was silent for a while. 'Let me see what I can find on the utilities front so I can rule out any direct lines.'

'And if not, what then?' Jonah asked.

'Then ED's going to have to plant a link,' Ebony stated.

'What, tamper with the computers?' I was aghast. 'Wouldn't they notice that immediately? They scan for malware on a very regular basis.'

'Normally yes, if you go through the regular computers, I want you to put something in the root hardware itself.'

That was even worse. How the hell was I supposed to place something on or in the computer.

'Sound's dangerous.' I tried.

'Only if you're caught,' she replied happily. Not a big help.

'Well, thanks. That's a real relief.' I answered laughing. 'I was actually thinking of you. Wouldn't a link give your location away?'

'Not if I do it properly.'

'Careful, Eb's,' Jonah interjected concerned. 'They found you before. They could find you again.'

'Not this time, big man. I've done my homework. No one will find me now. And if—just if—someone could, they wouldn't like what they found.'

There were darker sides to our little friend.

Ebony came back to us two days later. I was in the office I rented in the valley, pretending to run the business Ebony set up. Naturally she and her team were the driving force behind the actual work being done. They made it legitimate, I was just the front man. I do have IT knowledge, but nowhere near the level our wizard has. Mind you, I don't think anyone comes close to her.

'There is a dedicated line. It's underground though. Different from most. They really take their security seriously in the mosque. Way too much for an above-board religious organisation,' she explained.

'Can you hack it?' Jonah asked.

'No. Not without sending up loads of red flags. Somehow, I don't think they would go for the "engineer needs to check the line" scam. We can rule out any obvious intervention. It will have to be a plant.'

Disappointing. I'd hoped we could avoid actual physical actions here.

'Now what?' Jonah voiced my question.

'You need to get to the data on the server,' Ebony said. 'One of my guys will give Jonah an external drive that you can uplink directly onto the server. Then I can scrutinise the contents once I get it back. I investigated the mosque's purchases for the last three years and have a reasonable idea of what hardware they may have. I've adapted the drive, and it will automatically download a copy of whatever is on the server.'

'How sure are you?'

'Not very. But I did put different access hacks on the drive, so one of them should do the job. Then Jonah, you take it back with you. One of the guys will pick it up again.'

How long will the upload take?' I asked.

'That depends on how much security they actually have

directly on the backdoor of the server. Anything from five minutes to twenty.'

Not good news. But I didn't see any other options. Even though I was getting closer to the Imam, it was a long process, and we didn't have the luxury of time. We had been lucky, no one had discovered us yet, but Jonah was becoming restless. Sitting back while I burrowed in the terrorist group was not in his nature. He was a man of action.

It was time to take act.

Chapter Twenty-Eight

'Ebony sent me blueprints of a tunnel system under the mosque.' Jonah commented.

Once again, I was sitting on the bed in a hotel with the tablet on my lap talking to my partner-in-crime via Teams. Three days had passed since our last call. Three long days worrying about how to continue our quest.

To tell you the truth, I was feeling depressed. The events of the last weeks and months caught up with me. The implications of what we were doing, my brother's visit and the finality with which I'd broken from my family hit me like a brick wall.

It had been an adrenaline rush. The ultimate rebellion. Now, it was reality. And it sucked. It was irreversible, no longer a joke or a childish tantrum. I wanted to make a statement, well, I'd certainly done that. I hadn't thought it through. I hadn't considered the consequences of my actions. Ideology led me and I followed. It outweighed my common sense and ultimately led me to the point of no return.

And then there was my obsessive compulsion to seek recognition from my father. If not as his favourite son, then as a respected opponent. How naive is that?

'You still there?' Jonah brought me back to the present.

'Yes, I'm here.'

'Did you hear anything I said?' He sounded aggravated. Well, tough.

'Eb sent you some blueprints,' I answered just as irritated.

He stared at me through the tablet, then sighed audibly to make a point. 'The blueprints show a tunnel complex from the eighteen-hundreds that runs under this part of the city. Some of the tunnels have been filled in, others just closed off at the ends.'

I was intrigued, my attention instantly awakened. This could be just what we needed. 'Under the mosque?' I asked.

'Under the mosque.' He sounded smug. I guess it was allowed.

'Can we access it?'

'Tiny said the entrance shouldn't be a problem. It's under an abandoned warehouse. The other end—in the mosque—is where the challenge lies. She overlaid the archi-tecture design onto the old tunnel blueprint and the exit is slap-bang under the centre of the main prayer room of the mosque. She found mention of a subterranean floor under the mosque, but there were no detailed designs showing the actual layout of the floor.'

I accessed my memory. 'There are multiple rooms down there.' I answered. 'Subdivided by concrete walls. I've been down to the computer room once, because of the security audit I performed for them. There were four doors in the corridor. It stands to reason the entrance to the tunnel must be behind the walls of one of the other rooms. Bring up the overlays please.'

Jonah shared his screen and seconds later I saw the blueprints. The tunnels in red, and the layout of the subterranean floor of the mosque in blue. From memory, I envisioned where the steps down to the basement were, and the corridor with the four doors. The second on the left was the computer room.

The red tunnel ended in the first door on the left. The one nearest to the stairway. There was no telling whether it was visible in the room.

'I can't imagine the Imam isn't aware of the tunnels,' I commented. 'The architects of the mosque will have found the blueprints of the tunnel system.'

'That's what I was thinking,' Jonah agreed. 'Maybe they use the tunnels for something. Like a quick get-away or an extra insurance, something like that.'

'Could be. That would mean it's accessible. I expect it will be secured in some way. They will have surveillance on the door and the tunnel. It's a possible weak link in their perimeter. With all the security they have, I can't imagine they don't monitor that as well.'

'Then you're just going to have to deactivate that,' Jonah suggested easily.

'And how do I do that?'

'Fucked if I know. That's up to you, Gabe. I can't take care of everything. You'll have to get inside and make sure no one is looking.' Sometimes I could just strangle him. Just as well that he wasn't in the room.

His suggestion was easier said than done.

He was right, though. I would have to work something out.

'Okay. I'll work something out. So, say I get in, then what?'

'Then you let me in, and we get into the computer room and follow Tiny's instructions. After that I leave.'

'Just like that, huh?'

'Just like that.'

The opportunity presented itself ten days later. Ten long, long days.

Imam Musa asked me to put together a security measure offer for an affiliated mosque. He insisted I do the research and create the actual proposal in a separate room in his mosque to guarantee secrecy. I accepted of course and asked for solitude to be able to concentrate.

Now all I had to do was find a way to neutralise the security guy monitoring the cameras. Everything depended on it.

No pressure.

In my many travels during the hundreds of years I've roamed this dimension I've practiced a lot of your martial arts. One thing I've mastered is the art of stealth. It was about to some in handy.

On the designated day I entered the mosque early in the afternoon and started work on the proposal. I worked diligently, or so it seemed, up through the day and into the evening, only pausing for the obligatory prayers and the occasional meal. Ibrahim sat with me in the office for the first hour, but tired quickly and left. He returned to check on me several times, never in a structured routine. Once he found me missing and searched the mosque, only to encounter me in the main prayer room. I had taken the earliest prayer moment; one I knew he wouldn't officiate. I left the prayer room to continue my work just as he entered to lead the second wave of the congregation.

Back at the desk I waited for ten minutes, listening intently to the soft hum of the prayers. Content the others in the building were all engaged in the evening prayers, I left the office and made my way carefully to the control room that housed the screens for the many cameras in and around the building.

As so often happens, security is minimal where control itself is housed. Is it complacency or just arrogance? I don't know, but I see this too often. The guards are the ones who scrutinise the others, they themselves are inherently deemed to be trustworthy. So much so that there were no cameras at the door to the control room.

I softly opened the door and slid inside. There was one guard sitting in a wheeled swivel chair with his back to me. To his credit, he was concentrating intensely on the two rows of six screens in front of him. His gaze moved from one to the other, scrutinising the images of the praying congregation, the in and outside of the mosque and even the kitchen.

I silently moved closer on the balls of my feet. My hand moved to the back of his neck. There is a spot there where many of the human nerves come together. If the correct pressure is applied to the exact spot, then the body shuts down immediately and goes into a deep, dreamless sleep.

I caught the guard as he descended into unconsciousness and laid him down softly on the desk. He would be out for about half an hour, depending on his physical condition.

We were on a timer.

Remotely, I slightly realigned some of the cameras in the basement, in the tunnel, and aimed at the stairs leading down, then made my move. Staying out of camera range I carefully made my way down into the basement corridor. I opened the door to where I expected the tunnel entrance to be and slipped into the dark room.

It was pitch black. Just as well my eyes adapted better than yours. I can see in the dark virtually as well as in daylight. The room was bare, no furniture, nothing. Only another door opposite the entrance. It was a steel portal secured by big levers reminiscent of walk-in fridge catches. Just to be sure, I looked around the room for hidden cameras. None. I walked over, opened the catches, and pulled the big steel door open.

Jonah stood in the dimly lit doorway of the long tunnel, a big smile on his face and night goggles resting on the top of his head.

He moved into the room, and I closed the portal again. Jonah pushed the goggles down over his eyes and followed me out of the room into the dark hallway. Hugging the wall, we made our way towards the computer room where we quickly searched for the servers Ebony had indicated. It was an educated guess, but in her case, I expected it to be ninety-nine percent accurate.

Jonah pushed the goggles up over his forehead back to their earlier perch on top of his head and turned on the computer. The light of the screen illuminated the area enough and he was able to locate the USB port exactly where Ebony said it would be. This was the clandestine back entrance to the server. Most had one, if you knew where to look.

He plugged in the hard drive and pressed a key on the virtual keyboard that came up on the screen. It was now up to Ebony's software to hack into the system.

I watched amazed as the assembly code flicked over the screen in an almost Matrix manner. It was mesmerising.

Broken when the ones and zeros were replaced by a list of drives and folders.

We had no idea which ones we needed. Jonah looked at me quizzically, I shrugged and suggested the C or D disk. It was a guess, there were five disks.

'The "C" is where most of the program data will be according to Tiny,' Jonah remarked.

'Okay. The "D" it is.'

He clicked on the disk icon and the software started its work.

Suddenly my instincts flared up. Goosebumps covered my arms, and a feeling of dread took hold of me. There was someone else in the room with us.

Someone from home.

Chapter Twenty-Nine

'Well, well. If it isn't the wayward son.'

She came out of the shadows. A tall statuesque, beautiful young woman with olive skin, long jet-black hair collected in a plat that reached down past her waist, and mesmerising lavender eyes.

Naturally, I recognised her immediately. We were trained to identify our competitors.

We stood there observing each other. Behind me I could feel Jonah's surprise. Thankfully he stayed where he was, manning the computer.

She finally spoke again as she continued to scrutinise me. 'I thought you were taller.'

The muffled chuckle I heard from behind me stung. Jonah was going to have a field day on this. Well, he'd better get his act together and watch out for this new threat. She was a warrior from my world. Not someone to underestimate.

'Sorry to disappoint.' I answered flatly, the sarcasm dripping off my words and tone.

She walked closer, her eyes wandering over my body from my shoulders down over my torso, lingering slightly on my groin area and then down over my legs to the floor. I felt violated. My anger flared. The familiar heat started at the base of my spine and move up, radiating to my neck and up into the back of my skull. I could feel the red colouring my cheeks and forehead. She noticed and smiled slyly. This woman was starting to piss me off big time.

'Gabriel. Long-time no-see,' she said in a velvety voice.

'Can't remember we actually ever met,' I answered as coldly as I could.

'Not in person. No. But I've seen so many streams and images, I feel I know you.' Her voice and demeanour were overly sweet and friendly, flirty even.

I just smiled.

'You know her?' Jonah came up beside me and nodded in the woman's direction. Was that a glint of humour in his eyes?

I took a deep breath. Just what I didn't need; Jonah sticking his nose in everything.

'This is Aaliyah, Arand's daughter.' I said, keeping my eyes on her all the time. 'She's the competition.'

'Really, maybe I should change sides. She's quite the improvement on your family members I've met,' he joked. It brought a small smile to Aaliyah's lips.

I ignored him.

Aaliyah turned her attention to my partner. Her gaze travelled slowly from Jonah's feet all the way up his body to the big smile and raised eyebrows. I swear he winked at her. Did the guy have absolutely no sense of decorum. This was not the time to flirt. And she was not the woman to do that with.

'Who's the hunk?' she asked in a husky voice. Oh shit.

Are you kidding me? This was not what I needed. Not the right time.

Sighing, I rolled my eyes up to the ceiling.

I pointed to my partner. 'Aaliyah, meet Jonah.' They smiled at each other. I counted to ten in my mind. Then again, in an attempt to calm my anger. It didn't help.

Aaliyah reluctantly turned back to me. 'You're trespassing.'

I cocked my head in question. 'Depends on how you look at it.'

'Not really. This is my family's turf. You and your kin are not allowed here. Your family knows that, as do you.'

'Yeah, well I don't work for my family anymore,' I answered.

She smiled slyly. 'I heard about that. Not officially, of course. Your dad insists you're just taking a short break. A sabbatical, if you like.'

'I quit.' My answers were short and to the point. I didn't want to elaborate on my family issues with the competition.

She laughed. 'That's what the grapevine says.' Aaliyah paused. 'Still. You shouldn't be here.'

'Maybe not. But I am.'

'I could call in the troops and if my father doesn't kill you, we could always hand you over to your family. I bet dear old dad would like to have the prodigal son back again.' There was a cruel glint in her eye.

'You could. But you won't.' It was a calculated risk, there was something about her that I recognised.

'What makes you think that?' She crossed her arms over her chest and observed me, calling my bluff.

'Well, to start off with, you're too curious about what I'm doing. Second, you're quite the rebel yourself. And finally, you're not wearing your amulet. So, you can't call anyone.'

Anger flitted over her face. My turn to smile. I was right.

'You AWOL as well?' I asked.

'Not officially,' she answered reluctantly.

'A walk on the wild side?'

'Something like that.'

'Breath of fresh air?' Jonah asked. She turned towards him.

'Yes. Do either of you have any idea how constraining my family is becoming?'

'Your dad living the dream too, huh?' Jonah asked.

She looked puzzled.

He continued, 'he's starting to believe he is Allah?'

She nodded. 'Bashir is even worse. The boundaries between the image they project in this dimension and true life in ours, are rapidly waning in my family. They've started to believe the crap we tell the humans. Worse than that, they're adapting the Islamic customs and laws as their own back home. My brother wants to bring Sharia to our world, can you imagine?' She was fuming, her eyes burning with the fire of indignation. We let her rant.

'He wants to set our civilisation back thousands of years. Take away women's rights and make our lives hell. No fucking way. He actually petitioned my father to bring me in from the field so that I could "take up my place as a god-fearing female."'

We refrained from comment. It would be too dangerous. In her anger she was formidable.

'Me! A docile wife and mother of a brood of children. Are you kidding? Fuck. No. Pompous prick. I do what I want.' We believed her. This woman was a powerhouse. I couldn't imagine anyone voluntarily going up against her. I didn't have that choice. She was the enemy.

'What about your dad?' I asked apprehensively. 'What's his perspective on all of this?'

'He's stuck between the family and pressure from my brother's fanatics. Plus of course the constant rivalry with your family.' She shot a dark glare my way. Oh, so now it was my fault? The moment was short, her anger fleeting.

Her voice softened. 'He's not the man I used to know. He was such a happy and affable man. Now. Now, he's pulled apart by the pressure.'

Not exactly my perspective of the guy, but hey. What do I know? I wasn't about to share my opinion.

This was an interesting development. One that was also very welcome. My bluff about the amulet was a risky one. If she did have one—and I had no real way of knowing whether she did—then we could have been in deep shit. She could call in back-up and we would have been toast. Michael would have a field day if he got his hands on me. I had no doubt Arand would have handed us over; me alive, Jonah probably not.

'Why did you leave?' she asked, pulling me back to the conversation.

'As children we were told what we did was acceptable because we never interfered with the humans,' I explained. 'We reaped the souls after death. Whoever died, was recruited. The Establishment was created to offer the believers a way of moving to us of their own free will after their death. We were not instrumental in their death. Only in the resurrection. Our hands were not bloody.'

She nodded. 'Same here. Where is this going to?'

'Bear with me. Please,' I asked her.

I continued. 'I was in denial. Somewhere deep down

inside I knew something was wrong. Jonah set me on a path to further question these beliefs. I took a detailed look at The Establishment, what they actually do, and who's really in charge. It's not a human led organisation as I was led to believe. Our families run The Establishment.'

My words made an impact. Her brow creased and her full lips pulled tight not in surprise, but in anger.

'The Establishment is behind CWW.' I continued. 'The same members of the so-called neutral organisation are behind the recruitment of the CWW terrorists.'

'What makes you so sure?' I saw hesitant acknowledgement in her eyes.

'We set up profiles and applied to join the CWW. After the initial online screening, they insisted on a face-to-face meeting before our prospect was initiated into the organisation. The CWW contact our profiles were instructed to go to was always a priest. Without fail, the priests were all top recruiters in The Establishment.'

'What does that have to do with my family?' she asked.

I dropped another bomb.

'We think this interference is rampant in all divisions of The Establishment.'

She was silently mulling over everything I had said.

'You're claiming our families are behind the human religious terrorism?'

I nodded. She glanced at Jonah. He nodded too.

'It gets worse.' I added carefully.

'How much worse can it be?' Her nostrils flared; the anger was creeping back into her features.

I took a breath and held her gaze. 'A lot.'

'Big time.' Jonah added.

She took a deep breath and nodded for me to continue.

'Does it have something to do with what you were looking for?'

I nodded. 'We were searching for information on an alliance.'

'What alliance?'

'The one between our fathers.' This was the defining moment. Either she would decide we were idiots or her whole world would come crashing down, like mine had.

'You're shitting me. There is no alliance.' she tried to laugh it off. It didn't work. I saw more in her features. Something that surprised me. She didn't seem totally astounded. There was a slight hesitation before she spoke. One of recognition maybe?

'You may be wrong there,' I continued.

'What do you mean?'

'This escalation of violence between the two major religions in this dimension is no coincidence. We think they planned it, our fathers. The first attack by CWW, the retaliation by ISIS. Everything after that. It's all too convenient to be a coincidence. It all needs too much preparation as well. No way this is by accident.'

She was silent, contemplating what I said. 'You honestly think they set this up?'

'Don't you?' I asked incredulously. She was an intelligent woman, surely, she could see it. 'Think about it.' I urged. 'How did your family react to the CWW attack?'

'Bashir went ballistic. He called for an all-out attack. Like it really had anything to do with us. I mean, he should have been happy. The attack supplied us with thousands of new souls. Okay, most of them were women and children, but still. They were an unexpected and welcome influx. I didn't get why he was so mad. Another example of the persona switches. Islam was angry. That was to be expected. But why Bashir.'

'Identity issues again?' Jonah asked with a smile.

'Yeah.' She shrugged.

'What about your dad?'

'He was a lot more reserved, come to think of it. He didn't even seem surprised.'

'He wasn't.'

I let her come to the obvious conclusion.

'What does it mean?' She still tried to ignore what was staring her in the face.

'That they are working together.' Jonah interjected.

She reluctantly nodded. Her earlier strength seeped out of her posture momentarily, her shoulders slumped slightly. She noticed me studying her and squared her shoulders and lifted her head to stare at me.

'It means they are initiating a new Holy War between Christianity and Islam. The likes of which has never been seen in this dimension.'

'And that's why you left,' she concluded correctly.

I shook my head. 'Not exactly. I didn't know about the alliance then. Or the CWW. I left because of the lies. I believed the scam. That they came of their own free will. They don't. They're unaware of what lies in their future. The believers expect Heaven. They get Hell. It's wrong. Ethically and morally offensive. I couldn't be part of it, or condone it, any longer.'

'Novel thought. Especially from the son of one of the false gods.' She mocked me.

My turn to keep my mouth shut.

She turned to Jonah. 'What's his role in all this?'

'It was his quest to start with. To bring down The Establishment.' Another calculated risk on my part, one I was pulling Jonah into. There was no protest from him, so I guessed he was okay with it.

'All of it?' She raised an eyebrow. The whole Establishment would mean all religions, not just Christianity. That made our quest a direct danger for her family business as well.

'Yes,' I stated resolutely. We had gone too far to start lying. Besides, my very dangerous play was that she was more sympathetic to our cause than she should be. I hoped she respected honesty. Otherwise, we were in for a fight. One that could get very messy. The curved blades on her back and dagger on her left thigh looked extremely sharp and I was acutely aware mine—and Jonah's axe—were absent.

The only noise in the room was a soft hum from the servers. I was mindful of the time. We had a restricted window here, and no matter how interesting our conversation was, we had to leave. I was mulling over how to broach the subject when Aaliyah glanced at the computer screen.

The download was still progressing, albeit much slower than I hoped.

'There's no information on any alliance here.' She finally broke the silence.

I waited. Did this mean she had bought into our conclusions?

'I wouldn't expect my father to keep anything as sensitive as that in this dimension.'

She had a point.

'If there is anything it will be back home. Have you looked there?'

I shook my head. 'I can't go back,' I answered.

She cocked her head and her brow creased in surprise. 'Why not? You could evade the transporters if you used a different frequency and went through one of the smaller sites.'

'I would need an amulet. I smashed mine.'

'You did what?'

'I destroyed it.'

'Then you really can't go back.' The severity of my choice was dawning on her. I'd truly burned my bridges.

'Nope. And they can't pull me back either.' I added trying to keep the gravity of the situation out of my voice.

I observed her closely.

'There's more isn't there?' I asked.

She refrained from answering.

Different scenarios passed in my mind. What could she be hiding? There was a discussion going on inside her head, probably whether to confide in us or not. Why should she? Our families were rivals. Sworn enemies.

I stayed put. Jonah did the same, amusement on his lips. It was a waiting game. Not that we had the time for it, but there was no way we could push without adverse results.

She started to fidget.

We waited.

After about two minutes she couldn't take it any longer. 'What else are you looking for?'

'What else is there to find?' I turned her question around.

'What do you mean?' She was definitely avoiding my gaze.

'There's something you want to discuss with us, but you're reluctant,' I explained.

She looked away. The silence was loaded.

Finally, she spoke up. 'What you said earlier.'

I waited.

'About the stories we were told when we were children.'

'Go one.'

'That our fathers never interfered with humans.' I nodded.

'Well. We do.' She looked me straight in the eye. 'At least my family does.'

'In what way?' Jonah asked.

'We support the radicals.'

'ISIS?' Jonah asked.

Her turn to nod.

'How?'

'My brother Bashir. He's behind a lot of the fundamental attacks on moderate Muslims. Not those on Christians as far as I know. His efforts keep the violence and the benefits in the family.'

She sighed. 'It all started out as extra push to generate souls for our family. The fundamentalists fitted into our plans; they want to bring Sharia to the whole Islamic world population. They professed to punish anyone who didn't follow their strict rules. Because their reading of Sharia is so violent, this would no doubt result in more dead people, in souls. I don't think Bashir, or my father initially wanted it to really evolve into a Holy War.'

'They never contemplated that?'

'The ISIS attacks on western civilisation were useless to us. The harvested souls would not be our own. Your family profited from that, not us. We need Muslim souls. Bashir and my father fought long and hard about it. He forbade Bashir to continue that avenue, but secretly I think my brother never stopped. He identifies more and more with the fundamentalistic humans and with ISIS. His hatred of Christianity runs deep. It's more than just the rivalry with your family. He has radicalised himself.'

'That's why you don't believe our families are working together?'

'Exactly. My brother wouldn't agree to it.'

'Would he have to?' I asked carefully.

'What do you mean?'

'My father is a tyrant,' I explained. 'He doesn't care what his children think or want. He decides. Is it the same with your family?'

She shrugged. 'Yes, and no. He does have the last word. But father always wants agreement. He hates disharmony in the family. He strives for consensus.'

'And how is that working for him lately?' I asked.

'Not so well. The family is falling apart. Bashir's radicalisation. My stubbornness. My siblings are being forced to one choose a side. Even my mother has given up on my brother.'

'Trouble in paradise?' Jonah added his two cents.

She nodded. 'You have no idea.' Her brow creased and I saw pain in her lavender eyes.

I glanced to the screen again.

The download of one of the two drives we identified as potentially interesting, was up to ninety percent. Aaliyah glanced at the screen.

'You need the G-Drive,' she commented.

I looked at Jonah and shrugged. He keyed in the download of the G-drive and started the process.

'Tell your tech wizard to be careful,' Aaliyah added. 'It's encrypted and will send out a beacon if you try to decipher it.'

I stared at her. Why was she helping us? I didn't buy her story about the family issues. Not to the extent that she would betray them. I couldn't imagine anyone following my example. I didn't trust her. I had no reason to. That didn't mean I wasn't grateful for the help and the fact she hadn't called in the cavalry. Yet.

'Thanks,' I said.

'Why are you helping us?' Jonah asked, blunt as always.

'It's boring here. Time something knocked the cobwebs out of the Imam's eyes. At least it promises to be more interesting.' She smiled, chuckled a bit, turned and walked to the door.

'Good luck,' were her parting words as she opened the door and peered out to the hallway. Nothing alarmed her and she left the computer room.

The hairs on the back of my neck stood on end. My nerves screamed at me to grab the hard disc and get the hell out of here. I glanced at the screen again. The download was almost complete. I willed the blue line to move quicker. Ninety, ninety-three, ninety-five percent.

Finally, it reached the one hundred percent. Jonah removed the link and the server screen closed down automatically. He looked as jittered as I felt. As one, we moved to the door. I opened it to a crack and looked out into the dark corridor. There were no sounds. Nothing to indicate we were not alone. Still, I waited. Nothing.

I opened the door just enough to squeeze through and moved out of the way to let Jonah join me. We stopped moving and listened again. Still silent. We hugged the walls as we moved up the corridor to the adjoining doors. Jonah took the left one, back into the room with the hidden entrance to the underground tunnels. I followed to re-lock the steel door as he left. After that, I walked back to the dark staircase that led up to the security room, hoping the guard was still unconscious and that Aaliyah hadn't ratted me out.

The guard still lay slumped in his chair in front of the

battery of security camera screens, his breathing regular and deep. He wouldn't remember anything once he woke. Jonah didn't show up on any screens and I assumed he was in the tunnels on his way out of danger. I repositioned the cameras and left the control room. I had to get back to the office where I was supposed to be working on the security plan.

I hoped against hope no-one had been in to see me in the almost twenty-four minutes I'd been gone. I planted myself behind the desk and started typing with a vengeance. Not that I needed to, the offer was already complete, curtesy of Ebony, I just had to do something to calm my nerves. I was acutely aware of the goosebumps coating my body, thankfully my robe was loose and hid my rebelling nerves. Once again, I was thankful my kind didn't sweat.

Ibrahim stuck his head around the door an hour later. 'How's it coming along?' he asked.

'Good,' I answered in a calm and enthusiastic voice, fully back in my role. 'Just doing the final review.'

He walked around the desk to stand behind me and studied the screen over my shoulder.

'Can you walk me though it?' Ibrahim asked.

'Sure.' I proceeded to lead him through the PowerPoint presentation, the accompanying Excel with the numbers, and the PDF containing the details.

He seemed impressed. I'd discovered Ibrahim was by no means computer illiterate, though I suspected this was way above his level of understanding.

'Shall I print them out?' I asked.

Ibrahim produced a memory stick and handed it to me. That effectively answered the question. I hadn't expected them to let me link to a printer.

I downloaded the documents and relinquished the memory stick.

'Please delete the documents completely from your computer,' the Imam requested. I looked at him uncertainly, as would be expected with such a request, then proceeded to fully expunge any trace of the documents from my laptop. He watched me during the process, then took the computer and did a few searches to make sure there were no copies and that the files had been fully removed from the computer. He searched my computer bag and quickly frisked me. I underwent the security measures without complaint. Glad Jonah had the drive.

'Would you like me to present it to Imam Musa?' I asked, pointing at the memory stick.

'If he has any questions I will contact you,' Ibrahim replied, dismissing me.

I smiled in agreement and packed up my computer. Imam Ibrahim watched me intently. Of all the Imams, he was the least trusting of me. I stayed calm and collected. Exchanging the ritual thank-yous and goodbyes, I unhurriedly made my way out of the mosque and into the fresh air outside. I walked towards my car, placed the laptop in the passenger seat and looked back at the mosque as I walked to the driver's side. Ibrahim stood in the doorway, still watching me intently. I smiled again and got in the car.

I let out a sigh of relief as I drove out of the parking lot on to my studio.

It was all up to Jonah and Ebony now. As agreed, I would continue my undercover work in case the files didn't offer us anything we could work on.

I would have to remain vigilant. It was quite possible someone would find out there had been a breach, even with all the security Ebony had provided. And I had the distinct impression Ibrahim had me in his crosshairs.

And then of course there was Aaliyah.

Chapter Thirty

'Do you believe her?' Ebony asked. We were in a Teams meeting again, me calling from a hotel in Los Angeles where I was for a security convention.

'I don't know,' I answered.

It was strange and taxing to meet like this all the time, but we had to be careful. I didn't know whether I was being watched by the Imams. To be on the safe side, I stayed in character, even here in LA.

There hadn't been any fallout from our foray into the computer room. The guard was still employed by the mosque, and it seemed no one was any wiser about what we had done. Aaliyah hadn't shown her face either. I hadn't dared ask around about her presence. There was no reason for me to know, and definitely not to be aware of who or what she was, so we just left it there.

'She could be playing you. Getting you to lower your guard.' Ebony continued. Jonah nodded on the split screen.

'It wouldn't work. I have no reason to trust her, quite the opposite. At home, her family and mine are competitors.

Officially, they're at each other's throat. Besides I already told her what we were planning.'

That got me a definite scolding look from Ebony. She did not agree.

Jonah urged me onwards.

'I would expect the animosity would continue here. It's inbred. If we encounter each other, then we attack. It's no coincidence the religions we represent actively oppose each other. The antagonism from my dimension seeps into this world. Her behaviour is confusing.'

'You're saying she wouldn't be a plant working for your dad?'

'It's unlikely.' I shook my head to emphasise me opinion.

'Okay, not sent by your father. What about her family.' Ebony was playing the devil's advocate, pun intended.

'I can't imagine they would send anyone unless it's to kill me. Now they know I don't have the backing of my family anymore. I'm a lot easier to target. My dad might even thank them if they brought him my head.'

'That's reassuring,' Jonah chimed in.

'Yeah. Another danger to look out for. The other families don't have to fear my father's wrath.'

'Maybe that's her plan. Endear herself towards her family and yours by terminating you.' Jonah was ever the optimist.

'Time will tell. She hasn't done anything yet. But we'll have to watch out for her. Her story just doesn't sound believable.'

Jonah cocked his head in question. 'Not believable she would turn her back on her family, you mean?'

'Yes. And that she would go it alone.' I answered surprised at his question.

'Like you?'

Touché.

Maybe I wasn't the only one to grow a conscience, and a backbone.

'Let's take it a day at a time, and meanwhile just be very careful. I think we should assume she is not an ally.'

Jonah nodded, a smile on his lips. I wouldn't live that one down for quite a while. The guy loved to bait me. It was so easy. Too easy to pass up on.

'How is progress going on the files?' I decided to change the subject, the irritating smirk on Jonah's face was getting to me, even at this distance. And I did not appreciate Ebony's laughter.

She turned professional again. 'I've deactivated some of the boobytraps on the data. I need to look further, especially for the beacon your new friend told you about. Once that's done, I can get down to the actual data. I don't want to rush it. Just in case there's a mechanism to destroy the contents if I take a look.'

'Sounds good,' I answered, happy she was being careful. I'd grown very fond of her, not to mention she was worth her weight in gold with her special computer talents and contacts. It occurs to me how much she had already helped our cause. Not in the least by her extensive—slightly illegal—network.

'I'll stay undercover and find out what I can. I think Imam Musa is finally starting to trust me. The concept you set up for the other mosque went down like a storm. Ebony'

'Good. I'll be busy with the files. And some others stuff I need to do.' We both refrained from asking what that was. She would tell us if we needed to know.

'What about me?' Jonah asked expectantly. 'What can I do?'

I thought about it for a minute. We were still keeping

our heads down regarding the Christian side of The Establishment, trying to stay off the radar. Since my family knew of our partnership, things had become much more dangerous, and I still wasn't sure Jonah's new persona would stand up to deep scrutiny.

'Not much at the moment,' I answered much to his chagrin. 'You need to lay low. Stay out of the limelight.'

His face clouded and his fiery eyes shone under the heavy eyebrows. His lips pulled into a thin line. This was not going down well. I understood. He was going stir crazy.

Ebony noticed too. 'Hang in there, big man. You need to chill.'

His face softened a bit, but the fire was still in his eyes. 'Will do, Tiny.' I noticed he didn't acknowledge me, and that stung a bit.

'I mean it, Jonah,' she continued. 'Lie low. Your time will come. Now we need you to sit tight.'

I let her convince him, certain I wouldn't be able too.

'I don't want to lose you.' She played the trump card.

Jonah sighed and nodded his head.

I took the turn in the conversation as a hint and, after goodbye and good-luck, I signed off. It was time for the final prayers, so I had to get to the mosque.

I hoped Ebony would be able to persuade my partner to stay clear of trouble for a while. We would need to think of something for him to do to keep him occupied.

For his own safety, and ours.

An eruption wasn't what we needed right now.

Besides, I didn't have time for my partner's tantrums. The situation at the mosque was still precarious. I wanted to get deeper into the recruiting racket Musa had. The after-prayer meetings had moved from the open spaces outside the mosque into one of the smaller meetings rooms in the building itself, necessitated by the evolution of the subject matter.

The group of seven believers and the three Imams met twice a week. The "Sons and Daughters of Islam" was a regular topic as well as the increased tension between the Christian and Islam worlds. Atrocities on both sides were still rampant and even the most peaceful of people were polarising.

The authorities were helpless. Their efforts thwarted by the terrorist groups. The CWW was structured much in the same manner as ISIS. A conglomeration of small cells that worked within a very close framework which, though connected by a common purpose, depended on very boxed information. The cells didn't know the details of any of their brethren. Everything was on a need-to-know basis. Secrecy guaranteed invisibility. Even the small success the authorities achieved when they rolled up one of the CWW cells in New York backfired. They ran into a brick wall. Not even less-than-ethical interrogation tactics worked on the prisoners. They simply didn't know.

The unbridled violence in both camps fostered a massive influx in recruitment. Their influence gained enormous momentum and their numbers were rumours to be in the thousands. ISIS's previous popularity was eclipsed by their new-found Jihad resurrection.

Chapter Thirty-One

The phone rang. I picked it up and looked at the caller. Jonah. I was surprised because we'd agreed to a complete radio silence other than the Teams meetings. There must be something up, otherwise he wouldn't be trying to reach my mobile. With some trepidation, I answered the call.

'Yes?'

'Hello, Gabriel.'

The voice gave me goosebumps. It sent waves of alarm up my spine and into my brain.

It wasn't Jonah.

'Michael.' I answered in what I hoped was a calm and collected voice.

There was a hollow laugh on the other side of the line. This was bad. Michael obviously had Jonah, otherwise he wouldn't have his phone. Thankfully it was a burner with only one number on it. I hoped they didn't have Jonah's laptop and his connections to Ebony or Benedict.

'I would imagine this is quite the surprise for you,' my brother gloated. I declined to answer. He wasn't expecting one. 'Just in case you are wondering; your partner,' he spat out the word, 'is still alive. Though slightly banged up.' I heard a commotion in the background which corroborated his statement.

'For the moment.'

I didn't like the addition.

'If you want him to stay that way—alive I mean—then you need to come get him.'

'Why would I?' I tried.

Michael laughed. 'Don't kid yourself. You've gotten attached to your pet.' Again, there was commotion in the background. And a muffled cry. 'You'll come.'

He was right. I would.

There was no use in pretending indifference.

'Where?'

'That's better. The old port on Al Scoma Way. There's a dilapidated warehouse at the end of the street. We've cut the chain for you. Come into the hall through the black door to the left of the heavy truck entrance.'

'I'll need some time to get there. It's not close.' I had to stretch the time. I had to formulate some kind of plan. 'At least an hour with this traffic.'

'Don't dally, we're getting bored here and your friend is our only distraction.' Again, that laugh, followed by a grunt.

'Don't come, ED,' Jonah shouted in the background. Then I heard a deep thud and a cry. They had made their point. Any delay would be painful for my partner.

Michael hung up.

This was unexpected.

Michael had thrown a hell of a spanner in the works. I had no idea how he found Jonah. We were exceptionally careful after our previous run in. The only possibility that came to mind was Aaliyah. Had she ratted us out? Pointed my family to San Francisco?

It was moot. I had to do something.

Not that I had any illusions about the outcome of this meeting. Michael held all the cards this time. I deduced he would want to bring me home, preferably alive, where I could face my father's wrath. Not a good prospect. But neither was losing my partner. I had to at least try.

I grabbed my car keys and was about to leave when Jonah's words stopped me. Why had he called me ED? That was the name Ebony invented for me. He never called me that. It had to be relevant. There was no way he would have said that on a whim in the current circumstances. I deduced he wanted me to contact Ebony.

I started the agreed process to contact our computer wizard, very aware that this would cost time. Time, I didn't have. I said a silent apology to Jonah, but I was sure this was what he wanted me to do.

Three very long minutes later my second phone rang. I answered and Ebony was on the other side.

'What's up?' She sounded anxious. With reason. I never called her. All contact was initiated through Jonah.

'What's happened to the big man?'

'He's alive,' I reassured her, hoping I wasn't lying. 'But my brother has him. He's using Jonah to get me to meet him.'

'Okay. Big man spoke to you?'

'In a manner of speaking,' I answered. 'He shouted for me not to come, then he called me ED.'

'Good that you contacted me.' She was all business now. 'Where are they keeping him?'

'In a disused warehouse on Al Scoma Way, in the commercial harbour.'

'I know the place.' She never ceased to surprise me. 'Get there, someone will contact you before you enter the wharf. They will be in a black GMC Yukon SUV. Wait for them before you go in.'

I thanked her and hung up. Once again, I was grateful we had her on our side. She was a godsend.

I grabbed the keys and my phones and left the studio apartment for the garage and my car.

Forty-five minutes later I approached the wharf. The place was deserted. My phone rang and a car I hadn't noticed in the shadows, flicked its lights. Ebony's reinforcements had beaten me to the rendezvous.

I parked my car opposite theirs and exited. The driver turned on the headlights illuminating me. I heard the doors open and two burly men got out of the car and approached me. Two more stayed with the vehicle, machine guns in hand.

'You Ed?' one asked.

'Yes.' I nodded, going along with Ebony's nickname.

'We're the cavalry.' No one laughed. 'Do you know how many there are?'

'No. But I expect Michael will have brought at least four or five.'

'And they're not from around here,' he asked laconically. It was the understatement of the year.

'That would be correct.' I smiled at the comment.

'Our mutual friend told us.'

'Keep an open mind,' I advised. He nodded. I had no idea what Ebony told them, but it was about to get very strange for them.

'Wait for five minutes,' the leader ordered. 'Then you go in. We'll be in the shadows around you when you need us.'

'If I need you.'

'You'll need us.' With that last statement they returned to their car, turned off the lights and moved out.

I waited the agreed five minutes then slowly rolled my own car further on to my destination. I stopped at the gate and sure enough, the padlock on the chain-link fence had been cut with what I expected was an angle grinder. I pulled the chain out on one side and slipped through the half-opened fence onto the dark grounds. I couldn't see the SUV and had no idea where the cavalry was. I would just have to trust them, and Ebony.

There was no light other than the half moon. My eyes adjusted to the gloom, and I made out a dark foreboding building. Most of the windows I saw had broken glass and one of the big loading doors hung lopsided on its broken hinges. Next to it was a smaller black door; still big enough to let a forklift truck drive into the massive building. I opened that one, entered and left it ajar.

There were small emergency lights distributed over the building, some of which glowed weakly. They shed a disjointed light on the mostly empty floor space at the entrance of the warehouse. I moved into the cavernous space and followed the lights. The floor was interspaced with large metal pillars that held up the roof. Glancing up, I could see the moon and stars in places where the covering had long since rotted away.

The further on I walked, the more debris I encountered. Here and there I saw big wooden crates, their contents strewn on the floor. A collection of metal parts and occasional plastic containers with what looked like motor fluids. A rat skittered over the floor away from me, disturbed in its nightly hunt for food.

At the far end of the warehouse more lights were on. I counted three men around another hanging from a chain over a metal joist. No doubt that would be Jonah. Two of the others took turns striking him with what looked like baseball bats. Muffled grunts carried in the empty building.

My footsteps on the concrete floor were a dead give-away. Michael turned to watch me approach. I wondered how Ebony's troops would get anywhere near without alerting my brother with my resounding foot falls but decided to let that go. They would do what they could. Nothing I could do about that.

'You came,' Michael stated the obvious. 'Finally.'

I walked up and stopped about two metres from my brother. I glanced at Jonah. He was bleeding profusely from a cut above his left eye and his naked upper body sported an array of bruises and welts. They had really gone to town on him. He smiled wryly, cocked his head, and shrugged his shoulders as far as the chains would let him in a "what can you do about it" manner which made me think he was in better shape than he looked. Maybe not all the bruises were from this altercation.

Michael was gloating.

'I'm sure you're racking your tiny little brain trying to figure out how we found you so easily.'

I stayed silent. His ego wouldn't let him keep that a secret. He'd finally bested me, or so he perceived.

'You can thank your partner for this really.'

I looked at Jonah. He shrugged.

Michael held up the remnants of Jonah's "ticket-to-Heaven."

'The idiot kept the pieces of his identifier.' I glanced at my partner again. My brother continued, 'we can now trace even the smallest particle of our technology in this world. Even if it's broken, like this one.'

Dread filled me. If this was true, then they would also be

able to trace my transponder. That meant Ebony was in grave danger. Jonah's eyes turned hard, and his brow creased, convincing me he had come to the same conclusion.

I turned to Michael. 'What do you want?'

He smiled from ear to ear, so sure of his upper hand. Michael had the advantage, and he knew it. I tried to pick up any indication of Ebony's men but couldn't. I consoled myself that if I couldn't hear them, neither could Michael. There might be a surprise here after all. Now I just had to find out what was in store for my partner and me.

'Me?' he answered. 'I just wanted to get you here. Personally, I want nothing more to do with you. If I had my way, I'd slit your throat and be done with you.'

'So why don't you?' A tingling started at the back of my neck. Never a good sign. A voice in my brain screamed at me to get the hell out of here. Never mind Jonah. He was a lost cause anyway. Michael wouldn't let him live. I tried to ignore the pull the voice had on me. My body was rapidly descending into panic mode, and I didn't know why. It wasn't my brother. I hated his guts and his seemingly control of the situation. But that wasn't what was getting me up-tight to this extent.

'I would. But someone wants to talk to you,' he replied. His smug smile pulled his face into a vicious grin.

'I'm not going with you.' I stated.

'No. We expected that. Besides there aren't many who want you back home anyway.'

I was confused. How did that compute with Michael's earlier statement? The panic I felt intensified exponentially and it took all my poise and strength to stay where I was and project what I hoped was still an aura of calmness and inner power.

A familiar soft whine behind me froze the blood in my veins. It was the sound of a transportation.

I felt the presence as soon as the sound ceased.

I was glued to the floor, my body refusing to move.

Slowly I forced myself to turn around.

'Gabriel.'

I nodded. It was all I could do.

'Who's this?' Jonah demanded, much less impressed than I was.

'My father.' I managed to say.

'I expected more.' Jonah was never one to mince words. His callousness brought me out of my inertia and earned him another vicious blow to the torso.

I observed my father. His reaction was to smile. The humour didn't reach his eyes. They were black as coal.

'Ah, the rogue priest.' he said in his familiar derogatory manner. 'Michael told me about your strange "partnership" with my son.'

'Then you are not as disappointed as I am,' my friend answered dryly.

Father laughed. That hollow sound that froze my hearts as a child. It still affected me, though I noticed not to the extent it had earlier. I pulled strength from the callous posture Jonah portrayed to the whole situation. He was not impressed.

'You prayed to me,' my father said amused.

'No.' Jonah stated resolutely. The venom in his tone hard. 'Never to you. You're a fraud. A miserable con man.'

Michael step forward to attack Jonah. 'You miserable hump of meat. How dare you talk to your God that way.'

The disdain in my partner's demeanour was commendable under the circumstances. 'He's not my God. And never will be.'

Michael hefted his sword but was stopped by my father's hand wave.

Dad turned to Jonah. 'Much as I find you amusing, I'm not here for you, Priest. You are nothing but a diversion. A means to an end.'

He turned back to me.

'You disappointed me, Gabriel.' Great start. 'None of my children have ever left our family. I assumed it was a temporary phase you were going through. You needed something to focus your energy and attention on. You felt an urge to make a stand against your family, against me.'

This was not what I expected. I'd steeled myself for reproach, blame. Whatever.

'Initially, I didn't understand. What was it that had gripped you so completely that you were willing to throw everything away? Your prolonged absence made me wonder whether there was more to your rebellion than simply making a point.'

'It pained me to think there was something that made you would want to leave your home. Leave your family.'

I stayed silent. Outwardly, I refused to show the emotions that were raging inside me. His words were making a very unwanted impression. I didn't want to react, but hundreds of years of manipulation and conditioning kicked in.

'Your mother is heartbroken' Another stab in my gut.

I refused to take the bait and stayed mute.

'Because of her, and because you are my son, I have decided to look into your accusations.'

I raised an eyebrow.

'I realised I may have done you an injustice. You seem to be very passionate about all this, about the humans.' He waved his hand at Jonah. 'I will listen to you, hear what you have to say. Then, if there is merit to your words, we will look at our business from the perspective you now represent. Together we will determine how to go forward.'

Say what? Was I hearing this correctly? My hearts gave a jump.

'I know you have your doubts. I have not listened to you in the past, so you wonder why I would start now.'

I nodded. That was exactly what I was thinking.

He smiled. I wasn't sure that was an improvement, it was actually unnerving.

'The fact that you would be willing to give up your family, everything you stand for, for this cause of yours, shows me how serious you are. I commend that. You have found something you are passionate about. So-much-so that you place your future in the balance. It shows dedication. I can appreciate that.'

The big block of concrete in my gut was still there. It refused to move. Not convinced at all. The rest of me wanted to believe.

'If you are so adamant, then it merits investigation,' he continued.

'We will do this together. If necessary, make some changes and stamp out the dissent. I will listen to what you have to say.'

It sounded good. I wanted to believe him. Truth be told, I never meant to distance myself from my whole family, just him. Or maybe just the business. If we tried to come to an arrangement, I would be able to return home for visits. I could see my mother, my sisters.

I felt my resolve falter.

I was beginning to hope we could work it out.

'Take your place at my side again, as my favourite son.' My father pulled me out of my reverie.

I looked at him. His face was unreadable. No emotions, nothing.

I glanced to the side at Michael. His face contorted in a vicious grimace. He was silently laughing at me.

My heart sank as realization sank in.

I looked up at my father. 'It's always the last sentence, isn't it? You nearly had me, I almost believed you were sincere. Right up to the last statement. But you had to push it just that little bit more. Over the believable edge.'

I stared him in the eye.

'It's just another scam, isn't it?'

He remained silent.

'None of it was sincere. You'll never listen to what I have to say. Your mind is already made up. You've decided. As always. It's just you. There's no room in your world for other voices or opinions that don't echo yours.'

His lips pulled into a thin line as he stared back at me. Deep breaths and the fire in his eyes confirmed what I had deduced. This was just another manipulation. None of it was true.

'Well, I won't do it anymore. I will not be a clone in service to your ego.'

The silence was hard and could be cut with a knife. Even Jonah refrained from comments.

'I am your father.' He tried another approach. 'I'm the head of the family. You will do as I decide. I know what is best for our family.'

'You've never been a father to me,' I answered. His lies had burst the dam and all the resentment that lay behind rushed through my veins. 'A tyrant, yes. A father, no.'

Michael gasped. I ignored him.

My father's thin lips turned up in an amused smile. 'Your rebellion entertained me. It showed character. More than any of your other siblings portrayed. You dared—in your childish and ineffective way—to stand up to me. That reminded me of myself as a youngster.'

'Funny really. You—the wimp of my spawn—you are the one who resembles me most. You dared to think out of the box. You questioned what was put in front of you. Refused to blindly follow the directions you were given. That could be the sign of a budding visionary. I expected great things from you. That is why I chose to ignore your transgressions. That is why you were always my favourite.'

'But father?' Michael couldn't stop himself. Dad ignored him. He moved slowly from his position, past me, towards where Jonah hung from the chains.

'You were the only one of my children who had the balls to contradict me. They only one with the brains to question my decisions and think for yourself. The rest are nothing more than cattle. They blindly do my bidding.' The contempt for his children was astounding. He had never been a loving father, but the extent of his scorn was unprecedented.

'Desperate for my approval and acknowledgment, they debase themselves to the pathetic minions they will always remain. You were the only one capable of being my heir. I envisioned you and me ruling not only this dimension but ours as well. I see now that was a mistake.'

He stopped in front of me again. Now between me and Jonah. 'Your rebellion was not the result of a great mind; it was the ranting and raving of a spoiled child. You failed to channel your potential into the man and true heir you could have been. You disappoint me. More than any of the others. I expected more from you. Yet that which is most important in our culture is absent within you; loyalty; to your family, to me. You are devoid of that.' He looked completely disgusted.

'You confuse loyalty with fear, father.' I dared to contradict him.

'No. I don't. For me, they are one and the same.' His words cut deep.

'And now you pretend not to fear me anymore.' The patronising tone riled me; I wasn't the small, terrified boy I had been. Not even the same man as minutes ago. Who the fuck did he think he was? Debasing my whole family and me in this way. The fire ignited again and pushed up through my body.

'No.' I answered, squaring my chin, and standing up straight in defiance. 'You still frighten me. That hasn't changed. But what I fear more, is losing myself. And that, I won't do.'

He stared at me. I returned the favour. Where minutes ago, his intense gaze sent goosebumps up my spine and pushed me to cower in abject terror, now I identified it for what it was; a means to manipulate me into submission. I finally opened my eyes and what I saw was a man. No more than that.

A man, a head smaller than me, with a massive ego. A weak man, if truth be told, who's only strength was in how he dominated others by fear and intimidation. Jonah was right. He was a disappointment.

'So, this is your choice?' The anger in his face was barely contained. Hard lines were harder. Thin lips pulled to a granite line. But mostly it was the eyes. With my father they were clearly the famed window to his soul. His were black as coal. I saw absolute Hell and damnation in them. For me.

There was no turning back now. The concrete block in my gut anchored it all.

I refrained from comment. It was clear to anyone. It didn't need any more.

'Very well. It is on your head.' The words closed any doors that might have been open even an inch. There was no going back now. Not for me. But he couldn't let it lie. He had to have the last word.

'You are the son of a God. Why do you persevere in this nonsense?'

'You're not a God,' I interrupted him. A major infraction of respect in my father's eyes.'

He glared at me, even more than earlier.

'To humans, I am a god. I am their God.'

'No. You're not. You are a narcissistic, megalomaniacal, arrogant little man with a god complex. That's something completely different.'

His nostrils flared and his face coloured red. The muscles of his shoulders tensed; his hands bunched into fists. I thought he was going to attack me. His surprise was total. Never had anyone spoken back to him like this. And then one of his own sons to boot.

Michael raised his sword and took a step forward. He was stopped by my father's hand gesture again. It still worked with him. Me, not so much anymore.

Dear old dad squared his shoulder, forced the muscles to relax and a contemptuous smile came onto his thin lips.

'I am God.' He held up his hand to stop any reaction. It was superfluous. I had spoken my mind.

'To humans, I am God. They pray to me for redemption. They depend on me to deliver them to their afterlife. And that makes me God,' he continued, observing me closely.

I couldn't stop myself. 'They pray to the God they knew before you. All you do is hijack their souls and pretend to be the deity they worship. The afterlife they petition for is not what you give them. They ask for Heaven, and you give them Hell. You are not God.'

'Let's agree to disagree, shall we?' The smile intensified. It wasn't a nice smile. The venom dripped off the edges of the sentiment. Apprehension pushed goosebumps back onto my arms.

'If I am God,' he continued, daring me to contradict him. 'Then my sons are the angels.' An icy feeling started at the bottom of my spine and made its way up my back to the base of my skull. The hairs on my neck stood on end again.

'You choose to oppose me. Me, your father, your God.'

I couldn't speak. My gut constricted painfully in apprehension. The glint in his hard black eyes intensified, his vicious smile was full of amusement.

'And that makes you the fallen angel.'

Realisation hit me like a brick wall.

'I will have to rename you. You are Lucifer. You have chosen to oppose me and all I stand for. Everything the Church stands for. That makes you the Devil. I will make sure everyone knows your newfound purpose.'

Then he said the final words before he touched the amulet and was gone.

'This means war.'

The silence was total. No one moved. Not me, not Michael, nor his henchmen.

'You idiot.' Michael finally said. 'You could have had it all, and you threw it away. I pity you now. You have brought down God's wrath on yourself.'

'Dad's.' I had to have the last word. 'Not God's.'

Michael laughed. He turned to his henchmen. 'Kill the priest.'

The man on the right swung his bat up above his head and readied to bring it down on Jonah's skull. It never touched him. Instead, a small hole appeared in the man's forehead and purple blood seeped out of the gunshot wound. The corpse dropped the bat as it sank to the floor.

Michael turned to me in shock. Guess he hadn't expected reinforcements. The cavalry emerged from three sides, their guns aimed at the remaining henchmen and my brother. Surprise turned to fear, and Michael grabbed his amulet and disappeared. The remaining allies did the same, leaving behind their fallen comrade. I rushed over and grabbed the weapon he carried on his hip, just in time before the corpse evaporated into thin air.

One of Ebony's friends freed Jonah and he sank to the floor. His wounds were more serious than he pretended. I started to walk over to him when the realisation of what I had done hit me.

My legs felt like jelly. They wouldn't hold up my shaking body. I stumbled to the nearest metal column and slid down to a seated position, my back to the cold ore, reeling from the confrontation with my dad and his parting words.

The Devil.

It had seemed like a great joke when Jonah and I said it earlier. Now it had a completely different connotation.

'You okay?' Jonah asked as he looked at me from his own seat on the floor. Our benefactors continued to scan the hall. The sudden departure of our visitors was as unnerving to them as the purple blood on the dead man, the spots still clear on the warehouse concrete ground.

'No,' I answered truthfully. 'No. I'm not.'

'What did he mean by that last comment? About your newfound purpose?'

I looked at my partner. 'He means The Establishment will brand me as the Devil. All of Christianity will oppose me—us. Our quest to convince the righteous ones in the Church about this scam has just taken a whole new turn.'

He nodded. The realisation of the impact on our cause landed with him too.

Jonah looked worried. 'Do you think Michael was telling the truth? Jonah asked. 'About tracing your technology?'

My turn to shrug. 'I don't know. But we can't take a chance. We need to contact Ebony.'

One of the cavalry came over with a phone. He handed it to me. Ebony was on face time.

'Turn the phone to let me see how the big man is,' she asked. I turned the screen towards Jonah who attempted a smile. He failed miserably. I turned it back again.

'He needs a doctor,' she declared. 'What about you? You look pale.'

'I'm okay. Just a bit of shock, I think.'

'That was your dad?

'Yes. It was. Ebony, you need to get rid of the transporter I gave you. They might be able to trace it.'

'Way ahead of you, ED. It's been locked in a lead-lined, natural-rock container. Nothing is getting through there. I don't care how advanced your lot think they are.' I let out a big sigh of relief. Jonah echoed me.

'Besides,' she continued. 'The parts aren't so very different from ours. The materials have the exact same molecular composition as minerals here and I personally think your brother's allegation that they traced their technology is pure bullshit.'

'Wouldn't put that above him,' I answered relieved. 'But that does pose another question; how did they find Jonah?'

'We'll find out.' she answered. 'First thing to do now is get the big man taken care of. He's going to a private clinic. You accompany him and get a check-up as well ED, just to be sure. One of the guys will bring your car back to your studio and get you home after an all clear from the doc.' I refrained from asking how they knew where the studio was. There weren't many secrets from Ebony.

'Okay.' I answered.

'Now give the big man the phone, please.' I stood up and stumbled over to Jonah. He took the phone and tried to put on a brave face.

'I'm okay, Tiny.'

'Bullshit. You're going to the clinic.'

'Not necessary,' he tried. But it was a lost cause. Ebony could be very persuasive.

They talked for a few more minutes.

After the call, Jonah handed the phone back to its owner. 'No need to take me to the doctor,' he attempted.

'You're going,' the man replied with a chuckle 'I choose my battles wisely. No way in hell that I'm crossing Lady E.'

Ebony was so much more than a computer wizard.

I had the idea we were just scratching the surface.

Chapter Thirty-Two

'Ebony came round last night,' Jonah mentioned in the car on the way from the clinic to his new hideout. The wounds were healing well, and it was no longer necessary for him to stay under medical observation.

'How is she?'

'Good. Underground somewhere and enjoying herself by the sound of it. She's back online and searching for more info on The Establishment, as well as deciphering the data on the drive.' I nodded. Good to hear.

'I filled her in on what we discovered. It corresponds with her findings.'

We continued in silence.

'Oh,' Jonah added as an afterthought. 'One more thing she mentioned.' I looked at my partner in question. 'That gadget she was tinkering with.'

'Which one?'

'The one from your dimension.'

'The transporter?'

He nodded. 'Yes. That one.'
'And…?' I asked.
'She fixed it.'

Next in The Dominion Series

vinci-books.com/thestorm

There's an inter-dimensional war brewing. I'm slap bang in the middle of it... and it's my fault.

My family are killers, kidnappers, slavers. They steal the life essence of humans to reincarnate them into endless servitude in our dimension. It's up to me and my collection of misfits to stop them.

Turn the page for a free preview...

I AM the Storm: Chapter One

The rain came down in sheets, obscuring us from their view.

No one would see or hear us.

Not before it was too late.

For them.

Navigating the fence was easy.

Long ago it might have been electrified, but today it wasn't. Jonah cut the mesh, and I held it back as our five-man team entered the factory compound.

The crumbling buildings and roads covered an area of more than two square miles. In times gone by, this would have been a loud, busy place. Now it was empty and abandoned.

The hard wind echoed in the empty buildings, creating a hollow, haunting cry. while the incessant deluge hammered on the tin roof of the lower building and dripped loudly from crumbling gutters onto broken concrete floors. All the buildings—but one—were dark and foreboding, their cavernous empty hallways dark as hollow eye sockets in a skull.

We hugged the shadows, moving stealthily from doorway to doorway. Sly took point, followed by Jonah, two more of Ebony's crew and I made up the rear.

The lit building was up ahead to the right. Our destination was within its walls.

We had a date with some very bad people.

We shouldn't be here.

With my father on our tail, we should lie low, but we figured life was short and we had a job to do. Our quest was never more real than now. The escalating violence between the fanatics on both fundamental sides cost more and more innocent people their lives and their livelihoods. Fundamental Christians targeted innocent Muslims, and fanatical Muslims returned the favour. Like in every war, the greatest damage was collateral. Innocent people died. Not the zealots.

We couldn't go after the Christian kingpins now we were in their crosshairs, so we turned our attention to the soldiers. More accurately, to the recruiters.

Ebony fed us with information on new endeavours the ever-creative recruiters were fabricating to gather as many lost souls as possible and turn them into killing machines.

We'd noticed a clear increase in recruitment over the past month. They needed new meat to sacrifice to the cause. The recruitment efforts were becoming more brazen and had moved from individual enrolment to mass events. The dark web was full of them. And that led us here, to an abandoned factory on this miserable night in the pouring rain.

Sly held up his hand and we dropped into a crouching position. There was movement up ahead.

It was too early for the would-be recruits. They had

been told to come at midnight, now—two hours earlier—
only the recruiters and their thugs were in the compound.
You could debate whether the recruits were innocents, but
maybe we weren't too late to save some of them.

I could always hope.

We crouched in the shadow of a heavily damaged building. Bullet holes showed its most recent use as target practice. The windows and doors were broken, glass shards
littered the floor and made it difficult for us to avoid cuts as
we knelt on the debris.

Three shadows passed ten metres from us. They made
no attempt to conceal themselves, secure in the knowledge
that no one knew what they were up to. No one who
shouldn't be there.

Jonah glanced my way and looked mildly disappointed
when I shook my head. Not yet, my big friend. Patience.

Two minutes after the men disappeared into the dark,
we moved into the shadows behind the lit building. Sly took
out a small camera on an extension and slipped it through a
break in the windowpane. He scrutinised the image on the
hand-held and shook his head. No one there. We continued
along the side of the massive factory hall and slipped
through a dark recess into the building where a few
camping lights set out a path in the dark. Sly sent his
companions onwards to circle the entrance while Jonah and
I pushed further into the bowels of the ruins, following the
trail of lights.

Seven people stood in the centre of the cleared area.
One woman and six men. Heated words echoed in the
empty space as the Asian woman and the man we identified
as the leader argued over who would approach the recruits.
The rest stood by silently, waiting for an outcome. Finally,
the woman threw up her hands and stomped off back

through the hall to the exit, followed by her adversary's derogatory laughter.

My phone vibrated in my pocket, the agreed sign everyone was in position. We'd decided earlier to get in and out as quickly and quietly as possible. We would terminate the recruiters with minimal bloodshed and take their bodies with us to dispose of at a different location. The recruits had to come here and find an empty building without a sign of a struggle. One thing we did not want, was to make martyrs of the bad guys and push the recruits further into the Establishment's arms. We figured the would-be soldiers would leave in disappointment, hopefully disillusioned. The woman leaving didn't help. We would have to catch up with her later if she was still on the premises.

No loose ends.

The group dispersed, three moving to the opposite side of the clearing, one coming our way and the other two fanning out to the sides. I saw Jonah slink away after the man on the left, Sly tiger-crawled to where the guy on the right stood lighting a cigarette. That left me to take the one approaching, the would-be leader.

He was a tall man, rough looking, thin in a wiry manner. His cheekbones were pronounced with the skin stretched over what in this light looked almost like skeletal features. His frame was sinewy, but the manner in which he walked belied the first impression of a weak man. He wouldn't be a push over.

He passed where I was hugged the shadows, completely unaware of my presence, his attention on his phone.

Again, I felt the vibration in my pocket. I counted to ten, the determined amount of time before we all sprang into action at once. On ten, I moved up behind him, my garrotte taunt between my hands. A muffled sound caused him to stop and turn his head towards the right. I saw his body tense and quickly slid the thin piano wire over his head and pulled back. His body fell back onto me, unbalanced by the suddenness of the attack, his hands pulling at the thin wire that cut off his oxygen. I pulled harder as he scrambled to get his footing and, in a reflex, tried to grab me. I sidestepped, holding on to the handles and pulled even harder. The gurgling sound he made resonated in the quite building and seemed like a shout. In reality it was a whisper as the life ebbed out of him.

He stopped struggling and I gave another hard yank on the garrotte, breaking his neck with the sudden change in direction. He was dead.

I pulled the corpse out of the path of lights into the darkness.

To both sides of me I heard the soft sounds of something heavy being dragged over the concrete floor.

Three vibrations indicated my companions inside had taken care of their targets. Four additional answering vibrations filled the quota. Only the woman left.

We waited in absolute silence. Straining our ears to hear any sound. Nothing.

I picked up the body, threw him over my shoulder and started down the building, avoiding the lights, but following that general direction out into the open air of the night. Jonah joined me and I could only just make out Sly in the dark distance, we were making our way to the vehicles the recruiters had arrived in. The others were already there.

The bodies were unceremoniously dumped in the back of the cars.

There was no sign of the woman. We assumed she had left.

I felt relived. There was still some part of me that was reluctant to harm a woman, even if she was the enemy.

Sly and the others each took a car and left the compound. Jonah and I made our way back to the hole in the fence. Our own vehicles were located two blocks from the fence and needed to be retrieved.

'That went well,' Jonah commented.

I nodded. It had been a quick mission. One that the Establishment would feel. They lost six of their recruiters and a large number of would-be recruits in one sweep. It would be a blow. We had no doubt they would know who was responsible. It was too much of a coincidence after my father's visit.

Jonah crawled through the fence and stood upright making room for me to struggle through the small opening. Bending my knees, I ducked my head and held the wire to the side.

A sharp pain in the centre of my back and a second in my side pushed the breath out of me as I stumbled through the fence and fell at Jonah's feet. He was already pushing back through the mesh to confront a man brandishing the bloody knife I'd felt. Jonah rushed him—oblivious of the weapon—and tackled him to the ground. They rolled in the slick mud, both trying to get the upper hand. Jonah held onto the attacker's wrists, twisting viciously in an attempt to dislodge the knife. But the man was strong and pushed back.

I struggled to my feet, blood gushing from the deep wounds the hunting knife had inflicted.

I was almost upright when another figure brandishing a machete came out of the dark behind the fighters.

The Asian woman we had seen earlier raised the big weapon above her head, aiming for the big man's neck as he struggled with her companion. I dove back through the hole, rolled on the ground and jumped up behind her. With one hand on her neck and the other on her head, I quickly snapped her neck.

Her companion wasn't faring any better. Jonah let go of his wrist and chopped into the upper arm holding the knife. A loud crack announced another broken bone. Jonah caught the knife before it hit the ground and in one fluid movement brought it up in between the man's ribs, effectively stopping his heart.

We looked around, all senses attuned to any sounds of more unexpected company, both breathing heavily.

I was badly shaken. My hearts beat rapidly and out of sync, pushing massive amounts of adrenaline through my veins.

We scanned the area, our backs to each other in defence.

'No one,' Jonah whispered.

'Let's get out of here.'

'Hell, yeah.'

We shuffled towards the hole in the fence, one stood guard while the other slipped through. I figured we were far enough away from where the recruits would be, so we left the bodies. We made our way to the vehicles and drove off into the darkness.

My pulses were still raging.

I berated myself.

Our complacency almost got us killed.

I AM the Storm: Chapter Two

'We're screwed.'

'I wouldn't put it that black and white,' Jonah tried to lighten the sentiment.

'You wouldn't? And how would you describe our current predicament?' Ebony shot back, her stare daring him to contradict her.

'We have challenges?' he tried.

Ebony brought her hands up to her face, rubbed her eyes and sighed. She plucked at a strand of hair that had escaped her cap, sighed again, and looked at the ever-smiling Jonah.

'Okay,' she said exasperated. 'Let me summarise this. Make sure I have the right perspective.'

Jonah and I nodded. It seemed the safe thing to do.

Ebony turned and walked to the three moveable white-boards arranged in a semi-circle near the computer set-up. She picked up several markers in different colours and beckoned us over. Naturally, we complied. Failure would not go down well in her current mood.

She began to write on the central whiteboard, then turned to face us.

Why did I always have the feeling I was back in the school benches when she was like this? I felt disproportionately intimidated by the tiny five-foot-two computer wizard in front of me. I glanced at Jonah and saw he wasn't much better off. Not even with his six-foot-six, two-forty pound frame.

'Right,' she started.

We were all ears.

'Your dad,' she pointed to me. 'The self-proclaimed Christian God, is now aware that you've joined forces with the big man.' She pointed to Jonah. I nodded. She turned and wrote it on the central board.

'He declared war on you.'

'Technically yes, but I suppose we did that earlier...' I stopped talking. Her stare was so intense it almost made me stutter. 'Yes. Right. Not the time for semantics.' I felt the blush rise and cover my cheeks as I averted my gaze.

'You think?'

I refrained from answering. Jonah stayed silent. He didn't even gloat.

'He doesn't know about me yet,' she continued. We both shook our heads vigorously and she wrote the statement down in a new list on the right-hand board.

'Your family has technology that can transport them to wherever they want including cross-dimensional.' Again, the centre board.

'We don't have a way to trace them or be forewarned.' Centre board. 'They are also the driving force behind the Establishment.' Again. 'The Establishment basically has control over the Christian Church.'

I was about to say something when she added, 'and the

other major religions as well.' I nodded. My input no longer needed.

'Your dad will have informed the Establishment so basically we're at war with them too.' It was starting to sound very bleak.

'It's just the three of us,' She continued to write, not bothering to look at us.

'Not just us,' Jonah dared to contradict. 'There's the archbishop as well.'

'Archbishop Benedict.' She stated, turning to him with a cold stare. Jonah nodded enthusiastically.

'The guy you think is our ally, who you haven't heard from since you visited him months ago?' she commented with an edge.

'Well. Yes. But I'm sure he's on our side,' he stammered.

Another big sigh from Ebony. 'Shall we put him down as a maybe then?' Jonah nodded sheepishly. Benedict was added to the left-hand board under our names.

'Let's continue, shall we?' When neither of us commented, she picked up her narrative.

'Thanks to your archbishop, the big man's picture is hanging on every cop-station wall.' Jonah was about to say something but decided just in time to keep his mouth shut.

'And you,' she pointed to me again. 'Are quickly coming into the spotlight of the anti-terrorism squad.'

I was taken back. 'Say what? When did that happen?'

'Anti-terrorism has had their beady eyes on your mosque for a while,' she explained. 'They're probing your background along with the other "persons of interest".'

Shit. Not what I wanted to hear. That would put an even shorter deadline on whatever we could find at the mosque.

'And to top it all off,' Ebony continued. 'I still haven't

deciphered the contents of the hard drive you downloaded.' That really bugged her. Maybe more than all the other things.

She added all the comments to the boards. Our "good guys" list on the left board was pathetically short and the plusses on the right-hand board were even worse. The one list that stood out was the shit list. The centre board. Our challenges.

If you put it that way, it really was depressing.

She took a step back and studied the overview, then turned to us.

'We're screwed.'

We didn't contradict her that time.

I AM the Storm: Chapter Three

'So how did they find you?' I asked Jonah.

He glanced at me, his eyes dark and unfathomable. 'Not important,' he declared and went back to unpacking his duffel bag.

'It is actually,' I countered. 'We need to know, so we can avoid making the same mistake again'

He stood up straight and gave me his best intimidating stare. Under normal circumstances, it would unnerve even the strongest of men. Me, I was used to it. It didn't have any more effect on me than mild amusement. After all our months together, surely he didn't think it still worked?

'Where did they grab you?' I tried a different avenue.

His stare continued. I returned it with a smile.

'You're not going to give up on this, are you?' he asked. I shook my head.

'At the beach,' he answered sullenly, turning back to his bag.

I waited. There were loads of questions I could have

asked, but he knew them already. It was a waiting game now.

He finally finished unpacking and moved to the living room of his new apartment. I followed and walked to the kitchen, taking the groceries we'd picked up on the way here.

San Diego was nice. The town had a distinctive Mexican vibe, and it was more laid-back than San Francisco or L.A. The few people we'd met up to now seemed friendly. More open. Jonah had definitely already made an impact on the ladies in the apartment complex. With his big frame, powerful aura, and the mischievous glint in his eyes, he was undoubtably already the topic of pool-side conversations.

We thought it prudent to move him to a new location after the debacle in San Francisco. We weren't sure whether his previous address had been compromised, but we couldn't take the risk. There were too many people hunting him. I had to stay put in the Golden Gate City, my job at the mosque wasn't done yet. San Diego was Ebony's suggestion. Far enough from Frisco and on the beach somewhere.

I wanted to know how my brother Michael found my partner.

Jonah poured two mugs of coffee from the ever-present coffeemaker and handed me one. We made ourselves comfortable in the lounge chairs and sipped the black gold.

'I was surfing,' Jonah finally divulged. 'At twilight. The beach always emptied around six and I figured I would be inconspicuous then.'

I looked at him in surprise, my eyebrows raised. Inconspicuous? How in hell did he think he could ever be anything close to low-key? He wasn't built for it.

'Let's face it Jonah,' I answered him. 'You will stand out wherever you are.'

He smiled and cocked his head. 'You know what I mean.'

I did, but a bit of banter lightened the mood.

'Anyway,' he continued. 'They were waiting for me when I walked back over the beach. Two of them approached me from the side, one in front and another came up behind me. They boxed me in.'

'Did you recognise them at all?'

'No. Never seen them before. Though I did pinpoint them as your people.' There was a slight reproach in his tone. I let it go—for now.

'They made it clear they would take me, voluntarily or not. There were still a few people around and I didn't want anyone to get hurt, so I complied, and they took me to a van in the parking lot. They made me get in the back, and that was where I saw Michael.' The hatred was back in his hard glare. Well, I had the same sentiment for my sibling. No discussion there.

'I was about to wipe the smile off his face when everything went black.'

I thought about it for a few minutes. Michael must have known where to look. It couldn't have been a chance encounter. That would be too much of a coincidence. There was more. There had to be.

'How did he know where to find you?' I asked in general, not expecting an answer.

'How the hell would I know?' Jonah avoided my gaze. 'Maybe it was just a case of being in the right place at the right time.'

I cocked my head and observed my partner. The question had been a rhetorical one, no more than me thinking out loud. Why had he taken it so personally?

'I don't believe in coincidence,' I continued, eager to find out what he was hiding.

He glared at me. My answering smile didn't help to improve his mood.

'What are you implying?' He spat out the words. 'That it was my fault?'

'I'm not implying anything.'

I continued to observe his fidgeting. He stood up and walked back to the kitchen to replenish his coffee. He stayed there, his back to the kitchen counter. The big man felt my eyes on him and looked up. There was a mixture of anger and self-reproach in his features. I waited him out.

'I just went surfing,' he finally broke the silence.

'How often did you do that?'

'Few times a week. Always in the evening and on quiet beaches.'

'Was there a pattern? To your visits?'

He shook his head and took another sip.

'Was there anything different that day?'

'No. Nothing. Look Gabe, I've been racking my brain trying to find out how they found me. I have no idea.'

I nodded. Aggravating him further wouldn't get answers. We would have to approach the conundrum in a different manner.

'Okay,' I said in a more conciliatory tone. 'Let's backtrack and see if we can find any clues.'

He moved back to the living room and sat down opposite me.

'We have to assume they were staking out the beach,' I began. Jonah nodded.

'There are loads of beaches. Was there anything special about this one that made you go there?'

'Just the peace and quiet. The waves are okay, not as good as in other places. But it's almost deserted. I thought that would be safe.'

'You'd think. Right?'

I peered into my coffee cup. Nope. No answers there either. There was something nagging at the back of my mind.

'I know we can't hide your size, but I thought with all the changes, it would be difficult to recognise you,' I mused.

He nodded as well.

'Yeah. My own mother wouldn't recognise me clean-shaven with this blond hair,' he laughed.

'Not to mention with the tats gone,' I added.

The atmosphere in the room changed immediately. I looked up at him. His brow was creased, the eyes hooded. What had I said? I rewound the last thirty seconds. The tatts. Could that be what had such an impact?

The nagging voice slowly made its way to my consciousness to form the question I didn't really want to ask. 'When you surf,' I asked. 'You wear the wet suit, right?' The wet suit covered the tattoos. A necessity because the usual camouflage foundation washed off in the water.

He stared at me. 'Yeah. Of course.'

We were silent. I held his gaze, he couldn't. Not a good sign.

'Most of the time,' he added sullenly.

'Most of the time?' I couldn't keep the reproach out of my tone.

'Okay. Once. I didn't wear it just once. There was no one at the beach. I checked. It was deserted.'

'Fuck.'

He didn't react. The self-reproach was enough.

'Someone must have seen you,' I said quite redundantly. He refrained from his usual sarcastic replies.

'How long after that surf did they grab you?'

'Two days. I didn't go back to the beach the next day.'

'Well, at least we know.' It wouldn't help to rub in how reckless he had been, he knew. 'Let's just be grateful they didn't follow you back to the apartment. They could have found your laptop and made the connection with the mosque or Ebony.'

Grab your copy…
vinci-books.com/thestorm